FACE-OFF

SHADOWS LANDING: THE TOWNSENDS #1

KATHLEEN BROOKS

ALSO BY KATHLEEN BROOKS

Bluegrass Series

Bluegrass State of Mind

Risky Shot

Dead Heat

Bluegrass Brothers

Bluegrass Undercover

Rising Storm

Secret Santa: A Bluegrass Series Novella

Acquiring Trouble

Relentless Pursuit

Secrets Collide

Final Vow

Bluegrass Singles

All Hung Up

Bluegrass Dawn

The Perfect Gift

The Keeneston Roses

Forever Bluegrass Series

Forever Entangled

Forever Hidden

Forever Betrayed

Forever Driven

Forever Secret

Forever Surprised

Forever Concealed

Forever Devoted

Forever Hunted

Forever Guarded

Forever Notorious

Forever Ventured

Forever Freed

Forever Saved

Forever Bold

Forever Thrown

Forever Lies

Forever Protected

Forever Paired

Forever Connected

Forever Covert (coming Jan/Feb 2024)

<u>*Shadows Landing Series*</u>

Saving Shadows

Sunken Shadows

Lasting Shadows

Fierce Shadows

Broken Shadows

Framed Shadows

Endless Shadows

Fading Shadows

Damaged Shadows

Escaping Shadows

Shadows Landing: The Townsends

Face-Off

Targeted (coming April/May 2024)

Women of Power Series

Chosen for Power

Built for Power

Fashioned for Power

Destined for Power

Web of Lies Series

Whispered Lies

Rogue Lies

Shattered Lies

Moonshine Hollow Series

Moonshine & Murder

Moonshine & Malice

Moonshine & Mayhem

Moonshine & Mischief

Moonshine & Menace

Moonshine & Masquerades

PROLOGUE

Stone Townsend hefted his backpack over one shoulder and strode down the hallway of his middle school. School was over for the day, thank goodness. He wasn't bad at it, but sitting still that long when he felt the energy radiating up his legs wanting to explode, made the day go by so slowly.

Up ahead a group of the older kids—the eighth graders —had snared another victim. That group of basketball players were assholes who took pleasure in torturing those weaker than them.

"Are you going to cry about it?"

"You're such a dork."

"Nothing but a nerd. You know what we do to nerds, right?"

They all taunted their latest victim.

"I may be a nerd, but one day I'll be someone and you'll be nothing but the boys who peaked in high school. They're called pathetic losers in case you're too stupid to know that."

Stone's stomach filled with dread at the sound of his younger sister, Olivia. She was nothing but a slip of a fifth grade girl against the pack of eighth graders. Their routine was for her to walk over to the middle school so she could walk home with Stone since most of their other siblings had afterschool activities. She made an easy mark for the eighth graders.

The energy that he had tamped down all day sprang to life as he ran the length of the hall. The boys knocked Olivia's books out of her hands, sending them crashing to the floor, but Olivia refused to cower.

One of the boys dared to put his hands on Olivia's arm and Stone saw nothing but red. "Don't you touch my sister!" Stone roared.

He dropped his backpack on the ground and launched himself into the backs of two of the boys, slamming them onto the floor. Stone rolled off their backs, making sure to dig his knees into their kidneys as he stood up. He grabbed Olivia and shoved her behind him.

"If you want to bully my sister, you have to get through me."

Olivia touched his arm. "They're not worth it, Stone," Olivia whispered.

"Aw. Now the little dork is protecting her brother. Listen to her, Stone. I'll kick your ass and then shove your sister in a locker and laugh about it all the way home," the ringleader said as he high-fived his friends.

Stone squared his shoulders. He was a year younger than they were, but that didn't bother him. He'd been wrestling his older brother, Damon, since Stone first learned to crawl. Those assholes had nothing on Damon, who, thanks to his birthday, was now a freshman even though he was only a year older than Stone.

The ringleader tried to sucker punch Stone, but it didn't work. Stone used his forearm to block the punch and then let all that pent-up energy loose. He slammed his fist into the boy's face before kicking out and slamming his foot into the shin of another of the boys.

Punches were thrown. Kicks connected. Stone landed most of his, but took a couple of hits, too. He absorbed them the way Damon taught him and fought back. He made sure Olivia was always behind him until help arrived. Unfortunately, help came in the form of the principal who already didn't like Stone. Stone had been sent to the main office for disrupting class a few times, but that didn't make him a bad kid. He was just a bored kid. But in the principal's mind, they were one and the same.

"Stone Townsend. Why am I not surprised to see you involved in this mess?"

"My brother was defending me from these bullies," Olivia said, now stepping in front of Stone as if she could protect him. "I believe the school has a zero-tolerance policy on bullying. They need to be expelled per the student handbook," Olivia pointed out.

"There's a zero-fighting policy too, Miss Townsend. That means your brother will also be expelled."

Olivia frowned. "But that's not fair. Stone was defending me. They were threatening me. Is he not supposed to protect his own sister? In the legal system, defense of yourself or another is an affirmative defense, meaning . . ."

The principal crossed her arms over her chest. Stone knew that look. She was getting pissed. "Don't tell me about the law, Miss Townsend. Now, I believe a fair punishment would be three days of in-school suspension for all involved."

"My record," Olivia gasped.

"Not you, Miss Townsend. Unless you threw a punch?"

"She didn't," Stone cut in. Olivia could be stubborn and he didn't want her to go down for this. "It was just us boys."

"Good, then report at seven Monday morning to start your suspension," the principal instructed the boys.

"Come on, Liv." Stone put a protective arm around his sister and got them out of there as fast as he could.

~

"Wake up, Stone."

"Go away, Damon," Stone mumbled into his pillow. It was Saturday. His parents had already reamed him for the in-school suspension starting on Monday and given him so many chores to do that weekend his head was about to burst just thinking of them.

Damon, the eldest of the Townsend siblings, yanked the sheets from the bed. "You want to hit someone?"

"Right now, I want to hit you," Stone muttered as he tried to reach for his blanket. It was freaking cold in upstate New York in December.

"Good. Then hit me."

Damon reached into a bag he was carrying and handed a pair of hockey skates to Stone. "But you have to hit me on the ice."

"With pleasure," Stone snapped before grabbing the new skates. "Where did these come from?"

"I bought them for you. I thought you'd appreciate not wearing Dad's old ones."

"Where did you get the money for that?" Stone asked. Damon took on too much. Yes, he was the eldest of nine, but he wasn't their parent even if he acted like it.

"I've been shoveling driveways. Don't worry, you will pay me back. You owe me the next ten driveways. Now, meet me down at the pond. I'll wear Dad's old skates."

Stone watched his older brother disappear down the

hallway of their house. Stone stood to get dressed and glanced around the bedroom. Damon's bed was already made, while their younger brothers, Hunter and Kane, were still asleep in their bunk beds. Down the hall he was willing to bet the twins, Forrest and Rowan, as well as Wilder were also still asleep. Olivia would probably be reading a book while the youngest, Penelope, was probably already up with their mom.

Stone got dressed in warm clothes, grabbed the skates, and snuck from the house. He didn't want another lecture from his parents. Damon was skating around the small pond at the back of their property, waiting for him.

"Grab the snow shovel and help clear the ice," Damon instructed as soon as Stone had his skates on. A shovel was in the snow next to two hockey sticks that had seen better days and a black puck.

"What is all of this?" Stone asked.

"I figured if you had all this energy and fight in you, I might give you something to use it all on."

"Hockey?"

"Considering you just beat the crap out of the basketball team, I thought hockey might be the better team to join."

"I've never played before and you want me to join mid-season?" Stone was pretty sure his brother must have a concussion or something.

"That's right. We have a lot of work to do."

Stone shook his head at his brother as he cleared the pond. "You don't even play hockey and you're going to teach it to me?"

"*If you can't do, teach.* Isn't that the saying or something?" Damon shrugged and picked up a stick. "I might not know how to play, but I know how to hit. You might not be the best skater, but you'll be the toughest. Now, let's get to work."

. . .

Stone gasped for breath as he stared up at the gray snow clouds. Damon had just leveled him. They'd only been playing for ten seconds. However, the familiar school day feelings of annoyance weren't there. Instead, that bright fountain of energy he seemed to always have bubbled up to his lips. He grinned up at the sky. This was gonna be fun.

Stone got back up on his skates. They'd grown up skating on this pond. He could skate and he could hit. Now he just needed to put them together. "Catch me if you can," Damon taunted, giving him the middle finger and then taking off.

Stone pushed forward, his speed building as they shot across the pond. Damon tried to turn, but Stone predicted it and cut him off short. Stone slammed his shoulder into Damon's arm, sending Damon careening into a snowbank.

"Whoa! This is fun." Adrenaline spiked and laughter spilled out of Stone's mouth as he skated around the pond at full speed.

At first, they only skated and hit each other. Then Damon handed him one of the hockey sticks he'd found in the trash of one of the houses he'd shoveled that morning. "I think you're supposed to hold it like this," Damon said, showing him.

For the next hour, they worked on skating with a stick, which only made hitting your brother that much more fun. The next day they spent all morning hitting, skating, and shooting before chores. It was clear, even then, that Stone was a natural and he relished beating the crap out of Damon.

Come Monday morning, Olivia escorted Stone to in-school suspension where the hockey coach was waiting. She argued that a more appropriate punishment for Stone was to join the hockey team. The practices and the discipline would teach him more than sitting in a silent room.

The coach agreed and eventually the principal did too.

Middle school hockey that first season was a mess of too much natural talent and not knowing what to do with it. Stone had to work on technique and learn the rules of the game. He learned math, angles, speed, force, and a lot about puck handling. Something the others had been doing for years. But by eighth grade he was playing on the high school team. He was named captain as a sophomore.

The college recruits came then. By senior year he had more college offers than he could count. He was ready to accept one for a college in Boston when he overheard his parents talking in the kitchen one night.

"I picked up an extra shift," his father said. "But with renting ice time for Stone and all the travel for Olivia's academic team, and not even counting all the younger kids' activities, we can't afford Christmas presents this year. Hell, paying the heating bill will be hard enough."

"I told you I can help," Stone heard Damon say as their mother sighed with worry.

"You're already paying for Penelope to take dance lessons. It's not your job, Damon. You're their brother and our son. You're not their parent. You should be in college, not working as a mechanic and signing over your paycheck to us," his mother said.

Stone frowned. He wondered why Damon still lived at home. Was this why?

"They're my family. Of course, I'm going to help. And you know college wasn't in the cards for me. I'm not a good student but I'm great with my hands. I even have a client who wants to pay me a thousand dollars to customize his motorcycle. That could buy gifts for everyone and pay the heating bill," Damon argued.

"Thank goodness Stone is getting a scholarship. He can go to college for free," their father said, sounding somewhat defeated. "I don't like doing this, Damon. But if you could pay the heating bill, I'd really appreciate it."

Stone stepped back from where he was listening and went back to his room to signal for Hunter to follow him before they went and knocked on Olivia's door. "Come in!" she called out.

"Liv," Stone said as he looked at Penelope twirling around in her tutu that Damon had paid for.

"Hey, peanut," Hunter said to Penelope. "We need to talk to Liv."

Stone smiled at the youngest Townsend. "Damon is in the kitchen and I know he would love to see you dance. Can you go show him what you've been working on?"

Penelope ran from the room, eager to show off her dance moves. Stone took a seat on the floor and looked up at Olivia. Gone was the gawky pre-teen and in her place was a beautiful young woman who, as a sophomore in high school, got perfect score on her big pre-admission tests and had interest from several colleges.

"Did you two know Damon paid for Penelope's dance lessons?" Stone asked them.

"He did? Why?" Hunter asked before Stone filled them in on the conversation he'd heard.

They were silent until Hunter cleared his throat. He was getting close to making his decision about his own future now that he was a junior in high school. "I already know what I want to do, and it'll help bring some money in for the family."

"I thought you wanted to go to college," Olivia said with a frown as if realizing Hunter was about to say something she wouldn't like.

"That's what's expected of me, but I don't want to. I want to join the military. Just eighteen months and I can give some of the paycheck to the family."

"But college—" Olivia protested.

"Liv," Hunter said gently, "college isn't for everyone like it is for you."

"I can help as soon as I graduate this spring," Stone announced. "I've gotten interest from some minor league hockey teams, which is a big deal since I'm still in high school."

"Like hell. You're going to college." Damon sounded pissed as he stood in the doorway to Liv's room.

"Why?" Stone argued. "The only reason to go to college is to make a name for yourself in hockey. I'm already getting noticed. I can go now and start helping you pay the bills. Bills you've been hiding from us and paying yourself. Let me help." Damon shook his head, but Stone was determined. "I want this, Damon. I don't want to go to college. I just want to play hockey."

"Hockey won't last forever. What will you do if you get injured? What will you do if you don't get drafted?" Damon pointed out.

"What if I agree to take classes during the off-season?" Stone blurted out. Right now, he'd say anything to get Damon off his back.

Damon was quiet and then sighed. "You have to swear you'll do it."

"Cross my heart."

. . .

Six months later Stone was off to Boston to play minor league hockey. Damon, Hunter, and Stone had used those six months to work on strength training and endurance. When Stone hit the ice for his first game, everything felt like it clicked into place. He was fast. He was strong. He was smart about plays and he was called up to the big league after just one season.

True to his word, Stone took online college classes in the off-season, but after just one season on the pro team in Boston, his new agent, Finn Williams, got him so many endorsements he didn't have time to finish his degree. He sent money home to pay the bills and sent money to Olivia so she could eat while in college. With Hunter and Damon doing the same, their younger siblings grew up never knowing how rough and lean it had been just a couple of years prior.

Three years later, with a tremendous deal, Finn got Stone a contract in Chicago. There was never a time on the ice when Stone didn't feel as if that was what he was meant to do. Every workout, every hit, every win, and every loss, Stone knew hockey was his one true love.

That was until he got a phone call from Damon saying he thought it was possible that Olivia was being taken advantage of by some billionaire. That was when Stone realized all the work and all the money he'd sent home didn't mean anything when he wasn't also with his family.

He missed Damon. He missed Hunter. He missed Olivia. He missed his whole family, who were now scattered all around the world. It was time to come home, even if home wasn't Upstate New York anymore, but would be in Shadows Landing, South Carolina now.

"Finn," Stone said the second his agent answered the phone. "I know my contract is up this year. Get me on the Charleston team."

"Charleston?" Finn was not expecting that. "Why would you go from a top-ranked team to a much lesser ranked team? A team I'm hearing rumors might go up for sale in the next year?"

"My brother Damon is moving there and my sister Olivia is also there. I want to be near my family, Finn. It's been a decade or more since we've all been together."

Finn gave a shiver over the phone. "Your sister scares the crap out of me. Did you see the press conference where the opposing council started crying?"

He had and Stone couldn't have been prouder. "Make it happen, Finn."

"Stone, if they know you want to go there, they'll lowball an offer," Finn told him.

"Then we better not let them know. Do whatever, say whatever, and get me to Charleston."

Stone hung up the phone with a sense of peace he'd only found on the ice before. It was time for the Townsends to be together again.

1

Paris, France, six months ago . . .

Natalie's hands shook as she wiped her sweaty palms on the expensive navy-blue gown that hugged her finely tuned body. Her injury was healed, but this wasn't going to be her world much longer. She was ready to move on, even if they weren't ready for her to.

"You don't just get to leave. That's not how it's done," the voice from the shadows of the gala hissed into her ear.

"What are you going to do, arrest me?" she hissed back. Her eyes went to the man in the tuxedo who held the key to her future. Archie Tupper had fallen for her idea hook, line, and sinker. She'd talked to him in London just last week about her father and she'd heard the news today. Her father was out of the KHL, Russia's professional hockey league, and was now the head hockey coach for Archie's new NHL team in Charleston. Her father was on a plane over the Atlantic as they spoke.

"Your father—"

"My father is never setting foot back in Russia again. I'm retired. I'm out."

"You're not out until I tell you you're out," the voice from the shadows snapped.

"Watch me," Natalie challenged. It was a risk, but if she had nothing to offer, he'd finally let her go. "I'm moving to the States. I'm retired and will no longer be in Europe."

The shadow was quiet for a moment. "For now, I'll allow it. But only if you deliver tonight. You know what your target is. Now go get it for me, then we'll see about a vacation."

Natalie snagged a glass of champagne from a waiter and began to move through the crowded gala at the mansion belonging to the owner of a large vineyard. It was packed to the roof with ballet dancers, directors, and who's who of the socialite charity scene.

The directions had been whispered to her in the shadows. Second floor, corner room. All she had to do was find a file on the computer, take a photo of its contents, and leave unnoticed. Natalie stumbled on the bottom stair and spilled her drink on herself. She kept her head down and muttered as she walked up the stairs and located the room.

The door was locked. The hallway was busy with people drinking, laughing, and schmoozing. Natalie plucked a tool she'd been given from her ballerina bun and had the door unlocked in seconds.

A large computer sat on a desk that had to be worth tens of thousands of dollars. The wood was so ornate that it was a work of art. Natalie rushed over to it and entered the password she'd been given. She had no idea how they'd gotten the password, but it worked. The computer came to life. Natalie took a deep breath to stay focused. She had work to do and she couldn't let fear or nerves get in the way.

The file was easy to locate thanks to the incredibly

well-organized computer. That made her job easier. She took the photos, uploaded them on the secure link she'd been given, and then deleted them from her phone. She was about to rush from the room when a file caught her eye.

Her hand was surprisingly steady as she slowly moved the mouse and clicked it open. Names, figures, and items filled the spreadsheet. Some of the names were known to her. Others weren't. She glanced around the room before reaching into her bag and pulling out a compact. She opened it and lifted the powder case to expose a small thumb drive. This was the backup if there had been no cell reception. It was riskier since she could be caught with it on her person, but that didn't stop her now as she slipped it into the computer and copied the folder onto it before popping it back out and turning the computer screen off. Natalie thought about putting it into the compact, but stopped at the last minute when she heard voices in the hall growing closer. She grabbed a box of tissues and hurried to the large mirror in the room.

The door opened and she casually looked to see two security guards looking around. "Can I help you?" she said imperiously, her full diva attitude in place.

"This is a private, locked room. You need to come with us."

Natalie didn't even blink. She turned back to the mirror and held up her compact to apply her makeup. "First, I don't have to do anything. Don't you know who I am? Second, the door wasn't locked. In fact, it was open. Which is why I ducked in here after some handsy drunk spilled champagne on my dress. It's *couture*. Do you have any idea how much it costs?"

"What's going on?" Emile Lavigne, the owner of the

mansion and host of the event, asked his security guards in French.

"These men won't let me clean up after some asshole spilled his drink on me," Natalie replied in flawless French.

"You're not supposed to be in here," Mr. Lavigne said seriously, switching to English. He was around five foot eight with thinning blond hair and was dressed in a suit that made her dress look like rags.

Natalie rolled her eyes and turned back to the mirror to finish with her powder before pulling out her lip gloss. "Then don't leave the door open."

"The door was open?" Mr. Lavigne asked it casually, but there was nothing casual about it.

"How else would I get in here? I mean, it's a nice office and all, but it's nothing special." Natalie blotted her lip gloss and turned to him. "How does that look? You can't tell I had champagne spilled all over me, can you?"

"You look as breathtaking as you did when you played Giselle. But, to satisfy an old man," he said, putting his hand over his heart, "will you let my security search you?"

She raised an eyebrow. "That's a new one. Let me guess, they'll grab my breasts, and you'll get off by watching. I swear, I am so glad I'm retiring."

"You wound me. I would never take advantage. There's just sensitive information in my office that competitors would love to get their hands on."

Natalie snorted. "You think some wine competitor hired me to steal the secret recipe?" She held up her arms and laughed. "Go ahead. Search me."

One guard took her purse. He emptied it. He opened everything, including the now empty hidden space of her compact. The other guard patted her down, but froze when he reached her breasts. Natalie rolled her eyes. He cleared his throat and made a move to feel her up.

"Unlock your phone, please," the other guard who had just searched her purse asked. Natalie unlocked it and then reached to the side of her breasts where her strapless gown clung. She pulled the gown down to her stomach.

"Happy?" She felt violated as she let the three men stare at her breasts, but it worked.

Mr. Lavigne cleared his throat. "That's not necessary. You may get dressed."

"Thank you. I told you the door was open. If you want to question anyone, question the guy who left a moment before I got here." She resettled the gown in place, snagged her purse and held out her hand for her phone.

"It's clear," the man told Mr. Lavigne in French. With a nod of his head, the phone was placed back into her hand.

"What man?" Mr. Lavigne asked.

"Hmm?"

"What man?" he repeated.

"Oh, about five foot ten or eleven with dark hair and wearing a tux. I didn't see his face. He walked out of the room and straight down the stairs back there. He looked like these guys," Natalie said, motioning to the two guards who both matched the made-up description.

"I'm sure one of my men just forgot to shut the door when he was doing rounds. I am sorry for accusing you, Miss Novak. I beg your forgiveness. Please, enjoy the rest of the gala knowing you look breathtaking. Martin will take you to get one of my private label champagnes as an apology for your trouble." Lavigne gestured to one of the security men.

Martin would be doing more than that. He'd be keeping

an eye on her for the rest of the night. "Oh, not the private label that Blaze is the spokesperson for?"

"Yes, the very one."

"OMG! I'd love to try it, but can you get me Blaze, too?" She giggled as Martin escorted her away as she chattered about the Hollywood hunk.

The champagne was excellent and worth almost being caught. For the next two hours she circulated, networked, and fended off handsy men. Martin even had to step in once. She thanked him and flitted away. Finally, she could leave without suspicion. If they had found anything they'd have grabbed her. But she was good and always overlooked. Apparently, everyone just assumed there was nothing in a ballerina's head but tutus.

Natalie was done. She was out. She didn't care if they thought she was bluffing. She was retired from ballet and done with these shadow games.

When she got home, she unwound her hair and shook it out. The thumb drive fell to the floor and she hid it someplace no one would ever find it before she began looking for buildings in Charleston, South Carolina to buy for her future.

Natalie Novak walked the length of the mezzanine observation level she had installed in her new sports academy, N2 Sports Training, in Charleston. She had a soft opening a month ago, but it was already filling up with classes. She had put out the word and it had worked the old-fashioned way—word of mouth.

Natalie looked down through the glass ceilings of the various rooms from dance classes, to weight lifting, to speed drills, to a half court for basketball, to a half court for tennis, and a small indoor field for soccer and football drills. The building was a cavernous industrial building close to Faulkner Shipping on the edge of the city and had all the room she needed for multiple sports.

Each room varied in size, but was self-contained. The tempered glass ceilings gave the parents and coaches a place to observe without trying to cram into the hallways below. Up a level there were more rooms for private lessons. There were no observation areas inside them, but they mirrored the rooms below. Some were dance, some were training, but most were for therapy and rehabilitation. Natalie had installed an elevator so she could optimize the space on the top floor.

"Nat." Natalie turned at the sound of her father's voice and smiled as he walked toward her. His hair dared not show any of the gray he should probably have now that he was fifty-five years old. Instead, he looked like one of the hockey players he coached.

"Hey, Dad. Coming by to take a yoga class for athletes?"

Her father tried not to roll his eyes. He understood her mission—to use cross-training to help form an all-around elite athlete, but he still didn't get how dance or yoga could help his hockey team, even after the Russians relied on it in their training of young players.

"No. I wanted to give you a ticket to tomorrow's game. You haven't come to one yet." Natalie knew she'd promised to come to support him, but she'd been so busy she hadn't made a game yet.

"Thanks, Dad. I'll make it this time. I promise."

"Did the last of your certifications come in?" her father asked instead of pushing the fact that she'd not attended a game yet.

"They did. Working with the Paris doctors for the ballet company this past year really helped show me how to use the training in the real world." Natalie couldn't be prouder. Any training, physical therapy, or rehabilitation certifications she'd needed, she'd gotten. She had them in everything from weightlifting to Pilates to yoga and literally everything in between, including therapy and rehab. She was trained in the old tried and true methods as well as the most current and cutting-edge methods. "I can't wait to start getting more serious athletes here to train."

The little kids taking dance were great and paid the bills, but her heart was teaching free ballet classes on the weekend and working with elite athletes to really unlock their true talents. Elite athletes, as she'd been, had natural athletic ability that spanned more than one sport. She'd found when she trained them in other areas their natural talent seemed to adjust, grow, and then they unlocked the next level of their career. Those tiny muscles you worked in Pilates helped players avoid injuries and improved their footwork in football.

Her father smiled. "See. Aren't you glad I made you get your degree while you were dancing? Even if I had to listen to all those years of moaning and groaning about it," her father teased, but Nat knew he was incredibly proud of her.

She hugged her tough-as-nails dad and enjoyed seeing the fatherly side of him. "I am very happy you made me do it." It hadn't been easy. She was principal ballerina in London while working on a physical therapy degree with an emphasis on sports rehabilitation.

Natalie had found her interest in this area of practice when her best friend had been injured and had to leave ballet forever. Over the years of being an elite athlete, Nat had learned a lot about sports medicine, injuries, and rehab.

At this point, she probably knew as much as most doctors. She lived it. She feared it. She breathed it.

She'd been pushed to the max physically and mentally as a prima ballerina. Then, as her thirtieth birthday approached and those "prime" years were fading, she began to look to the future. Natalie had suffered a tibia fracture, not at all uncommon with all the leaping she did. The injury forced her to look to a future that didn't include ballet. So, she'd gotten her master's even while she was spending hours a day rehabbing. When she'd gotten the all-clear to return to ballet, she decided not to.

Instead, Natalie used the injury as an excuse to leave ballet when everyone was telling her she still had one or two good years left. Yes, technically, she did. But now she had decades of good years ahead of her. She was tired of the demands made on her as a prima ballerina. She didn't want to have to fight her way back to the top for maybe one more year of dancing. She was tired of fighting the trainers and the ballet masters too often giving bad advice or telling dancers to just push through the pain and dance. She was tired of the strict diets and the stricter practice sessions. She was also tired of all the extra stuff required of her—the galas, the fundraising, the mingling. To them she was an object, not a person. Now, she could make a difference off the stage. She could help athletes and inspire the next generation by teaching that athletics is for everyone. No shaming, just encouragement and education.

"Well," her father said, looking around at the full rooms below, "I'm really proud of you, Nat. I know you could have started this business somewhere bigger than Charleston, but I love having you close again."

Her father had coached hockey in Russia while she'd been in London. It was hard to get time together when both of their schedules were so demanding. Then, after what she'd been through, she wanted her father close, even if he didn't know about it.

"I love it here. The people are so nice and the food . . . it's a good thing I'm no longer a ballerina, that's all I can say. Plus, we get our weekly dinners together now. We haven't had that since I was a kid."

Her father had been a hockey coach for Russia's biggest professional team. He was a good coach, but then things started to happen to Natalie. The politics began to shift as well and Russia was no longer the location her father needed to be in. Her father would never know, but she had floated the idea of hiring him to the rumored future owner of the Charleston team. She wanted her father out of Russia and this was the best way to do it.

Archie Tupper, the billionaire rumored to have an interest in buying the failing Charleston Gators, just happened to support the Paris Ballet. Natalie met him at one of the many glitzy parties filled with patrons of the arts and the ballet theater. Natalie tracked him down at the gala and casually mentioned how she was going to move to Charleston and how her father was hoping to come back to the States, but she wasn't sure the Russian team would let him go without a fight. Archie had taken it as a challenge. Three months later, it was announced that the Charleston Gators had been sold to Archie Tupper and were going to be known as the Charleston Pirates. Archie used the press conference announcing the revamp to the team to also announce that he'd stolen Russia's best hockey coach.

Her father had moved to Charleston before she had. In fact, he's the one who found her the house she bought just a half mile from her sports complex. That had been during his offseason, but now they were both about to jump into the thick of it. She knew it would be harder to have her weekly dinners and why it was important to make the games.

"How is the team looking this year?" Natalie asked as they made their way downstairs.

She had two new clients lined up for the afternoon. One was a tennis player and the other was a college basketball star who would train with her whenever he was back in town. She'd just talked to his college coach that morning and set out a game plan for his training. It was cutting it closer than she'd like since it was almost October and basketball season started in November. But the player, Terry Clemmons IV, or Quad as he was commonly known, came home most weekends and he also had a fall break coming up. She'd be training him every day he was home and she couldn't wait.

"The team is shaping up. We had a pre-season exhibition game last week and it gave me a good look at who put in the work during the off-season. Townsend is looking good at center. I just need him to shape up off the ice. I wouldn't say he's breaking any rules, but he's not necessarily being careful either." Her father frowned. That usually meant he was upset because he saw promise not being capitalized on.

"You think you can get him to shape up?"

"I do. I've already started working on it. He's going to be named captain ahead of the next game. He has the leadership for it. I just hope that responsibility will make him focus more on the game and less on the bunnies."

"Ah," Nat said with a nod. She knew all about the bunnies. Ballerinas had tutu chasers. She could spot them in a second. When she told them what she did they'd look her over and with a smirk say, "I bet you're flexible," in such a dirty way it made her skin crawl.

"Yeah," her dad said with a sigh. "Townsend is a good guy though. I wish he'd focus less on bunny hunting and more on the game and the team. We'll see what happens when he's made captain for this year. On defense, I brought in two guys from Finland, Elias Laakso and Kalle Aho. They grew up a town apart and have been playing together since they were five years old. They went to separate pro teams, but I got them back together. They're perfect together on the ice. They don't even need to speak to play off each other."

"What about your wings with Townsend?" Natalie asked. The center led the team in faceoffs and directing the plays. The best teams had a good center-wing combo.

"Andrew Kenny, a Canadian, and Theo Larson, a young kid from Minnesota. Kenny is more experienced. He and Townsend fall in pretty well, but I'm actually surprised how well Townsend is taking to Larson. The team likes to give the rookie a tough time, but Townsend takes time to work with him. It's the main reason I'm making him captain should the team vote him in, which they will. I'll be interested to hear what you think after the game."

Natalie smiled at her father. He always asked for her opinion and respected it. He might disagree with it, but he always respected it. "I'm not the professional, but I'll let you know what I think."

"You're not a professional, but you can play, you know the sport, and more importantly, you know what a good athletic partnership looks like. You have to have that with a dance partner."

"True," Natalie said, looking up at the clock. "Sorry, Dad. I have to go. I have a client coming in. I can't wait to see the team." Natalie kissed her father's cheek and walked him out the door right as her client came in.

"Miss Novak?" the thirtyish woman asked. She was in a white tennis skirt, matching tennies, and a hot pink tank top with her brown hair pulled into a ponytail.

"That's right. You must be Rita Babic. Welcome to N2 training. Let's sit in my office for a moment and you can tell me what you're looking for in your training."

Natalie shook Rita's hand and led her to the office. This was it. All she'd been working for. It was time to start making a difference in athletes' lives.

2

Stone laced up his skates in the locker room before the last exhibition game of pre-season. This was the first year the new team owner had everything and everyone in place. The team was bought early in the calendar year while they were still playing at the end of last season, which made the end of last season a bit of a mess. Novak had been named the new coach and had met with players but didn't officially start until this season.

The guys had been pissed at Archie Tupper, the new owner, for pulling that move. It sank their post-season hopes since their old coach completely checked out and the team got nervous as to which of them would be staying and who was going to be traded. Stone had put Finn to work to make sure he stayed in Charleston.

Luckily, Finn said the first time he met Tupper he was told that Stone was staying. However, most of the team was let go or traded during the off-season. This was almost an entirely new group for Stone to gel with. A good team had to have good communication and that didn't happen overnight.

Coach Novak came in as soon as the season was officially over. And while it had technically been the off-season, there had been team-building exercises and workouts non-stop for those players who chose to stay in town and participate. Today Coach was going to announce who would be the captain of the team. Everything from the old team was scrubbed. It didn't matter that Stone started last season. It didn't matter who had been captain. He'd had to prove himself all over again. So far, he'd beaten out Karl Berg, the Swede who was now on the second line.

"Stone," Theo Larson, the kid who had just graduated from the University of Minnesota and was playing wing, whispered. "Do you think I have a shot at starting tonight? Coach started Jensen last game."

"You've had a great week at practice and a good showing in the last game. Just do what we worked on and I bet you can win that starting spot." Stone's thirty years seemed a world away from Larson's twenty-two. Theo reminded Stone of a little brother, and with his big family it was easy for Stone to fall into the big brother role.

Theo took a calming breath and looked over at Anders Jensen as if measuring up his competition. Stone was about to tell the kid to relax a little when the Finnish defense duo, Elias Laakso and Kalle Aho, strutted up in unison. They were inseparable, so much so that most people assumed they were twins. They were both big guys—about thirty pounds heavier than Stone's 200 pounds. Their legs looked like tree trunks and their wide shoulders took down opposing players with ease.

"You play with bunny. Do the good thing?" Elias asked with a grin as Kalle nodded with a similar smirk on his face.

"Good thing, yes?" Elias asked again when Stone blinked in question.

"What the hell are you asking?" Stone had no idea what the good thing was.

"If you did the good thing with the bunny," Nils Olsson, the backup wing from Sweden asked as Karl Berg, also from Sweden, made a gesture that finally cleared it up.

"Sex. We call it having sex." Stone laughed.

The Nordic players all nodded as if Stone were stupid. "Yes, sex is a good thing," Elias said slowly to make sure Stone got it.

"No, I didn't have sex with the puck bunny last night," Stone said, clearing up the conversation for the rest of the Americans in the room who were looking confused.

"I'd take a blowie from a beauty," Canadian third line defender Stewart Reilly said while all the Canadians on the team confirmed this.

"I'm always up for getting laid," Theo added enthusiastically.

"*Mohl bych šoustat*," the new guy from the Czech Republic said. Everyone turned to stare at him with confusion.

A whistle blew and sex talk stopped as Coach Novak strode in with his notebook. "Townsend. Let's go."

Stone stood up as the guys teased him about being called into the coach's office. He flipped them the middle finger as he caught up with the coach in his secondary office inside the locker room.

"Close the door."

Now Stone was starting to worry. Hopefully the puck bunny he'd been in that hot tub with last week wasn't someone's wife. She said she was single, but he'd learned bunnies could bend the truth. "What's up, Coach?"

"I'm starting you again at center. Andrew Kenny will be the starting right wing. I want to know your opinion on left wing. Larson or Jensen?" Coach leaned back in his chair and waited for Stone to answer.

"Well, Jensen has more experience, but he's also set in his ways. I've been working with Larson and we play well off of each other," Stone answered after thinking about it.

"He's young."

"So was I. The only way you'll get better is by playing. Jensen is great. I don't think you can make a wrong choice. However, I think Larson has a lot of untapped talent hidden under his nerves and he's hungry to prove himself. I'd say give him this opportunity. You started Jensen last game. Start Larson, then you can compare tapes and stats."

Stone held his breath. Coach wasn't a warm and fuzzy coach and he wasn't asking because he didn't know what he wanted to do. He was testing Stone and Stone knew it. The question was if he'd pass this little test.

"I agree. My plan was to start Larson tonight. Also,"— Coach reached into a drawer and pulled out a jersey—"don't screw this up."

Stone caught the jersey Coach tossed him. The material was heavier than most sports jerseys and harkened back to when they were called sweaters. Many players and fans still called them sweaters. This jersey was his. When he turned it to see the front, he saw the captain's insignia. He'd been captain before, but Coach Novak put him through the paces to prove himself and damned if Stone didn't feel proud of himself.

"I mean it. Lead on and off the ice, Townsend. Now, go tell Larson he's starting and Jensen that he's not. You're the team leader now. Show me that you can do it."

It was a challenge in a way Stone loved. Novak was tough but not an asshole. He pushed Stone but didn't beat him down. He pushed and challenged, but then let him shine. Tonight, Stone was going to shine.

Natalie stepped into the arena and took a deep breath. Childhood memories of the smell of so many ice rinks rushed back and made her smile. When your father's a hockey coach, it meant you knew how to skate almost before you could walk. The closest she got to the ice now were ice baths after intense workouts. Just smelling the hockey rink made her miss it.

Natalie took a sip of her beer so it wouldn't slosh out and headed down the concrete steps toward the rink. Her seat was in the front row. As she got closer, she saw a row of jerseys with TOWNSEND written across the backs. Apparently, the golden boy had a big cheering section. Half the jerseys in there had his last name on them.

Natalie stopped at the edge of the row and waited for the tall, dark, and brooding man to notice her so she could get by them to where her single seat was located. "Excuse me," she finally said.

"Sorry." The man didn't smile, but he didn't need to. He was handsome without it and when he looked at her it made Natalie suck in her breath. Sure, he was sexy, but there was a hard edge to him that just wasn't Natalie's style.

"Thank you," she said when he stepped out of the way and let her through.

Geez, it was a gauntlet of super sexy, yet very intense, men.

"Pardon me," one of them said with a wink as he reached out to steady her when she wobbled trying to slide past him.

She was almost to her seat when a beautiful woman cut her off and slammed both hands against the glass. "Hey, fifty-nine! Your dangles are limp just like your—"

Natalie's jaw about dropped, but the man next to her cut her off. "Olivia, stop scaring this poor woman trying to make it to her seat. Sorry, ma'am."

The *ma'am* thing should be a turn off, but when those Southern men said it, it worked. "Thank you," she whispered to him, waiting for that Olivia woman to stop pounding on the glass.

"Oh! So sorry. I get a little carried away sometimes," Olivia said with a shrug not looking sorry for one second. Her nails were perfectly manicured and painted red. Her black jeans were designer. Her tennis shoes were *the* shoes to have. But she was drinking beer, cussing, and wearing a Townsend jersey. Just one of the reasons Natalie loved hockey.

"No problem." Natalie took her seat and smiled when her dad caught her eye and winked.

"Hey, number fifty-nine!" That Olivia woman was up again pounding on the glass. "*Le douche de Quebec! Charleston fera pleuvoir des buts!*"

Natalie chuckled. The woman turned to her with a smile. "You speak French?"

"I do. I used to work in Paris. I've never heard an American chirping in French to a Canadian player before. Impressive."

"Well, he's from Quebec. I figured French was the way to go. I'm Olivia."

"Natalie."

"Nice to meet you. We'll chat more later. It's the face-off."

Natalie was pretty sure the guy next to Olivia with the sexy Southern accent crossed himself.

The center, Stone Townsend, lined up across from number fifty-nine. Natalie could see the trash talking from her seat. Face-offs always made her hold her breath. The arena music stopped, the whistle blew, then the puck was dropped. She could hear it hitting the ice along with the clap of the hockey stick slapping the puck. Stone won the face-off, passing to his left wingman and then they were off. It only took a minute for Natalie to see why her father liked Stone Townsend. He was a warrior on the ice. No slacking off. He fought every minute of the game. It was such a sight Natalie didn't even notice the way Olivia was pounding on the glass.

He skated smoothly and with grace even as he hit with power and brute force. She couldn't keep her eyes off Stone Townsend, even though the woman next to her talked as if she knew him. She was probably his wife, although most WAGs, or wives and girlfriends if being formal, were up in the family room. Either way, it was interesting to watch Olivia's multilingual chirps literally throw number fifty-nine off his game. As the game went on, Natalie found herself standing, cheering, and even joining Olivia in a little chirping *en français*. She couldn't remember the last time she had so much fun.

3

It was the final period. Stone was sweating, his breaths came hard as he skated to the face-off, but they were winning, thanks to goals from himself and Theo. The kid had about cried when he scored his first professional goal and Stone felt like a proud parent.

With only minutes left, he stopped before the red circle where he'd face-off against number fifty-nine. Olivia had beaten the guy down to the point he looked ready to throw his stick down and leave the ice.

Stone looked over to where Olivia was shouting in French. His sister was always elegant, but the petite woman next to her, also shouting in French, caught Stone's attention. She carried herself as if she were royalty, even as she chirped. She also couldn't be taller than five foot two. She was a tiny thing, yet she held herself equal to his tall and intimidating sister.

Stone looked over at number fifty-nine as he readied for the face-off. "Oh boy," Stone said, looking surprised. "Your coach actually left you in? Are you sure you should be out here?"

Then the puck dropped and that was all that mattered. Stone slapped the puck to the left and Theo did the rest. Stone shoved fifty-nine and skated past him to open another lane for scoring.

"Theo!" Stone called out when he broke free.

Theo passed the puck, but the opposing team got just enough of their stick on it to send it flying into the boards to Stone's right. Stone immediately changed direction and skated towards the puck as one of the defenders tied up Andrew Kenny, Stone's right wing.

Stone pushed his legs. He felt the muscles bunch and release to his command. All the hours of training and weightlifting paid off as he beat the defender to the boards. Stone could feel the defender closing in on him. He knew he'd be hit against the boards, but it was more important to get the puck out. He used his skate to pry it free from where it leaned against the board and then with a flick of his stick, sent it sliding for Theo right as the defender plowed into him.

The defender hit him from the right side. Hard. The defender's knee slammed into Stone's left inner knee. Stone's knee buckled and bashed into the boards as the defender shoved him against the glass.

The pain was immediate as he went down hard onto the ice. The pain was so quick and intense that he couldn't even scream. All his breath was stolen from his body in a split second.

"Stone!" He heard Olivia yelling from her seat nearby.

"Don't put weight on it!" yelled a voice he didn't know, but he was in too much pain to care where it came from.

He also ignored it and tried to stand up. That didn't work. The pain was so intense he felt like vomiting. Damn. This couldn't be the end of the season. Dr. Bartlett, the team doctor, was there in less than twenty seconds, but it felt like an eternity.

Karl Berg, the second line center went in to warm up as Anders Jensen and Nils Olsson, the second line wingmen, jumped over the boards to come help Stone off the ice. There was no way in hell he was going to be carried off the ice. Stone reached up and grabbed Olsson's hand. "Help me up. I'll skate off," Stone said between clenched teeth.

"Still trying to show off to get the good thing," Olsson said with a laugh, trying to make him feel better. The Swede was perpetually happy.

Jensen put his arm under Stone's other shoulder, but they didn't carry him off.

"We push you like a *lille barn*." And that's what they did. They pushed Stone while he skated off on his right leg as if he were a toddler. The second he was off the ice, the doctor told his teammates to pick him up.

"Shit, shit, shit," Stone cursed as they whisked him under the stands and back to the medical room. "What is it, doc? Can we fix it up and get me back out there?"

Jensen and Olsson shared a look that said they didn't think so, but screw them. Nothing could stop him from playing. "Just bandage it up and let me get back out there," Stone said as his teammates set him on an exam table and then quietly left as Dr. Bartlett, a young hotshot orthopedic doctor with a specialty in sports medicine, began to examine him.

Dr. Bartlett removed Stone's shin pads and socks then cut the leg of his uniform pants enough to expose Stone's knee. "Oh, crap. That's not how it's supposed to look," Stone muttered when he got a good look.

Dr. Bartlett touched the knee and Stone cursed and tried

not to punch the doctor. He really wanted to punch him when Bartlett smiled. "Patellar dislocation."

"My kneecap is out of place," Stone said with a growl. "I can see that. It's on the side of my leg, doc. Pop it back into place and let me get back out there."

"It's not that simple. Well, the popping it back into place is. Let's see what the MRI shows. If your ligaments aren't torn recovery time is considerably shorter. Let's not get caught up in numbers until we have all the results. Now, on the count of three." Stone prepared for the kneecap to be put back in place. "One."

"Dammit!" Stone cursed as the doctor put his kneecap back into place. "You said three!"

"I lied. Now, let's get an X-Ray."

Natalie saw Stone's knee bend in a way it shouldn't the second the defender slammed into Stone. Stone went down hard, but insisted on skating off with help instead of being carried off. She caught her father's worried look, but there was no time for him to check on Stone. He had a game to finish coaching. The team doctor would take care of Stone until her father could assess the situation.

Olivia was freaking out, to say the least. Her entire row cleared out and raced up the arena stairs. Yup, definitely a girlfriend who hadn't been accepted by the wife hierarchy yet to be invited to the wives' room. There was silence followed by clapping as Stone left the arena. Then the music was back on and it was as if nothing had happened.

Her father caught her eye when the buzzer sounded and motioned to the locker room with his head. Natalie nodded and began to make her way through the crowds towards the Pirates' private facilities.

She was stopped by security and then cleared when her father met her there to wave her through. "She always gets through," he told the guard who would make a note of her name in their list.

"How bad is the injury?" Natalie asked as she followed her father into the hallway.

"Dislocated patella. X-ray is clear, but doc wants an MRI to check the ligaments."

"Good. Hopefully it's just the dislocation and your physical therapist can rehab him and he'll be back in a month. Sorry, Dad. I know you hate when your players get injured."

Her father ran his hand over his head and nodded. "I feel so helpless. I just wanted to thank you for coming. But I'm sorry, I won't be able to get dessert tonight. Stone's family took him to the hospital with Dr. Bartlett. I need to go meet them there."

"Of course. It was fun to be back, though. Think you can save me a seat for the season?"

Her dad lit up. "Really?"

"As long as we get dessert afterward like we used to." It was one of her favorite memories from childhood. After every game, it was a father-daughter dessert night, even if it was eleven at night.

"Deal. I'm so glad you're here. I'll talk to you tomorrow." Her father waved down a security guard. "Would you please walk my daughter to her car?"

"Yes, sir."

"Dad," she laughed but didn't fight it. She'd told him she was a grown-up every day since she was thirteen, but it didn't sink in. He always looked out for her. "I love you."

"Love you too, Nat."

Stone had convinced Olivia to let him change into street clothes before she made Granger, her husband, use the sirens of his sheriff's SUV to drive him to the hospital from the arena.

"Oh, goodie. The Townsends are here!" the night nurse said with a big grin as Olivia's arrival sent nurses and doctors scurrying in fear.

"Jen! Thank goodness you're here tonight," Olivia said with a sigh. "Jen, this is my brother Stone."

"I know." Jen winked at him and he winked back, but he also didn't miss the wedding ring on her finger. "We met once when Granger was here. I'm friends with Kenzie Faulkner."

"That's right. Thanks for helping me out tonight, Jen," Stone said even as his knee throbbed. Kenzie was the wife of billionaire Ryker Faulkner, who happened to be one of Olivia's biggest clients. Over the past year, Kenzie and Olivia had become friends too.

"He needs an MRI immediately," Olivia said before introducing Dr. Bartlett.

"Olivia," Jen said kindly. "Dr. Bartlett works here. He knows what Stone needs. Wait here and try not to scare anyone or make them cry. I'll be back as soon as I drop Stone off at radiology and I'll get you into a room." The doors opened and the rest of the Townsends rushed inside. "Well, you know your way to the Faulkner suite. It's the only room large enough for all y'all."

"Yes, I know the way. Stone, be good. Do what Jen says."

Stone rolled his eyes at his sister. "When am I not good?"

Olivia just stared at him. Quite frankly, he was too sore and too worried about his career to get into the kind of trouble Olivia was accusing him of.

"Right this way, Stone. That glamorous MRI machine will just oil herself when she gets a look at your sexy leg." Stone laughed at Jen and Dr. Bartlett shook his head as they took off to get the MRI.

The MRI seemed to take forever. Luckily, they didn't need to wait too long for radiology to read it. Dr. Bartlett had stood over the radiologist's shoulder the entire time before Jen wheeled him back to the Faulkner Suite, so named after Ryker had donated an obscene amount of money to the hospital.

He could hear his family from down the hall. "Want me to help you into bed?" Jen whispered, causing him to laugh. He knew she was playing with him, and it was actually fun.

"Only you could get me into bed tonight, Jen."

"Good, because we're going to get kinky after I get you into bed. I'm going to tie you up and strap you down."

"Wait, what?" Stone wasn't laughing anymore as Jen wheeled him into the room.

Stone didn't have time to ask what she meant because he was swamped by his family and coaching staff. Hell, even Coach Novak was here.

Jen put her fingers to her lips and blew a sharp whistle. "I need to get Studly J. Muffin here into bed and do some nursing. Everyone out. Dr. Bartlett will come in and talk to those Stone wants in here at that time."

Olivia began to argue and Jen shook her head. "I have to strip your brother naked and I know for a fact he's not wearing underwear."

Stone had to duck his head to hide his smile. He was wearing underwear, but Olivia didn't need to know that. He needed a moment to compose himself anyway. The room cleared and Stone took a deep breath. "Thanks for that."

"Don't thank me yet," Jen said as she helped him into bed. "I do need you to take off your pants."

"Just like all the others. You're only trying to get into my pants. I'm disappointed in you, Jen," Stone said with a sad shake of his head as he pulled down the pants he'd worn during the game.

Jen left the room for just a moment and came back with a pair of scrub bottoms that had one leg cut off and a contraption he knew. It was a leg immobilizer. "Now, let's get kinky."

Jen had just finished getting his leg strapped into the torture device before Dr. Bartlett came in. "You know I have to share the results with the team. Do you want them in here or should I talk to them separately?"

"Just bring them all in. Won't do any good trying to keep the team or my family out."

Stone's heart began to race as he waited for his family and the coaches to come back into the room. His palms were sweaty, and suddenly it felt as if he'd eaten rocks from the way his stomach felt heavy with fear. He didn't want to hear *career ending*.

"Give it to me, doc," Stone ordered the second everyone was inside the room.

"Patellar dislocation with no injury to the ligaments."

Everyone sighed with relief. His head swam with it as he took several deep breaths. "Okay, what does that mean? Surgery?"

Dr. Bartlett smiled and Stone knew then it wasn't that bad. "No surgery. I want your leg immobile for a week. Then I'll re-examine you to see if you can begin PT. We'll strengthen those ligaments and muscles to keep your patella from dislocating again."

"Stone," Coach Novak said, "I'm glad it's nothing too serious. Now, doc, what time frame are we looking at before Stone is one hundred percent on the ice again?"

Coach took the words out of Stone's mouth. That's what he wanted to know too.

"Depends on therapy. Could be as long as six to eight weeks or as short as three to four."

"I want bi-weekly updates then. And Stone, I expect you at practices. You're still the captain after all," Coach told him.

That was another huge relief. "Of course. Thanks for checking on me, Coach."

"I'll send over a physical therapist from the hospital who works in sports therapy with me next week, provided our checkup goes well. She can work with Stone at the arena after practices," Dr. Bartlett told them. "I'll give your sister your care instructions."

"No. Give them to me," Damon said, holding out his hand. "He'll be staying with me while he recovers."

Dr. Bartlett handed over a pack of papers, gave verbal instruction, and then turned back to Stone. "You're free to go home. See you at practice in a couple of days."

Doc left and then the coaches did too after patting him on the shoulder. "Come on, let's get you home before the rest of the nurses get over their fear of Olivia and rush in to throw themselves at you," Jen said, coming back into the room with the wheelchair and a set of crutches. She handed the crutches to Damon. "If he acts up, you can hit him with these."

Damon's lips twitched with amusement as Jen helped Stone into the wheelchair. Olivia and her husband said their goodbyes and promised to check in on him the next day. Then the rest of his brothers left so it was just Damon and Jen to escort him out of the hospital.

"I have to admit. I'm disappointed," Jen said before a dramatic sigh.

"About what?" Stone asked. "You did get to see me in my underwear."

"That was not a disappointment. The disappointment was your sister. She didn't make a single person cry this time. I think marriage is making her soft."

Stone heard Damon choke on his laughter. Too bad Jen was taken. She would fit into their family perfectly. Kind of like how that sexy woman who had been in the seat next to Olivia would fit perfectly in his arms.

4

"I hope you can take that blasted thing off your leg and get back to your own house," Damon grumbled as they sat in one of the treatment rooms in the arena. "Seven days of you is enough."

"I love you too, brother," Stone said sweetly.

They'd played video games and Stone had worked out his upper body in Damon's gym while Damon squawked like a mother hen, constantly fussing that Stone was going to hurt himself again.

It had been a massive disappointment when his knee was still too inflamed to take off the brace two days ago. Doc had ordered two more days of immobility. That was two more days Stone had to wait to get back on the ice and he hated every single second of it.

Damon had driven Stone to every practice and sat through them with him before driving him back home. It was really above and beyond what any brother needed to do, but that was Damon.

"Seriously," Stone said after Damon scoffed. "I love you.

Thanks for taking care of me. I know I am taking up a ton of time when you should be working."

Damon grunted. It was the most he'd acknowledge his feelings. He wasn't a touchy-feely kind of guy. He was a grunt-and-nod kind of guy.

The door to the room opened before Stone could tease Damon about those pesky emotions. Dr. Bartlett strode in wearing a Charleston Pirates polo. "How are you feeling today, Stone?"

"Like I want to burn this contraption and get out on the ice."

Dr. Bartlett sat down on the stool and rolled up to where Stone was sitting. Stone's leg was straight out in front of him with his other bent at the knee. Dr. Bartlett began the long process of taking the immobilizer off as he talked about what he hoped to find.

The relief of having the immobilizer off felt so good. Fresh air was an underrated joy as it blew across Stone's leg, sour smelling from the sweat that had been trapped under the brace.

"This is looking much better, Stone." Dr. Bartlett poked, prodded, bent and twisted his leg as he murmured to himself. Finally, he set down the leg and smiled. "You can start physical therapy tomorrow morning at ten. I want you to wear the brace while you sleep for one more week. Then you can ditch it completely. I want you in therapy every day before or after practice. I have a great therapist who will meet you in the gym tomorrow and you two can set up your schedules." Dr. Bartlett stood and held out his hand. "Good luck in rehab. I'll continue to check on your progress. I want three weeks before we even start talking about playing in a game, so don't ask. Just follow your therapist's orders to a T and you'll be back on the ice in no time."

"Thanks, doc." Stone was so relieved. Three more weeks. He'd work hard and be out on the ice before he lost his starting position to Karl.

"That's great news. Are you going to go to the game tonight?" Damon asked as he glanced at his watch. The game was starting in an hour.

"I am. Leave me here. I can crash at Wilder's condo in town tonight so I can get here for PT in the morning. I'll have one of the guys take me to Wilder's after the game," Stone said of their younger brother. Wilder owned a chain of nightclubs all around the world, using his initials as the name WET. He was currently visiting one in London.

Damon nodded. "Straight after the game. No night out drinking."

"Yes, *Dad*," Stone said sarcastically even though he'd been thinking of doing just that.

Damon grunted but left. Stone took a deep breath and picked up his crutches. He might be sitting the bench, but he'd look good doing it. He had a spare suit here at the arena and the game was going to start soon.

It felt strange sitting on the bench in a suit and not in his gear. Stone didn't like it at all. He wanted to be exhausted. He wanted to be sweaty. He wanted to be pushed to his limits. Now he was just sitting at the end of the bench, cheering on his team. But he was captain and that's what captains did. They supported and led by example.

So, he cheered, helped coach, and made himself useful. That was until he glanced across the rink and saw the now empty row his siblings usually sat in. His eyes connected with the woman from the last home game who had been sitting next to his sister. He'd been in so much pain and fear over his future that Stone forgot to ask Olivia about her.

She gave him a little smile and a nod of her chin before her attention went back to the game. She looked like a million bucks in an understated way the puck bunnies never had. It wasn't the clothes. She was in a Pirates T-shirt with a leather jacket over it. It was the way she held herself. The way she appeared to be six feet tall when she was short enough for him to tuck under his arm. It was the way she wasn't bothered by the fact she appeared to be sitting at a game alone. Or the way the guy slightly behind her was trying to get her attention and she wasn't giving it to him.

The goal sounded and Stone's team cheered all around him, but his eyes were on that sprite of a goddess who was clapping and cheering, and not his team. That is, until Theo beamed with pride as he came into the box. "I can't believe I got another goal."

"You're doing great, kid." Stone forced his attention from the woman and went back to being the captain. He talked through some questions Theo had on plays and then Theo was back on the ice. What Stone would give to be out there with him.

Going to bars after games was not as popular as it had been. Social media had killed that for many of the more serious players who were concerned over their images. But, the private VIP section of WET? That worked. It was reserved for them after every home game.

What wasn't cool was being the only guy who had to take the elevator up to it. Once inside he was part of the team again. Wilder had set out several different VIP levels. The first was closest to the dance floor and was the place to be seen. There was a second VIP area on the second floor that was open. Meaning, there were no windows separating them from the people below. You could be seen, but with only a glass railing separating you from the dance floor below, you felt very much a part of the club. Then the third VIP area was where the Pirates were. It was across from the open VIP area and above the bar on the left side of the building. There was a small secret staircase that took servers straight to the bar to get drinks and bottles immediately to the VIPs. Also, while the second VIP room was open, this one was not. You could slide open the glass walls to make it open, or you could keep the reflective glass closed for privacy. There was even a third option. With a press of a button, you could lower the privacy mesh so you could enjoy the music and atmosphere with the glass open, yet still be completely private, which was what the guys chose to do tonight.

Music pumped into the VIP room as the players clinked glasses, talked, and drank. A couple of wives were there, but it was mostly the puck bunnies the single guys had invited up. And sometimes the not-so-single guys. The wives who were here were held to a strict code of silence. Meaning, if word leaked, their husbands would feel the wrath of it. Stone didn't approve of cheating, but monitoring the sex lives of his team wasn't something he felt comfortable doing. It was sadly a part of being with a pro-athlete. Some men had stronger personal values than others. Stone knew when he found a woman he wanted to be with, no puck bunny antics would ever change that.

"How's the knee, bud?" Andrew Kenny, his right wing asked, handing him a beer.

"Starting physical therapy tomorrow."

"Good. Karl is great and all, but you're my bud, eh?"

Andrew looked down at his phone when an alert went off. Stone felt his vibrate in his pocket. Most of the guys similarly looked down at their phones. "What the hell?"

"What is it?" Stone asked as he fished out his phone. Stone put his fingers to his lips and whistled. "Team members and wives only. If you don't play for the Pirates, leave now!"

The guys were all murmuring. Pouting puck bunnies were completely forgotten as the room was emptied to the players and the two wives who were there. The VIP hostess closed the windows and left the room in muted silence.

"What the hell is this?" Karl asked Stone. "Did you know about it?"

Stone shook his head. "I had no idea." He started down at the news release stating that Igor Belov, a Russian defenseman with a bad reputation, had just been traded to the Pirates.

"You're the captain," Karl said and then followed it with a Swedish curse that the rest of the Swedes nodded in agreement to. "Tell Coach we don't want him here."

"I heard he took off his skate and used it to hit his teammate in the locker room," Theo said quietly and clearly intimidated by hockey's most famous troublemaker for his antics on and off the ice.

"That's after he hit the Seattle player so hard he was out for the season. The guy didn't even have the puck." Andrew shook his head. Yes, hockey was aggressive, but that didn't mean they approved of dirty hits.

"He's slept with half the wives, eh? That's not a good teammate," goalie Dan Jones said as he pulled his wife closer to his side as if to protect her.

"The wives know all about him. His wife comes in and destroys the wives' club. She goes after the men just like he goes after the women. It's as if they try to create as much chaos as possible, yet they are always invited places and people bow down to them out of fear," Ellen Berg, Karl's wife, told them. Several of the married men began to look even more nervous. Wives held them together. They ran their lives so they could play hockey. Wives took care of moving when you were traded, took care of the children, the house, basically everything. Unhappy wives were worse than curses.

"Doors are always open because he's also the best defensive player in the league," third line defender Stewart Reilly said. Everyone cast a sympathetic look at the two Finish defensive players, Elias Laakso and Kalle Aho. One of them was about to be demoted.

"Excuse me." Stone pushed onto his crutches as he made for the private hallway that would lead him downstairs. He pushed open the door and dialed a number he never thought he'd dial. "Coach, it's Townsend. We have a problem."

"I do, too," Coach Novak said, sounding tired. "Is yours also a six-foot, four-inch two-hundred-fifty-pound Russian?"

Stone was a little surprised the coach actually said anything. He figured Novak would be the silent type. "It is. I'm with the guys. No one wants him here. They're afraid he'll tear the team apart from the inside. Why'd you take in him?"

"I didn't. Archie Tupper did. I can't overrule the owner of the team. Tell the men nothing is decided and as of right now the starting lineup does not change. You're the captain, and I'm throwing you to the wolves. Or wolf in this case. Look, Belov played under me in Russia when he was starting out. He knows I don't tolerate bad behavior. I have a call into Tupper. I didn't even get a heads-up. I found out just now. I know I shouldn't be telling you this, but in a way we're in this together. I need you calm, cool, and collected with the guys. Try to keep them calm until I figure out what the hell is going on." Novak sighed and the anger Stone had toward him for bringing Belov to the team dissipated.

"Thanks for being honest, Coach. I won't tell the guys anything except what they need to hear."

"There's a lot to being captain on one of my teams, Stone," Novak told him. "It's a two-way street between us. I need to know player problems before they're even a problem, and I need the guys to know they can go to you as well. You're not just a leader on the ice but off it, too."

"I won't let you down, Coach."

"Good, now get to bed. You have to rehab that knee in the morning."

Stone chuckled. It was only midnight. He wouldn't be going to bed any time soon. He had a team to settle down before he even thought about going home.

5

"It's so great to meet you. My name is Lulu. It might mean bunny, but don't be fooled. I'm stronger than I look, but I can also be cute and cuddly. Now, I can't wait to get my hands on you." Lulu looked like she might be twenty. She was tall and clearly athletic. She wore the in-style leggings and a crop top that was also a bra he saw women wearing for workouts. Her super blonde hair was in a high ponytail and she was way too perky. Sometimes fate played with you, but this time fate was waving a giant red flag in front of him.

"And you're a physical therapist who works with Dr. Bartlett?" Stone asked, slightly afraid to go near her. She was practically bouncing with energy.

"I'm one of them. Now, let's get to work. Hop up on this table so I can get a feel for you."

"I was kind of envisioning a big guy named Fred," Stone mumbled as he got on the table and leaned his crutches against the head of it in case he needed to make a quick getaway.

"Oh, that's silly. I know you had requested your trainer

work with you, but I am a physical therapist. Now, let's start with some stretching."

Stone nodded, but Lulu pushed him down and hopped on the table. "What are you doing?"

"Stretching you." Lulu took one leg and rested it on her shoulder and then leaned forward. Yes, this was a stretch, but Stone was more than a bit uncomfortable with her breasts holding up his leg as she leaned forward over him and looked him in the eyes. "You're so strong."

"Um, thanks." No, she was a professional. He needed to relax and focus on his rehab.

Twenty minutes later, Stone was not focused on his workout. His knee was throbbing and then there was Lulu. Lulu was batting her lashes and making sure she was touching him the entire time.

The door opened, and if his knee wasn't killing him, Stone would have leaped away as if he were a teenage boy caught with his hand up a girl's shirt. "Coach!"

Coach Novak must have seen the panic in Stone's eyes as his own eyes went down to where Lulu was on her knees with her face near his waist as she rubbed his quad under his workout shorts. While it was technically part of her job, the look, the location, and the unsaid suggestions all hinted at flirtation that Stone had done everything he could to make clear was not welcome.

"I need a word with Stone." Coach held open the door, the meaning clear. Lulu smiled and promised to hurry back before leaving. "What was that?"

"Her name is Lulu. She told me it means bunny. She's doing her job, but . . ."

"Yeah, your butt." Coach rolled his eyes. "You have the

right to choose your own therapist. Doc said his veteran therapist is out sick, so he sent this one. If Lulu doesn't work for you, I actually have someone I know would do a great job. Have you heard of N2 Sports Training?"

Stone knew that name. Why did he know that name? "Oh! Yeah, Quad Clemmons told me about it."

Coach looked at him strangely. "How do you know the top college player in the country?"

"He's from Shadows Landing. That's where I live."

"Oh. Well, ask him about it. I can get you set up for this afternoon if you want to go in and see what you think of it."

Stone sent a quick text to Quad and the response was instant and full of praise for the owner. "Okay, I'm in. Thanks, Coach."

Coach Novak paused and glanced at the closed door. "I'm surprised. I thought Lulu would be just your type."

So did Stone. The trouble was, it wasn't Lulu or any other kind of bunny that was getting his attention. It was the petite, elegant woman from the rink who haunted his every thought. He'd even contemplated going into the office to see who had that seat.

Stone shrugged. "Maybe off the ice, but not with my rehab. And maybe I'm a changed man."

Coach busted out laughing. "You? A changed man? What, do you want to settle down and have some kids now?" Coach laughed so hard that Stone was slightly insulted. Sure, he hadn't had a serious relationship since he came to South Carolina, but that didn't mean he *couldn't*. He just hasn't wanted to. Then, seeing the woman next to Olivia had changed how he looked at the women around him. He didn't want a superficial attraction or fling—it wasn't enough for him anymore. There was just something about her that demanded he do better, be better.

"I don't know about that, Coach. Let's just say my standards are a little higher now." As soon as Stone said it, he realized the truth in it. It had been fun having women throwing themselves at him, but they didn't care about him. They only wanted the conquest of a pro-athlete.

Coach stopped laughing and actually looked at him with approval. "Look at you becoming a leader on and off the ice. I took the team's worries to Tupper. He didn't care. He wants Belov on the team. He thinks it will be good publicity, even if Belov goes off the rails. It's your job to keep everyone else on track when Belov crashes and burns. Are you up for it?"

Stone cursed. He didn't want to do this. The team was just starting to gel and Belov was going to throw everything into chaos. "I don't think I have a choice if I want to keep this team from falling apart."

Novak looked thoughtful for a moment as if he wanted to say something, but wasn't sure he should. "Stone, what's your plan for after hockey?"

"After? I don't know for sure. My agent has been lining up endorsements like crazy so I can just retire, but I think I would get bored. I had thought about broadcasting, but I'm not really excited about that."

"Have you thought about coaching? I've been watching you with Theo. You're good."

"Me? A coach?" Stone chuckled. "I'm the example coaches hold up as don't be like this off the ice."

"Hmm. We'll see. You have a lot of good years left as a player though. Now, I want to ask your opinion on Belov. Tell me what you think of him and how he'd fit into the team."

Stone had been doing nothing but that since he read that Belov was coming. "Honestly, I'd put him at third line instead of first. He'll throw a fit—a big one. But he's got to prove himself as a teammate first. The trouble is, he's damn good. But his attitude is all wrong. If we can fix the attitude and get him to actually play as part of the team, he can earn the starting spot."

Coach nodded as if he were mulling over what Stone suggested. "It's an idea. I'll let you know about your appointment at N2. In the meantime, I'll send Lulu away because you have to go meet Belov. He's going to be arriving in fifteen minutes."

Natalie was working with Rita on strengthening her back to help with her tennis swing when Natalie's watch silently vibrated, letting her know she had a call coming in. She glanced at it and saw it was her father.

"Do you need to get that?" Rita asked.

"It's just my dad. I can call him back in five minutes when we're done. I want to finish with some stretches."

"That's nice that you and your dad are so close. He's the new hockey coach, right?"

Natalie nodded as she helped move Rita's arm to really work on stretching her shoulders and back out. "He is."

"I bet he's had to do a lot of traveling. Tennis makes you move around for tournaments, but you can be based out of one location. Being a coach means you're always on the move to better teams as you work your way up the ladder. Did you have to move a lot?" Rita asked.

"Not with Dad. When he started to move a lot, I went and lived with my mom. Then I moved around some as a ballerina."

"That's so cool. How did you end up in Charleston?" Rita asked as she grimaced when she deepened the stretch.

"My dad was in Russia—"

"Russia!"

Natalie nodded and moved to stretch Rita's other arm. "Yes, he coached there for four years while I was in London with the ballet."

"What is Russia like? I've been to London and Paris, but never Russia."

"Cold," Natalie laughed. She didn't like talking about Russia. It didn't hold good memories for her. "Okay, you're all set. I'll see you in two days?"

Rita rolled her shoulders and smiled. "Yes, thank you. I can't believe how much better I feel after just four sessions."

"That's great. I'm glad I can help. You'll crush your tournament next month."

Rita left and Natalie went to her office to call her father back. He answered on the first ring and sounded stressed. "Is everything okay, Dad?"

"I assume you saw that Belov is coming today?"

"Yeah. I'm sorry, Dad." There was more history there than anyone knew. He'd been a rookie under her father in Russia. Her father held little respect for Belov and Belov held none for her father. Her father dared tell the golden boy what to do—you know, he tried to coach him. Belov didn't want to be coached. He wanted to be God. "I don't know why Archie would do this."

"He thought I would love it since Belov played for me my first year in Russia. Too bad he didn't ask me first." Her father sounded tired and she didn't like that. He was so excited for this season and then Stone Townsend gets hurt and now this.

"Can I help?"

"Actually, that's why I'm calling," her father told her. "Stone Townsend needs therapy. He didn't mesh with the therapist from the hospital. I was hoping you'd see him this afternoon. Kind of an audition for you both since I know you're the one person who won't fall head over heels for him simply because he's a hockey player and he needs to see if you'd fit his style."

Natalie froze as if being caught sneaking into her room after curfew. She'd been watching Stone Townsend on the ice way too closely. If he didn't have a girlfriend, she'd be all over him if she ran into him off the ice. But it wasn't because he was a hockey player. She had to admit the first thing that caught her eye was his good looks, but then she'd watched him at the games. He was the first to give pucks and swag to little kids. He took silly photos with them and never seemed impatient with them. She also saw the way he worked with the players on his team. He led through example, not fear or ridicule. They teased, but he was always the first to lift them up after a bad play. Then there was that intensity on the ice. She had wondered what it would be like to have that intensity focused on her.

"Of course, Dad. I'm happy to help. Can I see the order for his therapy?" Natalie asked as she moved to her calendar to see when she could fit him in.

"I'll send everything over with him. When can you see him?"

"How's three to five? We can do a full evaluation if we both rub along well." Natalie froze, glad her dad couldn't see her blush. She'd love to rub along Stone, but he was two things: Taken and a patient.

"Great. I'll let him know. Thanks, honey."

"Good luck with Belov, Dad."

Her dad grunted and hung up. Natalie went to work researching patellar dislocations and already had a treatment plan in place by the time Stone arrived.

6

Igor Belov was an asshole. He was self-centered, arrogant, and rude. He loved to use his height as a way to intimidate people. Too bad Stone didn't get intimidated. By anyone. That's what happened when you grew up with Damon and Hunter as brothers. They didn't posture. They didn't threaten. They didn't warn you. They simply threw the punch and knocked you on your ass. Stone learned to hold his own at a very early age and he enjoyed the look of irritation Belov had when he couldn't get Stone to bow down to him when he strode into the locker room. As a result, the rest of the team didn't bow down either.

Stone could tell that bothered Igor, which led to more posturing. A fight almost erupted when Igor kicked out Stone's crutch and the team bolted up from the bench in front of their lockers to defend Stone. What Igor didn't know was that Stone could defend himself, even when on crutches. Igor learned that after taking a crutch to the gut.

Igor went down hard. The team all skidded to a stop as Theo handed Stone the crutch Igor had knocked from him. Stone moved to stand over Igor, who was cursing in Russian between gasps of breath. "There are rules you need to learn, Igor," Stone had said calmly. "First, you don't mess with me and you don't mess with my team. Second, you are a part of the team. This is not the Charleston Igors. Be a good teammate. Third, don't be an asshole and sleep with the wives and girlfriends. Let's work on those three first, then we'll get to the others. Practice is over, boys. I'll see you all tomorrow."

Stone strode out as much as was possible on crutches to where the trainer was waiting to drive him to N2. Damon was going to pick him up after the session to take him back to Shadows Landing. Stone had knitting club tonight and wasn't going to miss it. He was almost done with a hat that was going to be a Christmas present for Olivia.

N2 was an industrial building about a mile from Ryker Faulkner's shipping yard. From the outside, it didn't look like anything special. Although, the flowers in the planters set it apart from the other industrial buildings.

However, once inside, Stone was impressed. State-of-the-art flooring for athletic training was on the ground. There was a pair of ballet pointe shoes hanging over the front door as if they were a horseshoe for good luck. They must train dancers because there were some spectacular pictures of a ballerina on the wall. Her head was thrown back so all he could see was profile. One photo was taken mid-leap with her arms stretched above her head. Muscles rippled down her legs that looked to be a mile long from her pointed toe to her flexed pointer finger. She was one hell of an athlete. She was at least four feet off the ground as she effortlessly soared through the air.

Then there were pictures of other sports as well, but Stone's eyes kept going back to the ballerina.

"Mr. Townsend?"

Stone turned from the photo and froze. "It's you!" The woman from the hockey games looked surprised and he realized he'd just blurted that right out. "I mean, I've seen you at the hockey games sitting by the glass." Oh great, now he sounded creepy.

Her cheeks turned a sweet light pink and she smiled. "Yes, that was me."

"Wait," Stone looked at her and then turned back to the picture that had captivated him. "Is this you?"

"It is. I'm retired now." Stone could tell she was a little hesitant. She probably thought he'd make some wisecrack about it.

"You're a hell of an athlete."

She looked surprised and then smiled warmly. "Thank you. So are you. Your form on the ice is perfect for speed and to absorb and distribute hits."

This woman was too good to be true. She knew about hockey. "You know hockey?"

"Yes. I know a lot about sports. It is part of my job," she teased.

He had to know more. "Stone," he said, holding out his hand. "Are you my therapist?"

The woman shook his hand and Stone's heart picked up. She was so tiny but held herself as if she were six feet tall. He could tuck her right under his arm and she'd fit perfectly. She had slightly more curves now than in the photo, but the power in her grip and the cut lines of her muscles showed him she was still in great shape. She was in the same leggings Lulu had worn but wore a tank top with N2 Training written across it. The vibe she gave off was completely different from Lulu. This was no bunny. This woman was an athlete and carried herself as one.

"Natalie. I've been reviewing your injury, and I think you need less of a therapist and more training with some sports rehab thrown in. The key is to strengthen the ligaments and muscles around the patella to keep your kneecap in place, which should help prevent future dislocations."

"I'm ready to go. Get me back out on that ice, Nat, and I'll love you forever."

Natalie blushed a little and Stone wanted to smack himself. Real smooth, Stone. Real smooth. Let's not talk about love, sex, or dating until his knee was back and he was no longer a patient. Then all bets were off. Unless she had a boyfriend. Which she probably did.

"Did you bring your medical work?"

Stone handed it over and she read over it. His eyes went from the bun her brunette hair was in to the way she nibbled her bottom lip as she read. Lulu had nothing on Natalie. "What do you think?"

Natalie was quiet for a moment before closing the folder. "I think if we work every day, I can get you on the ice in three weeks. But only if you do everything I say, which you might not want to do. Most guys don't." It was a challenge, but three weeks sounded a hell of a lot better than six to eight, which was what Dr. Bartlett had estimated as the top end of his recovery.

"I'm up for anything, Nat. What's first?"

"First, have you ever taken ballet?"

"Excuse me?" Stone asked, confused. "What does ballet have to do with hockey?"

Natalie smiled. "So much, Stone. So very much."

. . .

If Natalie thought Stone Townsend was sexy on the ice, seeing him in athletic shorts and a T-shirt standing two feet from her was near orgasmic. He fit the persona of a Charleston Pirate perfectly. His hair was black. His eyes were a stormy gray. His scruff was just long enough to give him a very sexy pirate look. Then there was the way he smelled. Sandalwood, ocean, and something uniquely Stone.

However, the way Stone now looked when she asked him about taking ballet had her worried he might be like some of the other male athletes who had walked out on her for suggesting ballet as a means of training.

"Ballet is all about strength and footwork. So is hockey. I had to train to be able to stand on pointe for five to ten minutes on one leg, and then leap into the air and make it look effortless. My training is all about strengthening your knees and ankles so you can effortlessly hold a squat for ten minutes and then skate off at top speed. Your injury would benefit from ballet training in addition to the regular squat-based training you do for hockey with a little Pilates thrown in. If you think you're up for the challenge, that is." It was a gauntlet that Natalie threw down and hoped Stone picked up. She knew she could help him if he trusted her.

"Do I get to wear tights? I've been told I look pretty in pink."

Natalie couldn't tell if he was serious or not, but hell yes, she wanted to see him in tights. His legs were thick and muscled. He looked as if he could lift her with one hand. Plus, by the way his athletic shorts hung she would bet Stone didn't need to stuff his tights like many of the male dancers did.

"Pink would look good on you. But you have to earn your tights, so let's see how you do first." Natalie was surprised when Stone laughed. Male athletes were tricky. Some were like Stone and Quad, up for anything. Others fought her every step. They always knew better, they never had to prove themselves, or they wanted to be treated like a god. So far, Stone had not asked for any special accommodations so it was time to see how he held up to her training.

"Let's go, Coach. I can take anything you throw at me." Stone had a lot of swagger for a guy on crutches.

"Have you ever heard of barre?" Natalie asked as she moved into the training facility toward the ballet room.

"Yeah, I think I know what a bar is. Is working with me driving you to drink already?" Natalie tossed a smile over her shoulder at him before she opened the door to the room.

"Not that kind of bar. This kind of barre," she said as she pointed to the ballet barre. The look on Stone's face was comical. He was staring at it as if he couldn't contemplate what it was. "Don't worry. We aren't going to start at the barre. We're going to start on the floor and work our way up to the barre."

"You're the boss, but what can I do on the floor?" Stone asked as he followed her to the barre.

"Ballet is all about being symmetrical. Each leg is strengthened equally. There is no dominant leg as we have to be flexible enough to leap from our right or our left leg depending on what the choreography calls for. To do that, we train at the barre, equally on each side. However, you're not there yet. We're going to do floor barre for the next couple of days until your knee tells me it's ready to advance."

"I'm just going to be lying on the floor?" Stone asked as she took his crutches from him and leaned them against the barre before helping him to the floor where she had a workout mat laid out.

"Try it and let me know how you feel tomorrow. If you're not sore at all, we'll move to standing. Now, let's get started with some light stretching before we begin."

Natalie stopped him when he went into the normal stretches most athletes did. "You just lie there. Let me work, okay?" Stone gave her a smirk and she realized how that sounded in a sexual way. Oh no, she didn't see Stone as a guy to just lie there. He would be an equal bed partner.

Natalie swallowed hard and forced the thought from her mind. She'd trained countless athletes, why this one had such an effect on her she didn't know. But she was a professional and nothing was going to happen.

"Give me your right leg." Natalie helped lift his leg to stretch his hamstring, but then she moved it not just toward him, but outward then across his body. By the time she was done with stretches, he was sweating, but Stone wasn't complaining. "Now, let's get to work."

"That wasn't work?" Stone asked, incredulously.

"That was just the warmup. Let's see what you got, biscuit beater."

Stone snorted at the joke. Hockey players sometimes called the puck a biscuit. So, he had a sense of humor for sure. Then all thoughts of laughing ended as they got down to work.

"How does your knee feel?" Natalie asked after she helped Stone up from the floor.

"I don't know if I've ever been so tired from a workout before, but it feels good." She watched as he put some weight on it and smiled. "And my hips feel really good." He moved a little from side to side and his smile widened. "I might cry from exhaustion, and I might get a muscle cramp in my ass, but I feel good."

"I worked all those little muscles you don't even know you have, so they will probably be sore. Those little muscles help keep everything in place. If you think you want to continue with my training, let me know. We can schedule a standing time for you, but it's your call. It's important that you get the right person for you when you're rehabbing an injury." Natalie hoped it would be her. She knew she could not only help him heal, but improve his game overall.

"You're stuck with me now, Nat." Stone grabbed his crutches, and while he limped a little, he didn't need to use the crutches as they walked into the lobby.

Natalie stopped short at the sight of a man in jeans and a tight black T-shirt glaring at them. She recognized him instantly from the game.

"Hey, D. I'm almost done."

"Was she better than the other one?" the man Stone called D asked with no embarrassment at being overheard. In fact, he wanted to be overheard. The man seemed to give no shit about what she thought of him.

"So much better," Stone said with an easy smile that was completely opposite from the man standing across from him. "Look. I'm not using my crutches."

The man grunted.

"Stone, how is every day, including tomorrow, at five? That's the only slot I have open at the same time every day and I believe it's after your practices. If there's a game, we can work around it." Nat tried to give the same no-shit attitude about the serious guy staring at them. She was used to temperamental directors. This guy had nothing on them.

"Sounds good. Natalie, this is my brother, Damon.

Damon, this is Natalie."

Brother. That made sense. They had the same dark hair and when she looked closer, she saw Damon's dark eyes were not brown like she thought, but were actually a dark gray under his thunderous glare.

"Nice to meet you," Natalie said with a smile as she held out her hand.

Damon grunted and shook it before glancing at the photo of her on the wall. "That you?"

"It is."

"Were you with the London company?"

Natalie blinked with surprise. She was not used to being recognized outside the ballet world. "I was. That picture was taken when I was performing Swan Lake. I was Odette."

"I saw you in that performance," Damon said as if it weren't a strange coincidence. "You were excellent."

"Thank you," Natalie said, feeling as if a compliment from him meant a lot more than some guy at a gala who was just sucking up.

"When were you in London?" Stone asked.

"Visiting Penelope. I took her to the ballet. Come on, we better get going if you don't want to be late for your"— Damon paused and if she wasn't mistaken, his lips twitched a little—"class."

"Thanks again, Nat. I'll see you tomorrow."

"See you then. Don't be surprised if you're sore. Sore is good. Sharp pain is not."

Stone gave her a smile before leaving with his brother. Natalie looked around her training facility. Her evening classes were going to begin soon. She taught one, but the rest were with the other trainers. Maybe this hard class would get Stone off her mind? Who was she kidding? She was pretty sure nothing would take him from her thoughts.

7

That night, Stone walked into his house without crutches for the first time in over a week. Damon looked tough, but he was a softie under it all. So much so that he hadn't let Stone drive yet. However, after seeing him walking more comfortably, he finally related and let him drive to class tonight.

Stone felt the familiar tiredness of a good workout. He was ready to get to work, get stronger, and get better. He grabbed the bag sitting in his living room and headed straight for the garage. If he hurried, he could get his favorite seat.

The drive to downtown Shadows Landing was quick. The town itself was small. Stone had bought a house near Damon's off Palmetto Drive. Well, it was near everything. There was only one road into Shadows Landing, South Cypress Lane. If you stayed straight on it, you would pass some businesses like Lowcountry Smokehouse and his sister's law practice. Then you'd find two-and-three-bedroom homes going farther and farther into the countryside. If you turned right when you entered town, you'd be on Main Street. There was a museum with relics found while treasure hunting. There was the diner called Stomping Grounds, the courthouse, the church, Bless Your Scarf boutique, Harper's Bar, an art gallery, the historical society, an old building owned by the Daughters of Shadows Landing, the Pink Pig BBQ, and Gil's Grub and Gas. That was the entire downtown.

Main Street ended at the marina where you could turn left and head out of town on Palmetto. That road only went a couple of miles, ending at the Bell Landing Estate. Billionaire Ryker Faulkner and his wife, Kenzie lived on that road. Their next-door neighbor was Ryker's cousin, Trent, who was married to Hollywood actor and America's Sweetheart, Skye Jessamine Faulkner. Stone's sister Olivia also had a house there, but it was smaller with more of a cottage feel.

Across the street from those waterfront properties was the subdivision Stone, Damon, Hunter, Kane, Forrest, and Rowan all had houses in. After years apart, it was strange to have almost all the Townsends together in the same town again. Wilder lived in Charleston and the youngest, Penelope, was still flitting about in Europe.

Stone had been the toast of the town when he lived in Chicago. He was revered. People bought him drinks. There was always a table for him at any restaurant he walked into. Not so in Shadows Landing.

The town was founded by pirates, as he'd learned during his first visit. The ability to use a sword strangely outweighed his ability to score with a puck. They prided themselves on judging a person for who they were, not how much money they had. Which was why billionaire Ryker was treated the same as ghost-tour host and sometimes ghost whisperer Skeeter. It had been a bit of a blow to Stone's ego not to be fawned over, but now he loved it. Here he was, Stone Townsend the neighbor, not Stone the hockey star.

He raced after church to get a table at the barbeque joint. If he wasn't fast enough, though, he didn't get a table. The people teased him, joked with him, and included him but never treated him differently from anyone else in town. However, they also supported him unlike any town ever had. Harper's Bar was packed with people to watch his games, wearing his jersey and cheering him on. If he had a bad game, casseroles and desserts were left at his door with encouraging notes.

Tonight, he turned right onto Main Street and drove past Gil's gas station, which also had bait for sale and some really good boiled peanuts. He found a spot near the front of the church and parked. He grabbed his bag and met Miss Winnie and Miss Ruby on the sidewalk. The two were best friends and had been for over seventy years. They were an interesting duo. Complete opposites in looks. Miss Ruby was round and soft. Her black hair was sprinkled liberally with silver as she aged. Her ebony skin was beginning to wrinkle, but nothing like Miss Winnie. Miss Winnie might weigh a hundred pounds soaking wet. She was short, scrawny, and as pale as the plucked chicken she resembled with her wrinkles, especially at her throat. But Stone learned not to let their grandmotherly looks fool you. They wielded their knitting needles just like the daggers from the pirates who founded Shadows Landing.

"Oh! Look who isn't using crutches. Such a good boy. How is your rehab going? I heard you started seeing the same woman little Quad sees when he's in town," Miss Ruby said as the two joined him in slowly going up the historic stone steps of the church that was well over three hundred years old.

"I don't think there's anything little about Quad," Stone said with a chuckle. The kid, okay, young man, was six foot seven.

Miss Winnie made a clucking sound that closely resembled the chicken she looked like. "Once you change their diapers, they're always little."

"Remember that, Dare, when you and Harper give us a little one," Miss Ruby said not even turning around.

Stone glanced over his shoulder to see Dare Reigns carrying his bag and looking as if he were debating his next action. Which is why Stone started to pick up the pace.

Dare was an ATF agent and resembled some of the bikers who were Damon's clients. He was tall, had massive shoulders, and tended to growl or grunt quiet often instead of answering.

"This here is a moral dilemma," Dare said, stepping up to Miss Ruby's side and taking her other arm. "I could have blown by you to get the seat I know you want because that's the seat you know I want, too."

Miss Ruby patted his arm. "You wouldn't push by two old ladies and an injured man. You're a good boy."

Stone snorted and Miss Winnie smacked him. "Don't sass us. You're both good boys and we'll help you both with your knitting tonight. I'm almost done with my Duke of Dick. After that Regency show got everyone all hot and bothered, my Dukes of Dick are selling faster than I can make them. But I worked all week and now I have a little stockpile of them."

That would have sounded bizarre before spending a month in Shadows Landing. Now he knew that the knitted penises—in all sizes and colors—made the seniors thousands of dollars a month. He was no longer shocked to see them stuffing the balls with beans or making them little outfits. It wasn't any stranger than Miss Mitzy making cat sweaters or embroidering dirty little pictures and sayings.

Dare held the heavy, three-hundred-year-old door open for them and they entered the church. The church should have been modest for such a small town. A pretty stained-glass window maybe and some nice woodwork but this church had been founded by pirates. Gold candelabras, gold sconces decorated with jewels, and priceless artwork that had probably been stolen off European ships hung on the walls. Olivia told him that inside those candelabras and candlestick holders were daggers, pikes, swords, and other weapons from the eighteenth century that the women of the church to this day were all trained to use. It was the job of the reverend to teach them as soon as they reached a certain age. Ten seemed a little young but when all the men were away pirating back then, all of the ladies were expected to be ready for anything to protect themselves and their town.

Stone took his seat in the knitting circle. Dare took a seat next to him and gave him some serious side-eye.

"You're lucky you're injured or I'd knock you out of my chair."

"As if you could," Stone teased back. Dare was gruff, but he was a cool guy. He teased and Stone teased back. It was a good friendship.

"Hey, guys," Edie Durand said, taking the seat next to Stone as Miss Ruby sat next to Dare.

"Hi Edie. Would you mind helping me tonight while

Miss Winnie finishes her . . . project?" Stone asked as he pulled his latest knitting project from his bag. Edie smiled and immediately agreed. Edie was a widow who had recently remarried. Her husband, Tristan Durand, was a retired foreign government assassin who was now part of the sheriff's department. It was a strange coupling, but it worked. Edie was sweet as pie. Tristan not so much. But with Edie he was gooier than a fresh-from-the-oven apple pie.

Speaking of which, "Miss Winnie," Stone said, leaning forward to look around Edie, "when do I get my apple pie?" Miss Winnie and Miss Ruby made the best apple pies and used pictures of naked men with strategically placed pies as their marketing at county fairs.

Miss Winnie clucked again. "Everyone's seen you naked, Stone. Once a week, you're on some gossip page or another naked in a hot tub with your bunnies."

"Or naked on the balcony. That was a good one. Saw your pecker and everything," Miss Ruby said.

"It's a nice pecker," Miss Mitzy said absently. She was wearing a shirt with one of her 3-D cat heads knitted on it. "I'd go naked too if I had a pecker like that."

Dare grunted and rolled his eyes.

"Jealous? Don't you have a nice pecker?" Stone whispered to Dare.

"I can measure for you, Dare, if you want to know how you compare." Miss Mitzy looked way too excited as she held up a measuring tape.

"By the smile on Harper's face, I think we can all assume it's good," Edie said, keeping her eyes on her knitting. "No pecker measuring needed."

"Pecker measuring is always needed," Miss Mitzy grumbled as she shoved the measuring tape back into her bag. "How else do you know if size really matters? It's scientific research. Are you against science?"

Stone about stabbed himself with his knitting needle when he choked down a laugh. Poor Edie looked as if she were about to expire on the spot. Her mouth dropped open as she stared at Miss Mitzy.

"It's not science. It's personal preference," Edie said, her face turning red with embarrassment as she suddenly couldn't look at Stone or Dare.

Miss Mitzy shook her head. "It's about so much more. There's the ratio of length and girth and even debate over curvature."

"It's saying something about a pecker if it has nice girth along with length," Miss Ruby said casually.

"For sure, but it can be too much. Ever seen one where you just cross your legs and say 'not going to happen'? My cervix is fine as it is, thank you very much," Miss Winnie said as she tied off the last bit of yarn on her large Duke of Dick.

Stone cleared his throat and looked around at the roomful of women who were all nodding. "It seems we always talk about dicks. What about breasts? Do I get to measure those?"

"Now, here's a discussion I'm all for," Dare said, looking up from his boob scarf knitting project.

"You don't have to worry about breasts being so big they hurt you during sex," Miss Ruby pointed out.

"Oh, Miss Ruby, how wrong you are," Stone said as if he were a professor about to give a lecture. "Ever been smothered within an inch of your life? Breasts are very dangerous if your face is in them for too long."

"That's true," Dare added as the woman all rolled their eyes. "But what a way to go."

"And then there's the cute little breasts that sit all perky saying hello to you. The women seem to never wear a bra with those little strappy sundresses. That causes a painful case of blue balls when they perk up and wave their nipples at you," Stone said, going on in his lecture on breasts.

"It really begs the scientific question of whether there's even a bad set of breasts," Dare said seriously.

"Not that I've found," Stone answered a moment before a ball of yarn smacked him in the face.

"Countess of Cleavage!" Dare said with a snap of his fingers. "There you go, for your regency fans," he said, pointing to Miss Winnie.

"Duchess of Titties," Stone added.

"Baroness of Boobs," Dare immediately added.

"Knights of the Knockers," Stone said. "You could sell a whole troop of them armed with little swords."

Stone felt Edie shaking next to him and glanced over to see Edie's head ducked as she smothered a laugh.

"I could make them those really pretty regency gowns," Miss Mitzy said with a nod to Miss Winnie.

"Oh, that would be cute," Miss Ruby agreed.

"Pride and Privates," Stone said, jumping in. "You could do the whole cast. Mr. Dick Darcy. Miss Elizabeth Boobett."

Now Edie hooted next to him. "I can't. Stop!" Tears rolled down her face as she buried it in her knitting project. "But I so want the whole set!"

He'd never tell anyone on his team he was a knitter, but knitting class was by far his favorite night of the week. It introduced him to a world he'd never known before. Mostly retired women over sixty talking about life, love, friends, and family. Then he, Dare, and Edie brought their perspective to the discussion and found really good advice from the group since, as they like to say, "they'd been there, done that, probably at least twice."

"How is your knee doing?" Edie asked as she walked with Stone out of the class later that night. She'd stayed late to show him a certain pattern he wanted to do for the rim of the cap.

"It's a little tired today since I had physical therapy and ditched the crutches. But it works. Natalie thinks I can be back in three weeks," Stone told her.

"Natalie? Hmm."

There was a little smile on Edie's face he didn't trust. "Hmm what?"

"Oh, nothing. Just that my brother fell in love and married his physical therapist who helped him recover after being shot. He lives in Keeneston, Kentucky with Layne and their daughter now."

"And you think I'll fall in love and marry my therapist just because your brother did?" Stone shook his head, but the truth was his mind had been on Natalie for a while already. However, his thoughts hadn't been romantic, but lustful. Very, very lustful.

"Tell me about her. Maybe Layne knows her."

"She's a former ballerina who studied sports injuries and rehabilitation. I like what she's taught me so far. It's different from the way I normally workout by incorporating ballet into rehab to strength my knee."

"Makes sense. Those women must be crazy strong to do what they do. Let me know if you want Layne's input at all. I'm sure she'd be happy to help, but it sounds like you and Natalie are getting on well."

"I'll let you know after tomorrow. I might hate her then,"

Stone said with a laugh, thinking about how he was already getting sore.

"Good luck!" Edie called out as she crossed the street and walked toward her house.

Stone groaned as he got into his car. How did those little movements cause his muscles to be so sore?

8

"He's a player. Don't let him play you." Natalie's father's words played in her head as she walked back to her training center. After teaching her free ballet class that morning she'd run errands, cleaned her house, and filled her father in on how Stone's first session went. She'd made the mistake of saying she liked Stone and they got along well. That's when her father went off on Stone's off-the-ice antics, which led to her googling Stone on her walk back to the center.

She mostly just frowned as she saw the pictures of him with various women. Actresses, models, and bunnies, oh my! Good heavens but he looked glorious naked. Now she was definitely going to have trouble not picturing him naked during therapy. However, the playboy lifestyle wasn't for her.

The last class wrapped up at two so Natalie would have the training center to herself that evening. She unlocked the front door, flipped on the light, and walked to her office. At first it didn't hit her what was wrong. She just knew something was. The door cracked when she always locked it since clients' medical files were stored there. When she opened the door, it took her mind a moment to process the mess that greeted her. Papers were everywhere. Her desk was overturned. The plants were dumped on the ground and the dirt shifted through.

Suddenly, the place that had been her pride and joy made her feel fearful. Was someone still here? Who had done this? Why had they . . . no. No, it couldn't be that. No one knew she had it. No one.

Her hands trembled as she dialed 911 and reported the break-in. It didn't take long for the police to arrive. There were questions about what had been taken as she tried to wade through the mess to see what was missing. The trouble was, nothing was missing.

"Natalie!" she heard a deep voice shout from the door to the center. She'd only met him once, but she already knew his voice and was surprised by the relief it brought.

"Stone! Please let him back," she told a patrolman who nodded and left her office. Seconds later, Stone was by her side, his arm around her shoulder as if he could protect her from the mess of her office. She hated to admit it, but it was a relief to have him here.

"What happened?" Stone asked.

"I don't know. I came in and my office was a mess, but nothing was taken." Shit, shit, shit. It couldn't be *that*. But the more she tried to tell herself, the more she didn't believe it.

"And who are you and why are you here?" the tired looking man in the wrinkled suit asked.

"Stone Townsend. Natalie is helping me rehab an injury."

"Townsend? As in Olivia Townsend?" the man asked warily. Stone nodded. "Just what I need. Another freaking Townsend," he muttered.

"Detective Chambers," Natalie said, sounding annoyed. "Have you found anything?"

"Not really. You don't have a security camera, so that makes it difficult. With nothing missing, it's not a burglary but more personal. Do you have something someone wants? Or maybe a bad breakup?" He might look aloof, but his eyes told a different story as Natalie tried not to shift nervously.

"No. I'm just starting my new business and moved here not that long ago. No boyfriend. No time to date. I can't imagine what anyone would be after."

"Hmm. Well, we took fingerprints. I'll let you know if we find anything. Until then, you might want to think about installing a security system."

"Thank you, detective."

It took a moment, but the police finally cleared her training center. She turned and looked at the mess that had been her perfect office. Stone was inside setting her desk upright. "Stone, you don't have to do that."

"I'm happy to help, Nat. The sooner it's cleaned up, the sooner you'll be able to move on."

"Thanks. I appreciate it. Let's just get the worst of it, then we'll get you taken care of." Natalie watched Stone for a moment moving around her space. He didn't seem like trouble. He seemed to be an angel as they talked while putting furniture back in place and plants back into pots.

Stone didn't have many friends who were women. Georgie, the former bartender at Harper's Bar who married the sheriff's deputy, Kord King, and now ran her old family business worth millions more than Stone had, had been his first female friend. She wasn't interested in Stone sexually, as she only had eyes for her new husband. It had been really nice to have a platonic friend and he found that same easy banter with Natalie.

They talked about how she became interested in rehab and how Damon got him into hockey. They effortlessly flowed from cleanup to rehab. They were back on the mat in the barre room with Natalie's small hands on his leg showing him the proper way to do the leg lift she wanted him to do. There was absolutely nothing sexual about it, but Stone had never been so turned on.

It was strange, this potent mix of friendship and attraction. It was new for him. He never knew what most of the women he dated thought about except for sex, and they didn't care one bit about anything he said or thought except giving them orgasms. Natalie cared though. She asked him questions and asked him what he thought about topics ranging from sports to ethics. Before he knew it, it was dark outside and they were well past his session time.

"You have tomorrow off. I recommend a warm bath and some stretching."

Natalie held out her hand to help him off the floor. He was drenched in sweat and hadn't even lifted a weight. How was that possible?

Stone's hand engulfed hers. Her grip wasn't meek. It was strong as she actually yanked him up. She didn't feign falling into his lap. Strange. Electricity might be flowing between their hands and he wanted to move his hands all over her body, but she just yanked him up and let go. It was a bit of a bruise to his ego.

"Thanks, Nat." Stone looked around at how quiet and empty the building was. "Let me walk you to your car."

"Oh, I didn't drive. I don't live far, and I walk here when it's nice out."

"No, you're not." The order was out of Stone's mouth

before he thought about it. The look Natalie gave him would make Olivia proud. "Sorry. I just meant that your office was broken into today. What kind of gentleman would I be if I let you walk home alone in the dark?"

"From what I've heard, you're no gentleman," Natalie said, grabbing a light sweatshirt with a strappy back and pulling it on.

So, she'd been looking into him. "Trust me, sweetheart. I'm the epitome of a true gentleman." Natalie looked over her shoulder at him as she walked through the front door he held open for her and rolled her eyes. "I always make sure my women come first."

Stone grinned to himself when Natalie stumbled. His hands shot out to steady her. "See, I've always got you," he said, his voice dropping to the one he used in the bedroom.

"Please, I'm around men in tights that leave nothing to the imagination, grabbing me by my intimate parts, and holding me six feet or higher in the air. This little act isn't for me. I'm not some puck bunny."

Stone chuckled as he opened the passenger door for her. Most women didn't know what puck bunnies were. She really did do her research. "I'm pretty sure I can lift you easily into the air higher than any of them. Want to find out?"

"Not with your knee I don't." Then she winked and got into the car.

Stone laughed and rounded the car. "Do you miss it? Ballet?"

The teasing stopped as she gave him directions to her house and then stopped to think about the question. "Yes and no. I miss dancing. I miss the stage. I don't miss the long hours, the pain, the diets, and the pressure. Ballet is an interesting sport. It's predominately females but ruled by men. The directors, the choreographers . . . they're all men. Even the male dancers have more power than female ones. There are a billion females dying for a chance to dance, but so few men that they end up being able to make or break a woman's career. Same with directors. Not all of them, of course. But there are enough bad apples that you'll have your foundation shaken by them at least once. Only the strong make it to the next performance."

"I can see how that would be hard to handle." Stone wasn't laughing anymore. He'd always thought of ballet as light and fluffy, but apparently there was a dark underside.

"Oh yes. The threat of being recast if you didn't sleep with him, or being ditched for the lead role because you broke up with the male lead, or the director determining you couldn't dance because you were too fat when you were near starving all because of one guy's personal preference for skinny dancers. I don't miss any of that. But, the thrill of dancing your favorite ballet. The way you and twenty ballerinas can move in perfect synchronization. The rush when the curtain goes up and you hear the applause of the audience. The feeling of flying across a stage. That I miss."

Stone tightened his hands on his steering wheel. He wanted to go pummel every man who had tried to hold their power over dancers like that. Those weren't real men. They were scared little boys who were so insecure about being rejected that they blackmailed women into sex. They were cowards and deserved to have their asses handed to them.

"I'm sorry you had to deal with that, but now I want to see you dance. Damon said you were amazing and my brother is a very tough critic."

Natalie laughed. "Damon? A ballet critic?"

"Oh yes. He funded our youngest sister's ballet classes for a decade. Don't let any of our tough appearances fool you. All of us Townsend brothers were at every recital and performance."

"That's actually really sweet. Does your sister still dance?"

"No. She danced from toddler through high school. She stopped when she went to college. Now she's gallivanting across Europe, but she hopes to move back to the States in the future."

"Do you have lots of siblings?" Natalie asked.

Stone laughed as he pulled into her driveway. "You could say that. I'm the second eldest of nine."

Natalie gasped. "Nine! I'm an only child. I can't imagine."

"You met Damon. He's the oldest. Then me. Then Hunter. Then Olivia. You met her at the game."

Stone saw her brow furrow. "I did?"

"Yeah, you sat next to her. Olivia's husband, Granger, was next to her. You were both chirping in French."

"That's your *sister*?" she blurted, and Stone felt satisfaction at knowing she'd thought something else. So, she had been thinking about him and his relationship status.

"Yup. I'm not dating anyone right now."

"Oh." The tilt to her voice said more than the word. She was interested. Too bad she was off limits as his therapist. But when he was healed . . . "So, were all your brothers there?" Nat asked.

"Not all of them but most of them. Wilder and Hunter were missing. Wilder's been gone for the month on business but should be back tomorrow. Hunter missed that game but got back three days ago. Then you know Damon, who was at the end of the row, but then next to Damon was Forrest, then Kane, and finally Rowan. Let me get the door for you. See, I'm a gentleman."

Stone winked at her and walked around to open the door for her. The house was pretty. It was in a new subdivision near an upscale condo building. The house was a pale blue with a white door and white shutters. There was a small patio with a swinging chair on it with big thick pads that would be perfect to curl up into. It was feminine but not frilly.

"Thanks for the ride home. It did shake me up when I saw my office," she finally admitted as he silently walked her to her door.

"Let me give you my number. The arena isn't far away. If you need anything at any time, just call me. I live in Shadows Landing, but my brother-in-law is the sheriff. I can get here or get police to you in a heartbeat."

"That's not—" Natalie began to say, but Stone shook his head to cut her off.

"Let me be the gentleman, Nat."

She paused and then opened her phone. "Okay. What's your number?"

Natalie watched Stone drive off. The more time she spent with him the less she understood of him. Or more specifically, the more he defied her preconceived notion of him. When Stone left, she locked her door, made dinner, then climbed into a hot bath. She pretended to read, but the romance book she was reading had her picturing herself as the heroine and Stone as the hero. It was making her bath even steamier than the book.

Giving up on reading, she picked up her phone and stared at Stone's number. Her finger hoovered over the message button. "I'm not crossing the line. He needs my number to know if I have an emergency," she explained out loud to herself.

Here's my number if you need it. Thanks for helping me clean up my office. I'll see you Monday at five. Have a good day off – Natalie.

Natalie was about to put the phone back down and sink further into her bath when she saw bubbles form. Stone was writing back.

Happy to help anytime. So, are men who soak in the bathtub sexy? Asking for a friend.

Natalie almost dropped the phone thinking of him in the bathtub or more specifically them together in a bathtub. *Only if they send pics to prove it. Men who own their baths are sexy.*

A moment later a photo came through. Natalie held her breath as she opened it and then burst out laughing. It was a photo of Stone's head on a merman's body. *Come grab me by my tail. Splish Splash.*

Natalie settled into the warm water and texted with Stone until the water turned cold.

9

Two weeks of working with Natalie and Stone felt fantastic. It wasn't just his knee either. He walked taller. His abs were stronger. His legs were stronger. Then there was the fact that he smiled more easily than he normally did. There was also his heart. It was beating for Natalie in a way it had never done before. Before Natalie, Stone was usually bored with whoever he dated within a week. Now they worked out every day together. They talked constantly during their workouts and then at night over text. He'd been working on the barre and had even started adding in weightlifting. The texts. The flirty pictures, the funny gifs, the easy way he picked up the phone to send her something he knew she'd like. Natalie was constantly on his mind. While they'd never crossed a line, he was counting down the days until he was cleared from her care so he could ask her out.

Tomorrow, Natalie was going to meet him here to see how he did on the ice. Maybe he could be discharged sooner than he'd hoped. Now he was sitting on the bench watching his team play without him. Freaking Igor. He was tearing up the ice, scoring goals, and completely ignoring his team.

Stone glanced over at Coach Novak and saw his hands squeezed into tight fists. It didn't matter that Igor was scoring. He was hurting the team overall. The morale was low as Igor celebrated a goal by himself.

"It's quiet without your sister here, bud. She would put Igor in his place, eh?" Stewart Reilly whispered as Igor and Theo came off the ice. Theo sat down hard next to Stone.

"What the hell?" Theo hissed to Stone and Stewart. "Now Igor is playing offense and defense. That was my goal. Did you see him steal the pass to me so he could take the shot himself? This is bullshit."

The siren sounded, ending the game, and while it was a win for the Pirates, you wouldn't know it as the team walked quietly to the locker room.

"Townsend," Coach Novak said, halting him from walking with the team. "I got a report from Natalie. Sounds like you're doing really well. She's asked for ice time tomorrow. That's very promising. How are you feeling?"

"Well, I feel stupid for not knowing I had so many tiny muscles and ligaments in my leg. Natalie has worked with each and every one of them. How did you find her? She's amazing. I feel better now than I did before the injury."

"You don't know? She's—"

"Coach!" the assistant yelled as loud shouting erupted from behind the locker room door.

"Freaking Igor," Novak cursed before taking off with Stone right beside him.

Stone reached Igor first and yanked him off of Theo. Igor had been punching the kid in the gut.

"You have to grow some hair on your balls before you come for Igor." Igor smiled and Stone had it. He spun Igor and slammed him into the locker.

"Your play is selfish. You don't know your position. You are the problem here."

"What are you going to do about it from the bench, *captain*?" Igor taunted.

"Enough. Belov, in my office now!" Novak yelled after slamming his clipboard into a locker.

Stone tried to calm his team while they all heard Novak screaming at Igor, who seemed completely unfazed by the criticism. The players were no longer quiet. They were mad. The hope of a good season was quickly dwindling.

"I'm going to ask my agent to be traded," was heard more than once as the locker room quickly cleared.

The guys were off to WET without inviting Igor. "I'll meet you there," Stone said with a grimace. His mind wasn't on his team right now. It was on Natalie. Wilder had dropped him at the stadium and the plan was for Wilder to take him home from WET. Instead, Stone hopped in a cab and headed toward Natalie's house.

"Stop!" Stone called out when he saw the lights on at the training center as they drove by. "Let me out here."

Stone paid the driver and knowing this wasn't a good idea, he knocked on the front door. There was a pull for him to see her. Stone couldn't stay away if his life depended on it.

Natalie almost didn't hear the knock on the door as she danced. The slow, sensual, classical music filled the room as she danced freestyle. She stopped dancing as a moment of fear struck her. It was eleven at night. No one should be here.

Natalie picked up her phone and opened the security app. "Stone," she whispered. The reason she was dancing here tonight. Pent-up sexual energy was overflowing from her. Immediately after the game, she left to come here and dance off that energy.

Tonight, Natalie put into dance what she envisioned herself doing with Stone. Now she had to open the door to him and let him in. Natalie tried to calm herself as she walked to the front door.

Stone wasn't who she'd thought. He might have been the player her father said, but not with her. She'd seen nothing in the papers. He'd never come in late smelling of perfume. Instead, it seemed as if they were in constant contact. Their training ran late because they were so deep in discussion about life, desires, beliefs, or even which movie was the funniest. Then there were the sweet texts. *This made me think of you.* And it was a picture of the food she said was her favorite. Or there was a picture of her dancing and Stone would text *You're so remarkable.*

She'd had dinner with her father before the game tonight and it had been hard to keep the affection from her tone as she told her father how well Stone was doing. Her father was distracted though. Igor was causing problems.

Natalie unlocked the door and opened it to the sexual fantasy she'd been dancing to. "Stone. What are you doing here so late?"

Stone raked his hand through his hair in a nervous gesture that made her heart race even more than the sight of Stone's muscled body in a tailored black suit.

"I don't know. I just wanted to see you." He cursed under his breath and then took a look at her in her pink leotard with the see-through black scrap of a skirt that left very little to the imagination. He ran his hand through his hair again and whispered another curse. "I probably shouldn't be here."

"Then why are you?" Nat was poking the bear with the

tip of her pointe slippers, but it was too late. She'd opened the door and she didn't want to close it.

Stone swallowed hard. "I missed you."

"You saw me this afternoon."

Stone stepped forward until she was practically touching his chest. Natalie had to lean her head back to look up in his storming eyes. "I know. As I said, I missed you. What are you doing here so late?"

"Dancing off some excess . . . energy," she said the last word breathlessly as Stone's large hands ran down her arms.

"Show me," he said, his voice dropping to a seductive whisper. "Dance for me."

Natalie had never been so nervous to dance before. Her heart pounded when she took Stone's hand in hers and led him to her studio, almost stealing her breath. She'd danced in Swan Lake, Giselle, and Romeo & Juliet in front of huge audiences. Never had she been so nervous as dancing before the man who had somehow become so important to her over the past weeks. Her heart belonged to Stone, but he didn't know and she didn't have the words to tell him, so she would show him with her dance.

Stone was quiet as Natalie led him into the studio. She dropped his hand when they reached the middle of the room and headed to where her phone sat on the piano in the far corner of the room. Stone took the piano bench and picked it up. Silently he moved it to the wall opposite the barre and mirrors and took a seat.

He watched Natalie in the reflection of the mirror as she scrolled through her phone. He saw her finger hesitate and then she pressed something and stepped into the middle of the room. The first strands of the violin filled the room through the speakers. It took a moment for Stone to realize the classical music was actually a rearrangement of a very sexy pop song about love, longing, and desire. His breath caught at the realization and held it as Natalie began to move.

Stone saw the basic moves Natalie had taught him at the barre, but they were elevated beyond anything he was able to do. She floated, swayed, spun, and somehow made leaps that landed silently on the floor. Stone couldn't look away. His heart was in his throat as the lyrics of unfulfilled desire and longing that were missing from the classical music played out in front of him in Natalie's dance.

The music shifted to another classical arrangement of a song about sex and passion. Natalie seamlessly shifted to a more sensual dance as the lyrics that Stone and every man knew about laying down the woman you'd been wanting and making love to her played in his head.

Natalie slowly raised her leg until her toe was above her head. She'd told Stone the move was a *grand adage* and had been teaching him the strength and power used to pull off this move. Yet, as she looked at him with heat in her eyes, her leg up by her head, all thoughts of technique were lost and all that was left was the yearning between them.

Stone moved his legs wider apart on the bench to try to find some relief from the sensual nature of the dance. His breath caught as Natalie dropped her pose, took a step and a hop, threw her arms in the air, and leaped. Her legs outstretched in a move Stone had learned was called the *grand jeté*.

Natalie landed effortlessly on one foot and went into a spin that sent her gliding across the floor until she stopped between his legs. Stone had to touch her. They were in their own world in the studio in the quiet of the night. There was no right or wrong. There were only two people desperate to finally act on their desires.

Natalie placed her hands on his shoulders and bent backward into a swaying arch. Stone instantly brought his hands to her back to support her as she danced. She moved in his arms, spinning slowly within the support of his arms before leaning forward as her heaving chest met his.

Her arm slowly rose and the back of her hand caressed his cheek. His body pulsed with need as Natalie slid down his body until she sat on the floor, her cheek against the inside of his thigh, her arms wrapped around his leg.

Stone reached for her, but she spun away on the floor out of the cage of his legs. In one fluid move, Natalie placed an arm behind her, with one knee bent and one leg long. She lifted her hips, her legs arching over her head so that she ended the move standing in the middle of the room looking at him and breathing hard.

Natalie held out her hand and Stone stood, walking to her. He placed his arms on her back and they swayed together until Natalie broke off and spun around him, her hand dancing delicately across his shoulders as she moved. By the time she was back in front of him, she'd pulled the suit coat from him and left it in a heap on the floor.

The music started to build and as she made a move to spin in his arms, Stone grabbed the small bow on her hip. As she spun, the black skirt dropped to the ground as her leg wound up on his side between his arm and chest. Stone ran his hand down her leg until he reached her bottom.

Natalie looked up at him and he was lost. His large hands cupped her bottom and he easily lifted her into his arms. Natalie's legs wrapped around his waist, her fingers speared into his hair, as they looked into each other's eyes while Stone held her to him. Their heavy breaths mixed, flowed, then surrounded them until they were one.

Stone waited. They had never discussed their mutual attraction. It was so much more than sex. He knew that. He knew she knew that. But Stone needed this to be Natalie's choice. He needed her to choose him. If she leaned back, even a hair's breadth, he'd lower to the floor and step back.

If felt as if time stopped as the music flowed around them, building like his desire, until Natalie leaned forward. Her lips brushed against his like that scrap of a skirt whispered through the air when she spun.

The kiss lasted only a second, but it changed everything. Natalie leaned back just enough to look him in the eyes. The desire there reflected his, but now she was waiting for him to show that he wanted her too. Stone knew exactly how to answer.

His lips sealed over hers as he carried her to the barre. He felt the intake of Natalie's breath as her back pressed up against the cool mirrors. He used the inhale to deepen the kiss. The hesitation was gone. The question was answered.

Stone sat Natalie on the barre and kissed her. His heart about burst when he felt her small hands on his chest, undoing the buttons and pushing the fabric from his body. His pants were next until he stood before her nude while she sat on the barre in her leotard halfway down her body and pointe shoes.

Stone cast a glance at his discarded pants. He had a condom in his wallet, but was that moving too fast? He went to ask Natalie, but she slipped from the barre and placed her finger on his lips.

She kept her eyes locked on his as she removed her finger from his lips and shimmied from her leotard. She was perfect. Stone had mistakenly thought of her as delicate, but while she could portray elegance that was so delicate he could weep, Natalie was strong, confident, and so sexy he was momentarily frozen as he got his fill of her.

Natalie nodded to his pants and Stone reached for the condom. Mirrors surrounded them from front and back as he slid on the condom. He could see them from every angle as he dropped to his knees, kissing his way down her body until Natalie's moans mixed with the music.

Stone lifted her once again with one hand supporting her bottom as she wrapped her legs around him, bringing them fully together. Stone placed his other hand on the mirror to balance them as they finally came together.

Stone groaned into Natalie's neck and she clung to him, her fingers tightening into his back. Stone's eyes rose to the mirror just inches from his head, but it wasn't his own face he was looking into. His eyes caught where Natalie was watching them in the mirrors behind him. With each thrust, their eyes stayed connected until both of them closed them in ecstasy.

10

Natalie slid her hand into Stone's as they walked through the night toward her house. Her body hummed with the same energy as if she had her own standing ovation. They'd talked as they stood, clinging to each other in the post-glow of their lovemaking.

Stone had whispered words to her she'd never forget. He'd been so different from her previous lovers. Lovers who had been in the ballet world always seemed to treat sex as a quid pro quo for their careers.

Instead, Stone whispered about her beauty. About how he loved her curves, which would be the first part of her to be criticized by previous lovers. Then he'd whispered that he loved her strength, her kindness, her intelligence. If the lovemaking hadn't made her swoon, his words would have.

"Tonight was special, Nat," Stone said as he raised their clasped hand and placed a kiss on her knuckles. "I know I have a certain . . . reputation. But I need you to know this was different."

"I wouldn't have let you walk me home to spend the night with me if I didn't already know that." The relief in his eyes made her smile. "We've gotten to know each other so well over the past two weeks, and you never once made it feel as if I were only a conquest. I have to admit, I've been wanting this to happen."

"Me too, Nat. I was trying to wait until I was back on the ice, but then you made love to me while I watched you dance and I had to touch you. The second I did, I don't think a hurricane could have stopped us."

Natalie blushed in the dark as she looked up at Stone. Her house was just ahead and she knew their night wasn't over yet. There was still so much attraction between them. It would be impossible not to touch each other the second they got to her room. She was looking forward to showing him what she could do when they had a bed. "I had been dancing and thinking of you before you knocked. It was as if the universe was answering my dreams."

Natalie turned to walk up her drive and tightened her grip on Stone so hard that he stopped walking. "What is it?"

"I have porch lights. They're not on. I leave them on twenty-four/seven since I often walk to work and come home after dark."

"Stay here," Stone ordered. Gone was his sexy voice. In its place was the tone of the leader of his hockey team who expected her to do what he said. In this case, she was happy to.

She dug into her backpack and pulled out her phone. She turned on the flashlight and aimed it at her door. A door that wasn't even closed. It was busted open and had been propped closed as it was now hanging by only one hinge.

"Call the police," Stone ordered. Before she could stop him, he strode into the house.

Natalie placed the call but never took her eyes off the

door until sirens sounded and Stone walked back outside. "I didn't touch anything, but your whole house has been trashed, just like your office was."

A night that had started as a beautiful dream was ending as a nightmare. It was too much of a coincidence. Her office and now her home. That meant she couldn't hide her head in the sand anymore. She knew what was happening, what they wanted, and why.

Her body went cold in the warm night air. She shivered and Stone held her protectively against her as the first police cruiser pulled to the curb.

Someone knew what she had done, what she had taken. But who? It could be anyone whose name was on that drive and those were some of the worst people in the world. It could be Mr. Lavigne, or it could be . . .

"We'll clear the house, ma'am. But then we'll need you to come inside to let us know if anything was taken," an officer said, interrupting the fear she had of being drawn back into that world.

"Do you own a car?" Stone asked her as they watched the officers clear her house even though Stone had already done so.

"Yes," she said, glancing to the street. "It's that one."

"You're coming home with me tonight."

That got Natalie's attention. "What?"

"You can't stay here. It's not safe. When we're done here, I will nail your door up while you pack a weekend bag. You're not coming back here until the door is fixed and you have a security system installed."

Stone was being very demanding, but that was okay with Natalie. She didn't want to be alone right now and she didn't want to be in her house, knowing all her things had been gone through. If someone was looking for the drive, they hadn't found it yet. Natalie knew that with certainty. She'd already checked and it was safe. Now if only she could stay safe.

It took forever for the police to make their report, but they did help Stone secure the front door while Natalie packed. She came down with a giant suitcase, which would have Stone breaking out in a cold sweat. But the idea of her moving in for more than a night was exactly what he wanted.

"I didn't what to leave anything valuable behind, so I brought everything I could think of." Which would be most of her belongings. Stone had walked around the house with Natalie and the police. Nothing had been taken, just broken. It didn't take a detective to realize this meant it was personal.

Stone took the suitcase from her as she pressed the button on her key fob and opened the trunk. "That's fine, Nat. You can bring whatever you want to my house and stay for as long as you want."

Natalie gave him a look that clearly said she didn't believe that. "Right. I'm sure you love women hanging around."

"Honestly, I didn't in the past. In fact, you'll be the first woman to my home in Shadows Landing. But I think you've proved you're the exception. I want you in my life, Nat, and not only for one night."

Stone was worried when she didn't immediately agree. Most of the women he'd dated in the past would be picking out their sports car and jewelry for him to buy. "I would like that, but look how much trouble I have already brought to your life. This isn't a good way to start a relationship with a police report."

"Just adds a little excitement to our date night," Stone winked as he took the keys from her hand. "Do you want me to drive?"

Natalie nodded and he opened the door for her. Stone talked to her on the ride to Shadows Landing, but he could tell Natalie's mind was elsewhere. His was too, but he didn't want to show Natalie how worried he was for her. Instead, he worked at keeping her at ease and trying to take her mind off of what had happened.

"This is where you live?" Natalie asked as they pulled up to his house.

"Expecting more?" Stone asked, knowing most women would.

Natalie looked embarrassed. "I'm sorry. I totally expected some over-the-top mansion. Not a really nice family home."

Stone shrugged. "It's just me. I don't need a huge mansion. Plus, the money I saved from buying a nice family home instead of a mansion will let me retire anytime I want. I invest a lot and can buy four mansions if I really want," he teased. Money wasn't something he talked about much. But not only had he made enough to help take care of his younger siblings, he'd also saved enough that if he ever did get hurt, he could retire without blinking.

"My dad always says smart players are players who live in the present while saving for the future."

"Smart man," Stone said before getting out of the car and grabbing her bag. He should ask Natalie what her father did for a living. She talked about him a lot but always acted as if Stone already knew all those background details.

Stone closed the garage door and they walked into the house. He flipped on the lights and Natalie screamed.

"What are you doing coming home so late and with a

woman during the season and while you're in rehab?" Olivia was sitting with her legs crossed in a brown leather chair she'd moved to face the garage door.

Natalie stopped screaming as Stone put his arm around her. Tonight had been too much of a fright and now this. "Liv, this is not the time."

Olivia grinned slowly as she stood. "Oh, is this a bad time?" she asked innocently. "Like the night of my junior prom was a bad time?"

"Liv," Stone warned.

"Or practically all of my dates with Granger were a bad time?" Olivia sat back down and pulled out a book. "I think I'll stay here a while and read this really good book."

"I think I'm missing something," Natalie said, looking between Stone and Olivia.

Olivia set down her book and smiled sweetly at Natalie. "Oh, you're going to miss something tonight alright because there's been a penalty call for clitoference."

"What?" Stone asked his sister as Natalie snorted next to him.

"I'm twat swatting. I'm going with the full taco blocko."

Natalie began to vibrate as she tried not to laugh out loud. "Liv, what the hell?" Stone asked, getting irritated.

"Your sister is a muffin muzzler," Natalie said as she tried not to laugh.

"I created a real beaver dam here, bro." Olivia used her arms to make an X over her crotch and Stone groaned as it finally set in. Olivia just smiled wider. "I told you I'd get you back."

"This is not funny, Liv."

"Yeah, it really is." Olivia sat back down and picked up her book. "So worth not sleeping tonight."

"I take it Stone cock-blocked your dates?" Natalie asked as she gave him a look that clearly sided with his sister.

"Not just Stone. They *all* did. But Stone, Hunter, and Damon were the worst. So, I'm sorry if I ruined your night, but I'm sure you understand."

Stone was growling at his sister. "This is not the same, Liv."

"Oh no, this is exactly the same. Have a good night. Leave your bedroom door open too. No hanky-panky while I'm here," Olivia smiled and looked down at her book.

Stone took Natalie's hand and ignored the way she warmly said goodnight to his traitorous sister. He took her upstairs, into his bedroom, and closed the door. "This is funny? I can't have sex with my sister right downstairs."

Natalie finally let go and laughed loudly as she shook her head. "Solidarity with my girl. No sex tonight for sure."

Stone felt his mouth drop open. "You're agreeing with her?"

"Your sister scares the crap out of me. There's no way she needed you to cock-block her dates. Although, it's really sweet you love her enough to look out for her."

"Wait," Stone was confused. "So, you agree with her, yet also think it's nice that I did it?"

"You got it. Now, how do you feel about snuggling with our clothes on?"

Stone growled again, but when he lay down on the bed with Natalie in his arms, it was honestly one of the most real experiences of his life. He felt her breathing, her heart beating, the smoothness of her skin, and the warmth of her body against his. It was romantic, comforting, and somehow incredibly intimate even while they were fully clothed.

When Stone finally drifted off to sleep, his dreams were filled with the smell and feel of Natalie.

11

———————

Natalie slowly came awake when she smelled coffee brewing. Sleeping in Stone's arms had given her the best night's sleep she'd ever had. She hadn't thought it was possible after what happened at her house, but seeing how much Stone loved his sister and how much Olivia clearly loved him and then spending the night protected in his snuggles . . . well, it was enough to melt a girl's heart.

Arms were still around her, holding her to the large and hard body behind her, which meant Olivia was making coffee. Natalie reached to the bedside table and glanced at her phone.

"Oh crap!" Natalie yanked herself from the warm cocoon of Stone's arms and began grabbing her things.

"Get out, Olivia," Stone muttered into his pillow with his eyes still closed.

"No!" Natalie said, rushing to put on her shoes. "I have a class to teach in thirty minutes."

"It's Saturday," Stone told her, still not opening his eyes.

"I teach free ballet classes to children. I can't miss it. Don't worry, I have my keys. You sleep." Natalie snagged the keys from the table beside Stone's side of the bed, but his hand shot out to stop her.

"No way you're going alone. Give me a minute to change."

"No time!" Natalie yanked her hand free and made a run for the stairs.

Olivia was pouring coffee into a travel mug. Natalie figured it was Olivia's since it had the scales of justice on it, but she snagged it anyways. "Thanks for the coffee!"

"Hey. That's mine!" Olivia called out as Natalie yanked open the door leading to the garage with Stone hot on her heels.

"Payback for clam jamming me last night. See you at the next game!" Natalie shouted over her shoulder even as Stone leaped into the car wearing an undershirt, slacks, and no shoes to avoid being left behind.

"You couldn't wait for me to put on my shoes?"

"Sorry, but this is my favorite class and I can't be late. I teach free ballet to kids eight and under for an hour and then kids up to age twelve for an hour after that. It's important to the community and it's important to the sport of ballet for kids from every situation to have access at an early age if we want the sport to continue."

"I understand. I work with a charity that teaches hockey to kids. I can go lift weights while you teach the class. The weight room isn't that far from the dance studio. If you yell, I'm sure I could hear you."

Natalie shook her head as she sped toward Charleston. "Sorry, but all the rooms are in use today. I work with my ballet classes and all my other instructors are packed from eight in the morning to five at night on Saturdays." Natalie grinned as she looked over at Stone. "But we can get your workout in earlier than normal today. You can help me with the classes and then we can skate to evaluate how you're doing on the ice."

The look Stone gave her made it hard not to laugh. He looked as if she suddenly spoke a different language. "You want me to help with class? Babe, I don't know anything about ballet."

The *babe* got her. It was so natural to hear and it made her feel things she wasn't ready to feel—like hope for a future together. "I've spent two weeks, six days a week, teaching you ballet. You will be able to hold your own. Besides, it will be a big deal for the boys in the class to see you. Bullying is common for boys who want to dance."

"Sure. I can help with that. And show them the proper respect for their partner." Stone no longer sounded as if it were torture to help, so Natalie would take the win.

The rest of the drive to her training center was in complete silence except for the sound of Stone stomping on an imaginary brake. She might have driven a little quickly to get there on time.

"You can't be serious," Stone said, holding tights in his hand that didn't look to be longer than his arm. There's no way they'd fit.

"You can't dance in pants," Natalie said with zero sympathy.

"It'll leave little to the imagination, babe."

"Just wear your undershirt out and it'll cover it. Besides, all the boys wear them and you're to project confidence and show them wearing tights is cool. It's no different from swimmers or divers wearing speedos."

"Yeah, but I'm a hockey player." Seriously, the tights wouldn't fit his calf nevertheless his whole leg.

"Today you're a hockey player who dances ballet. I'll meet you in there."

His traitorous girlfriend left him alone in her office as she rushed to class. *Girlfriend?* Where did that come from so suddenly? They'd had sex. Once. He never called the girls he slept with his girlfriends. However, Natalie was the only one he'd snuggled all night and the only one he wanted to have sex with every night in the future. Girlfriend. He tried it out, "This is Natalie, my girlfriend." It had a nice ring to it.

Stone pulled off his slacks and held up the tiny tights. "Let's do this."

It took several minutes to get them on. Stone hopped around on one foot. He yanked, he pulled, and he fell onto his butt. In the end, he lay on the ground and wiggled them up and over his hips while doing a glute bridge.

"I can't believe they fit," he murmured.

Stone strode out of the office in his undershirt, gray tights, and barefoot. Women stopped and stared as he passed them. Crap, did his tights split? He got his answer when he walked into the dance studio and finally saw himself in the mirrors at the same time the mothers did. Suddenly he was very aware of all the faces looking down on him from the viewing area a floor up.

The tights showed every line of his thickly muscled legs. Legs that showed the power of a hockey player along with his manhood and even which testicle was slightly bigger than the other. Stone, and every other woman there, all stared at it. Damn, tights did a package good. It had never looked so nice.

Stone grinned when he caught Natalie staring. She shook her head and clapped her hands. "Ladies and gentlemen we have a special guest taking class today."

"Who is he, Miss Natalie?" a little girl no more than six

asked. Her black hair was braided with beads on the ends in pink, white, and teal.

"Nia, this is Mr. Stone. He plays hockey for the Charleston Pirates."

"But this is ballet," a little boy with moppy blond hair pointed out.

"Hey, kids," Stone said, squatting down to their level. "I'm excited to see you dance. I'm taking ballet because it makes me stronger and helps with my skating."

"You're old," a little girl said as she swished her tutu from side to side.

"You're never too old to learn something new," Stone said, trying not to laugh. He loved kids. It was a byproduct of being an older brother to so many younger siblings.

"And what great advice. Let's all learn a new dance move together." Natalie clapped her hands and the kids all lined up. She smiled and led Stone to the middle of the back row and class was on.

Stone felt surprisingly proud of himself for being able to keep up with little kids. The second class was harder though. But it was in that class he could really see the impact of having a strong male figure show the boys that ballet was cool and could also help with other sports.

Stone was taking pictures with the kids when a man entered the studio and simply stood by the door. Stone was immediately on guard. The man didn't look at the children. He didn't have a kid running up to him and tugging his hand. He further didn't look at Stone. The messy, fifty-plus-year-old man, a little ragged with an ill-fitting suit and windblown hair, was only staring at Natalie.

Stone glanced back to watch as Natalie looked up to see

the man. Her face went pale. She froze for a split second. Then she plastered on a smile as she waved the last family from the studio.

Now it was just Stone staring at Natalie and the man, who were both ignoring Stone. "Get rid of him," the man said, not bothering to look at Stone.

Stone stood up to his full height and towered over the man. "Let's see you make me."

"I don't negotiate with men in tights." The man had still not taken his eyes off Natalie.

Stone felt her hand on his arm and he looked down at her. "It's okay, Stone. We know each other. Why don't you finish taking photos with the kids and parents and change? I'll be out in a minute and we can go to the rink." When Stone didn't move, she added, "Please." That did him in.

"Only if you leave the door open."

Natalie gave him a nod of agreement. Making his feet move was the hardest thing Stone had done. He didn't want to leave Natalie, not when something clearly was going on that upset her. But he had to trust her. She'd asked him to leave, and he would.

Natalie crossed her arms over her chest and stared at the man she'd never wanted to see again. "What are you doing here?"

"That's not a nice way to greet an old friend," the voice that had always whispered into her ears from the shadows said.

"You were never a friend. You extorted me into becoming a spy, Agent Naylor."

"I didn't extort you. I simply encouraged you to serve your country."

Natalie felt the anger she always felt around CIA Agent Aaron Naylor. "What do you want?" she asked between gritted teeth.

Suddenly she felt eyes on her. She didn't need to look up to know that Stone had listened and left the room, but he still kept an eye on her from the parent observatory above the studio.

"I hear you've been robbed, twice, yet nothing was stolen."

"How did you hear that?"

Naylor grinned but didn't respond.

"So what?" Natalie asked flippantly.

"So, I think you took something that wasn't yours and now you're paying the price. If you come back and work for me, I'll protect you. You just need to tell me what you took and why someone is after it."

A cold chill raced down Natalie's back. "No. Now get out."

Naylor just shrugged, put his hands in his pockets, and rocked back on his heels. "You know the number to call if you get into trouble. Until then."

Agent Naylor turned and slowly walked off with his hands in his pockets and a jaunty whistle. Asshole.

Natalie glanced up to find Stone looking down at her. She forced a smile and walked to her office. They both needed to change. No matter what a mess her life was, she still needed to help Stone get back to his.

12

Stone had to admit he was scared. He didn't like that Natalie was keeping something from him, but he knew she'd tell him eventually. That wasn't what was bothering him. Right now, he looked out at the ice and was scared. What if his knee dislocated again? What if he lost speed from his injury? What if he could never take or give a hit again?

Natalie was next to him in a borrowed pair of boy's hockey skates the equipment manager found for her. "Ready?" she asked as she stepped out onto the ice without hesitation.

"You know how to skate?" Stone asked, feeling like a coward for delaying stepping on the ice.

Natalie laughed and did a spin that gained quite a bit of momentum. "Yeah, I did grow up in Minnesota, you know. It's kind of a requirement there. Then there's my dad. He wouldn't let me get away without knowing how to skate."

"Your dad?" Stone asked.

"Will love to see you on the ice again, so let's see what you've got. Come on, Stone. I promise, your knee is strong enough to handle skating."

Something about the way Natalie said that made Stone believe it. He placed his uninjured leg on the ice and then his injured leg. He stood for a split-second realizing there was no pain so he pushed off and began to glide on the ice.

"How does it feel?" Natalie asked.

"Actually, really, really good. I don't feel any pain. I don't feel any stability issues. In fact, I feel strong and really balanced." Stone pushed off harder and picked up speed.

"Okay, hot shot. No showing off. You're still rehabbing. I want you to just skate around slowly for twenty minutes or so and then we'll examine your knee for any swelling or pain."

Natalie easily caught up with him and grabbed his hand in hers, forcing him to slow down. He didn't know the last time he held hands with a woman and skated. It felt romantic. His two favorite things combined into one: Natalie and skating.

Natalie asked him questions about how he was feeling, asked him to try different moves, and then the alarm on her phone went off and she made him stop. They were standing in the middle of the ice and Stone was feeling something he'd never felt before—deep, heart-filling happiness.

"I've never seen you look so relaxed and happy before," Natalie said as she looked up at him with a genuine smile on her face before placing her hand over his heart. "You really love hockey, don't you?"

"I'm beginning to wonder if I love more than just hockey." The words were out before he overthought them. They were the truth. He was falling for this spitfire of a woman. He bent his head and kissed her. He figured he'd let actions show Natalie what he was feeling.

The kiss was reverent. Loving. Toe-curling.

Transcendent. Well, until a sharp whistle and a yell broke their kiss.

"Nice puck bunny! This one can even skate!" his brother, Hunter, yelled from where he stood grinning with their other brother, Wilder, who was giving him the thumbs up.

"She's not a puck bunny!" the person who had blown the whistle was now yelling.

"I know she's not, Coach Novak," Stone said as he pulled Nat against him and placed a quick kiss on her forehead even as she groaned. "She's the best therapist around and I'm lucky to call her my girlfriend, too."

"A smart puck bunny finally snared you!" Hunter gave another whistle.

"Stop saying that!"

Stone was shocked when Coach Novak stormed toward Hunter. "Coach?" Stone had the feeling Coach Novak was about to punch his brother for some reason and between Hunter and Wilder, he was going to punch the wrong bother. Wilder owned night clubs. Hunter was in the Special Forces.

"Dad, stop!" Natalie yelled at the same time.

Hunter, Wilder, and Stone all froze.

"Dad?" Stone asked slowly, looking between them. "Wait, what?"

"You didn't know he's my dad?" Natalie looked at Stone as if he had just suggested puck bunnies were actual floppy-eared, furry bunny rabbits.

"No! I didn't know he was your dad. How was I to know that?" Stone quickly dropped his arm from where he had it around her shoulder.

"N2 Training? Natalie Novak?" she said slowly.

"You never told me your last name and neither did your

father. He only told me he knew someone who could help me."

"What is it with you and therapists?" Coach Novak yelled as he stomped onto the ice. "Keep your hands off my daughter! I warned you, Nat, to stay away from him. That he was a player."

"Dad," Natalie said slowly, even as she placed her hand around Stone's waist who instantly put his arm back around her. He'd protect her no matter what, even if it meant losing his job. "He didn't take advantage of me. We both want this."

"How long has this been going on?" Coach Novak demanded.

"About sixteen hours, sir," Stone turned to look down at Natalie, ignoring the parental rage stalking him. "You knew about my history and moved forward with me anyway, even against your father's warning. Why?"

Natalie gave him a little smile as if saying it was obvious. "Because I met the real you. Not the player on and off the ice. I met a man who treats me as an equal, who works hard, who cares, who is respectful, and who helped me teach classes of children. That's who I want as my boyfriend. That is, if you still want me since I'm your coach's daughter."

"Natalie," her father groaned as he stopped before them and placed his hands on his hips and glared at Stone. "This man hasn't had a serious relationship in his life."

"That's not true," Hunter called out as he and Wilder joined them on the ice. "My brother can be an ass."

"Yup," Wilder said. "So many wedgies growing up."

"He can be a player off the ice," Hunter said, ignoring Wilder.

"Open bunny hunting season for sure," Wilder agreed.

"But he's had two serious girlfriends who wrecked him,

which is why he hasn't had any since then," Hunter told them.

"Broken fucking hearted." Wilder wiped away an imaginary tear and Stone wanted to punch him.

"He's also the best big brother there is. He helped raise us, pay for our sports and hobbies, get our sister through law school, and helped finance Wilder's first club. Stone wouldn't say girlfriend unless he was serious, and nothing deters him when he's serious. His all-star career tells you that." Okay, so maybe he wouldn't kill Hunter.

"Best big brother ever. If he loves your daughter, nothing will stop him from loving her with his entire being, whether you approve or not." Okay, so now Stone didn't think he'd murder Wilder either.

"No one is talking about love. They've only been together for sixteen hours," Coach Novak snapped.

"Oh, I know," Hunter said with an all-knowing smirk. "But did you notice how Stone pulled your daughter closer to him when I said the L word and didn't run for the hills?"

"Totally in love, even if they don't know it yet," Wilder added to really drive the point home.

Actually, they were right. Stone wasn't pulling away. He wasn't grimacing. He wasn't breaking out into a cold sweat. In fact, he was drawing Natalie closer to him. Maybe it wasn't love yet, but there was something special here and Stone knew it.

"Is my daughter worth your career?" Coach Novak asked and Stone swallowed hard as Natalie protested. The yelling, the arguing . . . Stone didn't hear any of it. Instead, he really thought about the question.

It settled in his heart and mind just as it had when Damon had brought him out to the pond that day and introduced him to hockey. It was a feeling and he just knew.

"Yes, she is. I would like to continue to play for you and be a good captain for my team, but if you can't tolerate me on the team, I'll call my agent right now."

All talking stopped. Then, at once, his brothers were talking him out of it, as was Natalie.

"You can't do that!" Natalie half gasped and half yelled.

"Why not?" Coach Novak asked his daughter. "Because you don't care enough for him for him to ruin his life?"

Stone didn't dare to even take a breath. He didn't want to miss a single word Natalie said. It was strange how, in a split second, his mind had flooded him with memories, of fighting to get on the school's hockey team, of knowing it was a fight worth having, just like this was.

"Just the opposite, Dad. Because I do care enough for him that I don't want to see all the hard work, dedication, and love he has for the team and his career tossed aside for me."

Coach Novak put his hands on his hips and looked between them both. "So, Natalie will sacrifice her happiness for Stone's career, and Stone will sacrifice his career for Natalie." Stone was about to say more when Coach Novak's scowl broke into a broad grin. "Finally! You've both figured it out. Relationships are sacrifice, compromise, supporting each other, putting someone besides yourself first when needed . . . all the things I messed up on with Natalie's mom. But it just took two weeks for you both to figure it out. Damn, I'm good!"

Stone saw Natalie's brow crease in confusion, but when he saw Dr. Bartlett stride out with a huge smirk on his face and high-fived Coach Novak, Stone understood it. He just didn't believe it.

"What's going on?" Natalie asked.

Stone shook his head and smiled. "They set us up. Lulu wasn't a therapist, was she?"

"She is a therapist," Dr. Bartlett said trying not to laugh. "I couldn't risk injuring you, but I told her to go full stereotype and she ran with it. I've never laughed so hard as watching the security footage."

"Dad?" Natalie asked now seeing what had happened. "You set us up? Why? Why not just have me train him to begin with?"

Coach Novak rolled his eyes in a way Stone had seen Nat do before. "You never listen to me when it comes to the men you date, so I used basic reverse psychology. I knew if I told you both that you'd be perfect for each other, neither of you would give it a fair try. I knew you two were perfect for each other as soon as I met Stone. How many times did I try to get you to come to team events? How many times did I tell you the guys you dated were only looking at using you for your career? How many times did I tell you that you needed someone with your work ethic and not looking for a shortcut in life? How many times in the past two months have I talked about Stone and you shrugged me off?"

Natalie looked guilty and bit her bottom lip even as she smiled at being called out. Then she held up her hands and laughed as she leaned against Stone. "Fine! I concede. You are right. I would have instantly been against him and never given him a chance."

"And you," Coach said, turning to Stone. "All those freaking bunnies and your antics. You needed someone who wouldn't put up with that. Someone who would push you but support you at the same time while not being a 'yes' girl. So, when you got injured, I saw my opportunity and enlisted Dr. Bartlett to help me."

"I thought it could be fun and Erica, that's the therapist

you actually saw, took it and ran. She came up with using the name Lulu as a sly play on puck bunnies. With you running from the room, it let Coach Novak send you to Natalie without raising any suspicion."

Stone could be mad, but why would he be when Coach Novak and Dr. Bartlett set Natalie and him up? They got both him and Nat to get out of their own ways so they could be open to learning more about each other and falling in love without the pressure of a known setup.

"You know what that means, right?" Coach Novak asked his daughter.

"I can't mess up his knee or the whole team will hate me?"

"Well, that goes without saying. It means he better start coming to our after-game dessert outings. We're off for the next two weeks before our first game. Preseason is done, but our first game is next week on October 8th. After the game, you will join Nat and me for a family tradition."

It wasn't asked, but Stone didn't mind. He'd be happy to. Especially if he could play at that game. "What about after I play during that game?"

A chorus of "NO" filled the air from Coach Novak, Natalie, and Dr. Bartlett.

"But I thought I was doing well. I have one more week left and I'll be on the ice again. Next week is the game," Stone protested. The fact that Dr. Bartlett and Coach hooked him up with Natalie was forgotten for a moment.

"One more week," Natalie said, putting her foot down. "The game is in four days. Not enough time. I will say I think you can start skating every day and start light practices for the next couple of days. No contact!"

"I agree," Dr. Bartlett said, piling on. "I've reviewed all the reports Natalie has sent in and I see you're comfortable on your skates, but I'd like to see you go slow so you're strong and ready to give a hundred percent when the time comes. Right now, I think we put you out there and you could give us seventy-five percent."

"You'll play scared. You'll worry about your knee. I agree with them. One more full week," Coach said with no room for argument.

"I'll miss opening night." Stone hadn't missed an opening night ever.

"It's against New Mexico. It's not one where we'll need you. But then we play Tennessee. We'll need you in that game. Get stronger and surprise the hell out of Tennessee when we take you off the injured list at the last second."

"You have a point, Coach." Stone nodded and felt that determination come back. He'd earn his start again. "I can start to practice though?"

"Monday. You can practice on Monday. Tomorrow you can come and get some slow skating in again. Now, go have a good weekend. And, Stone," Coach said, stopping from where he'd begun to walk off the ice before turning to look at Stone, "you hurt my girl and I'll cut you to death with your own skates and watch you bleed out on the ice."

Hunter leaned over and high-fived Coach Novak. "I can respect that."

"Respect," Wilder agreed. "But our sister might be an issue there. She kinda loves her big brother."

"She scares the crap out of me," Coach Novak said with a shiver.

"Really?" Natalie asked as she looked around in surprise. "I like her."

Stone grinned. He'd found a woman who could not only stand up to Olivia but liked her. Maybe he should just drop to one knee and ask her to marry him. Actually, that idea didn't seem so out there but now wasn't the time. It was time to get out of there and spend the night with Natalie. Now that his feelings had been pointed out to him and he'd been forced to really examine them, he wasn't scared of seeing if it was love.

"If Coach gets you both for after game desserts," Wilder said as Coach and Dr. Bartlett left, "you all need to come to Harper's tonight for family dinner. You two lovebirds can canoodle later."

Natalie giggled even as she rolled her eyes and looped her arm through Stone's as they skated off the ice. "I'd love that."

So would Stone. He hadn't brought a woman home in years. Yes, Nat already knew Damon and Olivia, but spending the evening with all his family and friends seemed so much more serious than a quick introduction and a miserable night of cock-blocking he'd gotten from Liv.

Stone took off his skates and watched Natalie joke with his brothers. Yup, she was something special. Stone was looking forward to dinner as he took her hand in his and they all walked outside together. He was ready for serious. He was ready for more. He just hoped Nat was too.

13

Natalie had never had a big family. She was an only child, but she felt as if she were already part of the Townsend family. Wilder and Hunter joked with her and told embarrassing stories about Stone as they walked from the arena toward their parked cars.

"Stone, I do have something for you though," Hunter said after telling a very embarrassing story about Stone getting rejected by a girl in fourth grade. "It's in the truck."

"I'll get the car and drive it over here," Natalie said, reaching into her backpack purse and pulling out the keys.

She was parked about a hundred yards away. Natalie thought that Hunter might want to talk to Stone about her and wanted to give him space to do so. She knew she would need all of their approval to really become Stone's girlfriend and she was okay with giving them the space to discuss her. She'd do it too if she had her girlfriends here. Plus, she had never been a clingy girlfriend, much to the displeasure of several past boyfriends who needed to be fawned over *constantly*. Natalie had her own life to see to and couldn't constantly be some guy's full-time ego-stroker. However,

Stone didn't seem to be that kind of guy, even with his history of puck bunnies. He had his career, she had hers, and so far, they'd both been supportive of each other without being obsessive. Their relationship had a feeling of trust because of that independence.

Natalie frowned as she approached her car. She should tell Stone the truth. They were getting serious now, and maybe he wouldn't freak out. Natalie wasn't able to finish her thoughts as someone burst out from behind her car in a ski mask. Natalie screamed as they grabbed her. She felt a hand squeezing her arm and yank her towards him.

Three angry Townsend voices seemed to boom around them and Natalie knew they'd come to her rescue.

"Where is it?" a man growled as he moved to grab the straps to her backpack.

"Where is what?" Natalie asked as they played tug with her backpack between them.

"The list of secrets, you bitch. I'll kill you if you don't hand them over." The man pulled a knife and Natalie figured the bag wasn't worth her life. She let go quickly and the man fell back against her car, rolled to his side, and sprinted to the van that was speeding toward them with the side door open.

The man leaped into the getaway van as Stone rushed to her side. Hunter and Wilder were chasing after the van, but they were no match for it on foot. The van skidded out of the arena parking lot and tore down the road, out of sight.

"Are you hurt?" Stone was asking.

He probably asked her more than once, but she'd been watching the van. "I'm okay. Hunter, did you get a plate number?" Natalie asked as Stone kept a protective arm around her, making her feel safe enough to focus on what had just happened without completely freaking out.

Hunter and Wilder joined them slightly out of breath. "Yeah, I got one," Hunter said as he pulled out his phone and sent a text to Stone with the plate number. "Maybe Granger can run it for us?"

"I'll send it to him right now," Stone told his brother as he sent a text to the sheriff of Shadows Landing who was also his brother-in-law.

Natalie waited for him to send the text and then asked to borrow the phone. "I need to make a call and the guy stole my phone. It was in my bag."

"Your dad's number is in my phone contacts," Stone told her and handed his phone over.

Natalie stepped away and dialed a number that was not written down anywhere in this world. "Flower shop," a woman answered.

"I need to order a flower delivery," Natalie said.

"Client number?" the woman asked.

"B19992003," Natalie whispered since the guys kept glancing her way.

"What order would you like to place?"

"Three sunflowers, please," she said, sending the code for a compromised asset who had been contacted three times.

"Your delivery will arrive shortly."

The line went dead before Natalie could say thank you. She went into the phone's settings and deleted the number from all records before walking to the guys and handing Stone his phone back. "Thanks."

"I got your car hotwired," Hunter told her and sure enough her car was now running. "Damon will be able to get you a new key."

"Thanks," Natalie sighed. It wasn't the fact her life was threatened that was upsetting her.

"It's okay, you're safe now." Stone hugged her, mistaking her being upset as a result of the attack.

"I know," Natalie said, swiping at a tear. "But now I have to cancel all my credit cards and . . ." She took a deep breath and let it out slowly. "Go to the department of motor vehicles."

Stone groaned. Hunter hissed. Wilder made the sign of the cross.

"If you move in with Stone you can go to the one in Shadows Landing and they're really nice. They'll even take your picture over again until you're happy with it," Hunter told her.

"Seriously?" Okay, that alone might be worth moving in with Stone.

"She even has fresh baked cookies with her most days," Stone whispered.

"You're kidding, right?"

Stone shook his head. "I came from Chicago. Trust me when I say I understand how alien it all is. This is temping you to move in with me, isn't it?"

"Cookies and a flattering DMV photo? Yeah, I'd move in with whoever just robbed me to get that."

Natalie was only partially kidding. She'd never had a good driver's license photo in her life. Actually, they were downright embarrassing. Her last one had one eye open and another partially closed and her nose was scrunched up. The DMV worker took it when she sneezed and wouldn't let her have a new one.

"Wow, way to make a man feel special," Stone said dryly. So dryly that Natalie didn't know if she'd actually hurt his feelings or not. By the way Hunter and Wilder were trying to hold in laughter, she might have actually hurt Stone's feelings.

Hunter threw his muscled arm over her shoulder and pulled her away from Stone. "My brother finally got his head out of his ass and picked a good one. I can't wait for you to meet Kane, Forrest, and Rowan." Hunter held open the passenger door for her and smirked at Stone as if Hunter was the real gentleman there.

"Oh, you think I'm the one who has his head up his ass about women?" Stone asked, eyeing Hunter as Wilder let out a snort of amusement.

"What does that mean? Women love me." Hunter puffed up his chest and gave Natalie a wink.

"Maggie." That's all Stone said. Wilder was struggling hard not to bust out laughing, especially after Hunter's smirk fell into a frown.

"She's not a woman I would ever want to date. She's a walking pink puff of monogrammed fluff."

Natalie took in the way Hunter was now pouting like a toddler who got his toy taken away, the way Stone was smirking, and the way Wilder was clearly struggling not to say something he really wanted to say.

"But under those pearls she's hot," Wilder pointed out.

"I wouldn't know," Hunter said stubbornly. However, Nat saw the way his jaw tensed. Oh, he knew she was hot and it bothered him. She couldn't wait to ask Stone about this Maggie. "I don't pay attention to silly women who only care about their cute little dresses and their sorority."

Wilder finally had a laugh escape as he shook his head. "I can't wait to see your face when reality hits you. Nat, we'll see you at the bar. Let us know if you need any help with whatever happened here today, okay?"

"Thank you, Wilder. See you all soon." Hunter closed her door as Stone got in behind the steering wheel and handed her his phone.

"You can start canceling your credit cards on the drive home."

Home. It wasn't her home, but it sounded really nice to hear. Like a warm fuzzy blanket on a cool fall night. Home. Natalie looked over to Stone as he drove out of the arena. What would it be like to love and be loved by someone as intense as Stone? She bet it would put that fuzzy blanket to shame. It would be more of a bonfire of her heart, and she loved a good bonfire.

"Who's Maggie?" Natalie asked as she listened to the hold music for her first credit card company.

"Maggie Bell lives in Shadows Landing and helps her parents run their family estate. Her parents run the bed and breakfast part, but lately Maggie has been taking over the event hosting, like weddings and corporate meetings."

"And Hunter doesn't like her because she's a girly girl?" Nat asked, trying to understand.

Stone's lips split into a huge grin. "He doesn't like her because, while she is a total Southern belle come to life, she's not intimidated by him at all. She dishes his BS back to him faster than he can shovel it. The best part . . . Maggie is an Olympic sharpshooter. She's a total badass, but Hunter judged the book by the cover. Maggie gets great pleasure out of watching my brother shove his foot in his mouth. She's told us not to tell him, even when he's giving her crap. She just smiles and lets him dig that hole deeper and deeper."

Natalie laughed. She could just picture it. "I hope I get to meet her tonight."

"I'm sure you will." Stone turned serious then and she knew the talk of Maggie was over and it was time to talk about things she wasn't ready to say. "What's going on, Nat? Your business, your home, and now a mugging? That's not a coincidence."

"I can't say." Natalie hoped her serious tone would put an end to the discussion, but it didn't.

"Can't or won't?" Stone asked, too perceptively.

"Can't."

Stone paused in his questioning and the annoying hold music played loudly into the silent car. "What kind of trouble does a ballerina get into? Tear the wrong woman's tutu?"

"I can't say, but someone will be coming to help. Then it'll be taken care of and we won't have to worry about it anymore." At least Natalie hoped that is what would happen after making her call.

"How would it be taken care of?" Stone asked.

Natalie shrugged. "Don't know. Don't care. It will be someone else's problem after tonight."

"Nat . . ." Stone started, but finally an agent came on and Natalie ignored Stone's unasked questions and began the process of getting her cards replaced. Yes, she was still going to have to deal with this, but hopefully she'd be able to turn it over to whoever was showing up soon from the CIA. Natalie just wanted to get on with her new job, her boyfriend, her father, and life.

14

Harper's Bar was *the* hangout spot in Shadows Landing. There was a fine dining restaurant next door, the diner down the street, and the two competing barbeque joints in town, but it was Harper's where everyone went to watch the games and chat.

Harper Faulkner Reigns owned the bar and was married to Stone's knitting buddy, Dare. She'd hired a bartender, Georgina "Georgie" Greyson, who was now married to sheriff's deputy Kord King. However, Georgie was no longer tending bar there. She was busy running her family businesses, which from what Stone could tell, meant she managed a lot of money. He was happy for Georgie, but he sure did miss the bourbon old-fashioned cocktails she'd made him.

Every week, the Townsends met at Harper's for dinner and drinks. They'd play pool, throw darts, and hear the town's stories. Even though they might have scared the residents when they first moved in, the town was warming up to them. Okay, maybe it was because the Townsend brothers were no longer trying to protect their sister Olivia from bad dates. She'd married the one guy in town who didn't cower from them. Granger was a good guy. Even Damon had admitted that to Stone. Of course, they'd both deny it if Granger ever asked. They had to keep him on his toes.

Stone pulled to a stop on Main Street and waited as Natalie banged the back of her head against her headrest. "That's what I'm saying. It was stolen. It needs to be canceled." There was some more headbanging and then, finally, Natalie sighed with relief. "Thank you. Yes, express shipping would be great. No. I don't want to take a survey." Then she hung up and looked around as if just realizing they were parked.

She leaned forward and squinted. "Is that man carrying a turtle?"

Stone looked out the window as three guys entered the bar. "Yep. That's Turtle."

"I know it's a turtle. Why is he carrying it?" Natalie asked.

"No, I mean, yes." Stone laughed and shook his head. This town was something else. It was no longer strange to see Turtle carrying a turtle or Gator wrestling an alligator. That was just Shadows Landing. "The man is carrying a turtle, but in addition to carrying said turtle, the man's name is Turtle."

"Oh. What's his real name?"

Stone thought back. "I don't know. I don't know if anyone knows."

Natalie giggled and opened her car door. "I can't wait to meet him. This is so different from ballet hangouts where everyone is super dressed up and competitive."

"Yeah, you won't find that here." Stone opened the thick wooden door to the bar that had more than a few bullets lodged in it and let Natalie walk right into Shadows Landing.

Stone paused and let his eyes adjust to the slightly darker interior. He slid his arm around Natalie's waist and directed her to the bar. He needed a drink before he joined his family, who were all staring at him or, more specifically, at Natalie.

"I don't understand the words comin' outta your mouth," Gator said really slowly to a guy Stone had never seen behind the bar before.

"He ain't speakin' English, that's for sure," Turtle added.

The third man, Skeeter, nodded. Skeeter spoke to the pirate ghosts of Shadows Landing in addition to giving ghost tours. Stone had thought he was making it all up until he felt the cold rush of a ghost pinching his ass. Skeeter said it was Anne Bonney and Stone was a believer.

Stone turned to the man behind the bar who couldn't be more than twenty-two years old. His hair was a mix of a wet mop and a mullet. His clothes were . . . well, he could have just rolled out of bed or he could be fashionable. It was hard to tell.

"Hey guys," Stone said to Gator, Skeeter, and Turtle. "This is my girlfriend, Natalie. Nat, this is Gator. He removes the alligators that wander into town. This is Skeeter. He knows everything about the history of Shadows Landing." Stone would let his ghost-talking abilities be a fun surprise for later. "And this is Turtle. He's . . . Turtle."

"It's nice to meet you all," Natalie said with a kind smile, but her attention was on the turtle Turtle was holding. "Um, does your pet turtle have something on his shell?"

Turtle grinned and held up the turtle. "Bro!" Stone said, his smile splitting his face. "That's my number!"

"Miss Mitzy made it for me. She copied your team

colors, red and black, and put your number, seven, on it in white. We're ready to cheer for you when you're back on the ice," Turtle said as more people gathered to see the turtle in a sweater. "Plus, I think Tank is happy to cover up his shell. It's still pretty banged up from where Mean Abe tried to rip it off."

"Who is Mean Abe?" Natalie asked.

"A right ornery alligator," Gator told her. "Now, can someone get me a regular beer or I might turn into Mean Abe. This fella don't understand the word *beer*."

Stone turned to the bartender and smiled. The bartender looked as if he were bored. "Can I get these guys three beers, please?"

"We're not in a beer era right now. I'm really feeling Fall with some hard cider. No cap, it's a hard cider era." The bartender tossed his head and his light brown, slightly curly hair flowed off his eyes for a split second before falling back into place.

"See, what language is that?" Turtle looked near crying.

Stone knew. He knew it in three different languages. It was Gen Z. "Hey man, I'm Stone. What's your name?"

"Kyler," the bartender answered as he got to work with a pile of herbs.

"Well, Kyler. This isn't going to be a W for you or for the hard cider. Three beers for them. Nat, what do you want?"

"White wine, please"

"Great, and I'll take an old-fashioned." Stone finished the order and Kyler looked at his phone. "Did you get that?"

"Bet."

"Bet what? Am I betting that I'm getting a beer?" Gator was near hysterics.

Kyler moved at sloth-like speed to get the beers. He topped them with a slice of mango and Skeeter cursed. A cold breeze started to swirl, moving some of Kyler's curly hair. Not that he noticed. A white wine appeared with a strawberry made into a flower at the rim. Natalie seemed pleased, so that was good. The old-fashioned on the other hand came with more herbs than a garden.

"Is this lavender?" Stone held up his glass with a posy of flowers and herbs in it. It would be great if he were traipsing around the woods in the eighteen hundreds or if he were smudging a house of evil.

"It elevates the drink." Then Kyler walked off to the other end of the bar.

"Hey fam! I see you met my fam!" Stone turned to see a massive manbun and the owner of it, Timmons, smiling. Timmons worked at the Bell Estate. Stone had never met a happier guy. "Bruh!"

Kyler turned and gave Timmons a flip of his hair. "The bartender is your brother?" Stone asked.

Somehow Timmons's smile widened even further. "Yeah. He's here for a couple of weeks. He travels the world and bartends to pay for it. He stopped by to see me and earn a couple of bucks. Then he's off to Paris to concoct cocktails at some big fashion shindig. He slays at making drinks, right fam?"

"This all makes sense now," Gator mumbled as he took the mango from his beer with a look of disgust.

"I'm sorry this is how we met. It's not our finest hour," Skeeter said to Natalie as he glared at the mango adorning his beer.

Stone put his arm around Natalie and led her to the side-by-side tables the Townsends had claimed about ten feet from the tables the Faulkner family had claimed. Olivia spotted them first and was instantly up and out of her chair.

She ignored Stone and hugged Natalie. "Hunter and Wilder told us what happened. I can't believe you were mugged!"

At least Stone wouldn't have to recount the story. The entire family already knew about it. Olivia pulled Natalie to the table and introduced her to Forrest, Kane, and Rowan. Stone let his gaze wander to the two tables between the Townsends and the Faulkners. The knitting club sat at the one closest to the Faulkner family, knitting and gossiping. But the table that got Stone's attention was the one just now being taken.

Maggie, her brother Gage, and another man and woman were walking to the empty table right beside where Hunter was sitting.

"Natalie, I'm so sorry that you had to be introduced to us through Stone," Hunter teased. "If you want to see real men in action and not dancing around the ice in their little skates, come hang out with Kane and me. We don't flinch at hits like Stone does."

Stone enjoyed how Natalie leaned against him in a silent show of support. "You should come to one of my classes, Hunter. Really put your muscles to the test," Natalie said sweetly.

Stone smiled down at her. Natalie was going to make Hunter cry and Stone was going to make sure to be there to video it. "Hey, Hunter. Your girlfriend is here," Stone said with a smirk.

Hunter looked confused until he looked over his shoulder at Maggie. "She is not, and will never be, my girlfriend."

Natalie looked over to see Maggie staring daggers at Hunter all the while smiling sweetly.

"Thank god for that," Maggie said in her sweet southern

voice. "I like my boyfriends to have brains and enough balls to respect women and what they can do."

Hunter laughed, but it held no humor. "I respect the hell out of women. My sister Olivia is a badass. What I don't respect is a woman who only cares about her frilly dresses and pearls. Oh, look, you have a monogrammed matching bag."

"You're such an idiot, Hunter. Don't you know my sister —" Maggie cut her brother off from finishing his sentence.

"Has guests," Maggie said with a sweet smile that was meant to scare the crap out of Hunter, but he only rolled his eyes at Maggie in response. "Allison Mullins and William Weisz. Al, Will, this *lovely* man is Hunter Townsend."

Will Weisz looked to be in his late sixties and had a twinkle in his eye as he looked at Hunter. "Oh, I remember Townsend. Sergeant First Class now, is that right?"

Hunter looked confused until all of a sudden the confusion cleared and Hunter jumped up from his seat to hold out his hand. "Sir, it's great seeing you again." Hunter turned to Stone and the rest of his family. "He was my instructor at Army Marksman school. He taught me action shooting and made me into the fine shot I am today."

"Townsend is a hell of a shot. I only know a few who could beat him. One of whom is sitting at this table," William told them. Stone saw everyone look to Maggie, but his idiot of a brother looked to Allison Mullins.

"Ms. Mullins, are you with the Army?" Hunter asked.

"Me? Oh, yes, I'm on the International Rifle team. But I'm not the one who could—"

"Allison is set to qualify for the summer Olympics," Maggie said before Allison could out Maggie as the team captain and apparently the one person at the table who could outshoot Hunter. Stone had been curious as to why

Maggie kept cutting people off when Hunter tried to challenge her, so Stone had looked her up. The first search result had been her position on the Olympic sharpshooting team as a college student. Maggie had a very impressive résumé that included an Olympic medal, six US national wins, and just as many world wins. On the pro shooting circuit, she was considered one of the best, regardless of sex.

Natalie shook hands with the table of really neat people. Gage had his master's in business and was working for a big company in Charleston while also trying out for the Olympic shooting team for trapshooting. Then there were the two guests at their parents' bed and breakfast. William was the coach for the Olympic team and Allison was one of their best. Second best, to be specific.

"Aren't you going to tell Hunter that you're the best sharpshooter at the table?" Natalie whispered after meeting Maggie and instantly taking to her. She was warm, kind, and not pretentious in any way.

"Nope," Maggie gave Nat a wink. "It's more fun like this."

Maggie was called into a discussion over which drinks to order when Natalie felt someone move to stand next to her. "Personally, I would love to see her whoop his ass in shooting."

Natalie jumped at the unfamiliar voice. When she turned her head, she saw a woman who wasn't that much taller than she was with curly blonde hair, a sweet smile, and mischievous eyes. "Who are you?"

"Flower delivery."

"You? You're who Naylor sent? I thought there'd be a team to take out whoever is trying to get to me, but Naylor only sent you?" Natalie hissed with anger. She'd expected a team to come in and take over, not some girl-next-door.

"Naylor's an ass, but I'm pretty good at what I do. Just like you're good at what you do. Look, I'm here to assess the situation and extricate you if necessary."

"No," Natalie snapped in a whisper. "I am not leaving. I wanted this handled, not to give up my job, my family, and my boyfriend."

"Boyfriend? That wasn't in the file. Who is it?" the CIA agent asked, looking way more interested in that gossip than in the fact someone had attacked her.

"Stone Townsend. That's not important. What is important is that you catch who is behind this."

"Oh, Stone. Good choice. Hunter and Maggie are totally together. You know what they say about enemies to lovers? They're going to burn this town down when they finally get together. Damon is too broody for you, but Stone is perfect. You both have that pro sports thing going on."

"Who the hell are you?" Natalie whispered again.

"Cassidy?" Ryker Faulkner stopped from where he was walking back to the Faulkner table with two drinks in his hand. At that pronouncement, the entire Faulkner table turned then shot up and rushed over to hug the woman. "What are you doing in Shadows Landing?" Ryker asked once all the hugging and introducing to Natalie was done. Apparently, her flower delivery CIA agent was one Cassidy Davies from Kentucky who was related to the Faulkners of Shadows Landing.

"I'm friends with Nat and was so excited to see her business up and running that I came to check it out and see my cousins," Cassidy lied smoothly.

Ryker leaned closer as the Townsends, Faulkners, and Bells all mingled together chatting, so that just Natalie and

Cassidy could hear him. "Bullshit. Let me know if you need anything."

Ryker left and Stone came with a drink in his hand that he gave to Cassidy. "I don't even know what this is. We have a guest bartender this week."

Cassidy took a sip and frowned. "Anyone who loves bourbon would be pissed with all this . . . stuff. But it somehow works."

"It's elevated," Stone said so seriously that Natalie suddenly laughed. "That's really nice that you came out here to support Natalie."

"That's what friends do."

Natalie grinned, but it was fake. Ever since she left the arena, things had gone to pot. Now all she could do was sit back and see what one woman could do.

15

Stone had so much fun that night with his friends and family that he momentarily forgot it appeared someone wanted something from Natalie. Stone drove them home after the bar and listened with a warm happiness as Natalie talked about his friends and family. He liked to hear what she thought of them and laughed when she, too, noted Hunter and Maggie seemed to have more chemistry than they could handle together.

"Is he the only person in town who doesn't know about Maggie?"

Stone pulled into the garage and turned off the car. "Yep. We've all looked her up after one of their arguments. It's clear as day that Maggie was hiding something in their foreplay-like arguments. We all laughed our asses off when we saw it and agreed Hunter needed to learn his lesson, so we never told him."

Stone paused as he opened the door to his house for her. Together they walked inside and settled in the kitchen. Natalie chatted happily about the night, but Stone noticed she didn't talk about her "old friend" who had stopped by.

"That was nice of your friend to come for a visit. Was it a surprise?"

"My friend . . . oh, Cassidy. I talked to her earlier and didn't know she would come so soon. It was definitely a surprise."

"Did you know she's cousins with the Faulkners?"

"She mentioned knowing people near Charleston, but I didn't realize they were from Shadows Landing." Natalie was lying and she wasn't very good at it.

Stone crossed his arms and leaned a hip against his kitchen island. "You know I've met her before."

Natalie went pale. "Really? How did that happen?"

"She and her cousin Greer danced with Damon and me at Ryker's wedding to Kenzie."

"That explains why she said you were a good choice for me. She said Damon was too broody." Natalie laughed, and while Stone didn't doubt that conversation had happened, he still felt that Natalie was keeping something from him.

He was going to ask more, but then Natalie grabbed the waistband of his pants and rose up on her toes to kiss him. "I think you're pretty perfect for me too."

Natalie's lips were warm on his. At first, she was hesitant, giving a little brush of her lips against his. Stone's hands instantly went to her hips and Natalie was encouraged to increase the pressure. Stone was lost when the tip of her tongue traced the crease of his lips.

He would like to say he had enough control to make it upstairs, but the farthest they made it was to the couch. Part of his brain realized Natalie was distracting him from asking about Cassidy, but when she shoved him back against the couch and stepped between his legs, he didn't care. He could ask her tomorrow.

Stone stared at Natalie as she slowly took her clothes off

before reaching for his shirt and pulling it over his head. Stone reached for her hips and lifted her easily into the air. Natalie laughed as he slowly lowered her so she was straddling his lap. "I could have done that myself," Natalie said as she ran her fingers through his hair.

"You were taking too long." Stone raised his hips and Natalie sank onto him.

They groaned together as she began to set the pace. Stone's head rested on the back of the couch. His hands explored Natalie's body as she moved up on him, chasing down her pleasure. He'd never seen anything sexier than when her head dropped back, her eyes closed, and she found what she'd been chasing. She flew off the cliff and he was there to catch her, just like he would do in life. This was different. This wasn't just sex. This was so much more.

Natalie didn't know she could simultaneously feel both amazing and awful. Making love to Stone had her on cloud nine, but she felt guilty too. She knew he wanted to know about Cassidy and she couldn't answer his questions, so Natalie distracted him.

They'd gotten up early and made love again before Stone got ready for his first practice. Now Natalie sat in the stands of the Pirate's arena, watching Stone struggle not to skate all out. She had a whistle and would blow it when he began to skate too fast or make cuts too hard. The good news was he was doing it. There were no signs of pain or decreased movement. In fact, he was looking better than ever.

"Stone's looking good."

Natalie jumped in her chair and lashed out with

something that was a combination of a punch and swatting a bug.

Cassidy blocked the hit and laughed. "We need to work on that punch. My little sister who's about to start kindergarten can do better than that."

Natalie looked to where she sat in the middle of a row in the middle of the arena all alone. "How did you get in here without me seeing you?"

Cassidy shrugged, but it was the pleased smirk on her face that told Nat she enjoyed her little trick. "I've looked into your police reports. Your CIA file is being sent to me as well. I've also started asking around to see what I can find out. Gossip, even in spy circles, is major currency. And trust me, I'll find out. I am the queen of gossip. If all else fails, I'll have to ask my grandma for an apple pie to bribe someone with. I get more info from that than any mole or bug. I wanted you to know I put up security cameras and some tougher locks as well. Here are your new keys to your house and office."

"That's it? What about the people after me?"

"Don't worry, I'm working on it. I'll get to the bottom of it. I promise." Cassidy's phone vibrated and she looked down at it and answered. "Grandma! I miss you too. I'm seeing the family in Shadows Landing. Do you happen to have a spare pie or two you could ship down today?" Cassidy paused. "Really? Are they as good as yours?"

Natalie could hear an older woman laughing over the phone and smiled. Cassidy's grandmother sounded . . . interesting.

"Okay, I'll ask them. Thanks Grandma." Cassidy hung up and stood. "Looks like I need to pay a visit to Miss Ruby and Miss Winnie. Also, tell Stone to watch Belov. While your name has been suspiciously quiet, Belov's name has come up several times."

"What should I do?" Natalie asked.

"Stick close to Stone and Shadows Landing." Cassidy was gone just as fast as she appeared.

Stone stepped off the ice feeling lighter than he had in weeks. He was only skating at fifty percent and it already felt ten times better than before. Andrew Kenny and Theo, his wingmen, had noticed and were asking him questions about his training the second they entered the locker room.

"Could we go with you?" Theo asked as Andrew nodded.

"You'd give barre a try?" Stone was surprised. They'd been giving him shit about becoming a ballet dancer and wearing tights and tutus.

"After seeing you today and knowing you weren't even skating at full speed, hell yah, bud," Andrew answered.

"I go too, yes?" Kalle Aho asked in his Finnish accent. "I get spot back from that rotten tree top. I have *sisu*, I won't give up."

It took Stone a second to figure out Kalle wanted to get his spot back from the rotten Belov by working hard to earn it back. "Of course, Kalle. I'll talk to Natalie tomorrow and let you know at practice."

Stone hadn't told them he was dating her or that she was Coach Novak's daughter. He didn't want any talk of her in the locker room or he feared Coach might pull a Belov and stab someone with a pair of hockey skates.

"Townsend. Office. Now," Coach Novak snapped and then disappeared back into his office.

"Coach doesn't look happy with you. Any idea why?" Theo asked in a whisper.

Yeah, Stone had a pretty good idea why he didn't look happy. It probably had to do with the fact Stone was dating his daughter. A daughter who had spent the night having sex with him.

Stone knocked on the office door and when Coach Novak snapped, "Come in." Stone opened the door and walked into the office before closing the door again. He didn't want his teammates hearing him getting ripped to shreds for dating Natalie.

"Yes, Coach?"

"First, my daughter is freaking amazing. You looked great in practice today," Coach said, somehow managing to sound both proud and pissed. "You'll start against Tennessee on Saturday."

"I can play Tuesday," Stone began to protest, but Coach glared and Stone snapped his mouth closed. "Thank you. I can't wait to be back on the ice."

"How does the knee feel?" Coach asked, finally taking a seat.

"Really good. I can't wait to see what skating at a hundred percent is like tomorrow. Actually, Theo, Andrew, and Kalle want to join me in training with Natalie. Is that okay with you?"

"It's okay with me as long as Natalie is good with it. I have to say, after seeing you today I am tempted to make it mandatory team training, but that's not why I called you in here."

"I know," Stone said, ready for a punch to the face.

"You do? Then tell me."

"It's because Natalie is staying at my place. I could lie and say I haven't touched her, but, well, that would be a lie. I'm sure as her dad, you don't want to know—" Stone didn't get to finish as Novak reached across the desk and grabbed

Stone by the jersey, yanking him up to his feet and bringing his face close to Stone's.

"You what?" Novak growled.

Oh shit. He hadn't known. "I love your daughter," Stone sputtered. He could see Novak's surprised look mirrored Stone's. "Please don't tell her before I can tell her."

Novak dropped his hold on Stone and sat back down. "I was going to talk about Belov and his wife. They're making a mess of the wives, and we can't have that. But I guess we'll talk about your . . . feelings for my daughter instead." Novak cleared his throat. "You actually love her? Not just trying to score another woman?"

The L word had always freaked Stone out, but this time it made him smile.

"Oh geez. You have the goofiest look on your face. You actually do love her." Suddenly Novak grinned and rubbed his hands together with a laugh. "Damn, I'm good! I knew you two were perfect for each other."

Stone finally took a breath. "You were right, Coach. Can't thank you enough for that. Now, tell me about your problem with Belov and I'll try to come up with a way to fix it."

16

Natalie was almost finished with Rita's training session, but it was hard to focus. It was Monday and Nat still hadn't moved out of Stone's house even though her door was repaired and her house was safe to go back to.

Instead, Stone had insisted she stay with him and they could carpool into Charleston together. Natalie hadn't put up a fight. She had just curled back up into his strong arms and nuzzled closer to his chest. She didn't want to go home. She loved this time with Stone. She loved the way he made her laugh. She loved the way he made her feel treasured and so special. She loved . . . Stone.

"Was my footwork that good?" Rita asked with a laugh.

Nat realized she was standing there, staring at Rita's feet with a goofy grin on her face. "Your footwork is improving. Next week we'll get a little fancy and try some new moves to see how you do."

Natalie put her cool, professional self back in place. She liked Rita, but Natalie wasn't going to tell someone else she loved Stone before she could tell him. Or should she not tell him? Stone was pretty notorious for not being serious with women. Would the L word send him running for the hills?

"I'll see you Thursday. Thanks for everything, Natalie." Rita gave her a little hug and then headed out the door, leaving Natalie standing in the middle of the room alone. Her mind was still spinning when Cassidy strode in.

Gone was the sweet and happy-go-lucky Cassidy. In her place was a pissed-off and slightly terrifying Cassidy. Her eyes were narrowed, her lips were pursed, and she strode quickly into the room with an open bottle of water.

"I'm here for my workout . . . eeek!" Cassidy pitched forward, her water splashing Natalie as Cassidy fell into her.

The cold water soaking her brought Natalie's mind snapping back to the present. "What the hell?" she sputtered.

Rita popped back in, looking worried. "I heard a scream. Is everything okay?"

"I am such a klutz. I tripped and spilled my water all over Miss Novak. Not the best impression to make." Cassidy gave a sheepish grin as she began using a tissue to try to clean up the dripping water.

Rita's face looked momentarily pinched. "Do you need help cleaning up?"

"No, I'll just change and bring in a mop. Thanks though, Rita."

Natalie waited for Rita to close the door before turning on Cassidy only to find a hand over her mouth.

"I'm so sorry. Let's go to your office to talk about my training and then you can dry off."

Cassidy strode from the room and was already in Natalie's office with the door closed by the time Natalie caught up to her. When Natalie opened the door, Cassidy was slowly scanning the room with a device. She lifted a lamp and plucked something from under it. "Go ahead and change, Miss Novak. We can talk when you're dry. Again. I'm so sorry."

Natalie wanted to say more, but Cassidy put a finger to her lips and continued to scan the room, stopping and plucking bugs from her office. At first, Natalie hadn't known what they were, but then she'd gotten a good look of one mixed in with the mulch of her potted plant. Natalie had planted more of those than she could count and instantly recognized it.

Natalie changed in the bathroom and found a bug under the towel rack. She flushed it down the toilet and went to join Cassidy in the office.

Cassidy was now sitting on the chair with a clear water bottle full of bugs. It looked to be at least six. "Someone has been hiding behind her tutu," Cassidy said seriously. There was no girl-next-door sitting in her office now. Now there was a CIA agent wanting answers.

"They're good at hiding things," Nat answered before taking a seat on her couch across from Cassidy.

"What exactly did you do for Naylor because there's no real file on you?" Cassidy asked. Natalie didn't answer. She'd been instructed not to tell anyone anything she'd done. "Are you selling secrets on the black market?"

"What!?" Natalie was so shocked it just burst out.

"Naylor won't tell me what you did to become a CIA asset, but he wants to know and possess whatever it is you have or you know." Cassidy was deadly serious. Natalie could tell this was an interrogation, not a friendly chat.

"I have insurance and that is all I will say."

"Is it worth being killed for?" Cassidy asked.

"Yes, is it?" The deep voice made Natalie jump to face

the now open door. She noticed Cassidy didn't jump, nor did she even turn around.

"Hello, Nico."

"Cassidy," said a very dangerous-looking man who entered her office and closed the door behind him.

"What brings a mafia boss to an athletic training center?" Cassidy asked, the sweetness back in her voice. But that didn't keep Natalie from catching the word *mafia*.

"*Former* mafia boss. My extended family in Italy has been talking about secrets of theirs being stolen. They want retribution."

"I thought you went legit?" Cassidy asked, almost as if she were bored.

"I am legit. But when the family starts worrying and talking about hits where my friends live, I look into it."

Cassidy smiled. "You thought it was Ryker."

"Wait." Natalie tried to understand what was going on. "You're really in the mafia?" she asked Nico.

"Eh," Nico said with a shrug.

"And you two know each other?" Natalie asked, pointing to Nico and Cassidy, who both just shrugged again.

There was a knock on the door, and then it opened. Stone walked in and glanced at Nico and Cassidy. "Looks like I'm late to the party."

"Stone Townsend, the star center of the Charleston Pirates. It's an honor to meet you." Natalie watched as Nico held out his hand to Stone and Stone shook it. "Nico Saccone."

"Nice to meet you, Nico. What's going on?" Stone asked.

"I had just wanted some girl talk with Natalie before I leave town."

"You're leaving?" Natalie asked Cassidy. No, Cassidy was

the one here to protect her. What would happen if she was left alone?

"Our mutual friend is insisting I come to visit. I'm off for a little bit, but will be back soon."

"I'll walk you out," Natalie said, leaving Nico and Stone in her office. "Naylor is pulling you?" she whispered as soon as they were outside.

"What did you do for him, Natalie? Like I said, there's no paper trail for me to really follow, and he's been very vague about it." Cassidy asked again. "Let me help you."

Natalie didn't know what to do or say. It was clear Cassidy was knowledgeable, but she also worked with Naylor and Nat didn't trust him at all. "Why did you spill water on me?"

"I didn't know if it was safe to talk in there. I got you into your office and cleaned it up so we wouldn't be overheard. Please, Natalie. Let me help you. What do you have? Where is it?"

Natalie stood quietly by Cassidy's rental car. She desperately wanted to trust someone. She just didn't know who. "I'll think about it. I was hoping the CIA would help, but clearly they're not going to. It makes it hard to trust you, especially when I'm in the mess because of the CIA."

"It must be bad because Nico wouldn't be here if he wasn't worried about a hit on one of his friends. We know at least the Italian-American mafiosi know about you having insurance. I don't like leaving, but you know how to contact me if you need me. I'll get back as soon as I can. I don't know what Naylor wants, but I've been ordered back to DC. Stay safe, Natalie. Trust the Townsends and the Faulkners. Even Nico to a point."

"To which point?" Natalie asked as Cassidy got into her car.

"To any point that will keep you alive. I'll be in touch."

Stone stared at Nico Saccone as if they were sizing each other up over a face-off on the ice. "What are you doing here?" Stone decided to go with bluntness over tact. Nico seemed as if he'd appreciate it.

"Family business. Just needed a chat with Miss Novak."

"Someone needs training?"

Nico just smiled looking all the world like a politician. "What exactly is your family business?" Stone asked.

"I have an appointment I need to get to. It was great meeting you. I look forward to seeing you on the ice." Nico turned and left Stone standing alone in Natalie's office. Something wasn't right and he was going to get to the bottom of it.

Natalie stood watching the car drive off until she heard the sound of someone walking behind her. The next parking spot over had a sleek black luxury car parked in it. "I am here only to help, Miss Novak."

"Cassidy said as much, Mr. Saccone." Natalie turned to see the handsome man in his custom Italian suit standing patiently with his hands in his pockets. "I wonder, why did you come to see me?"

"Rumors are there's someone selling criminal secrets that were stolen from someone very powerful. That person is willing to do anything to get it back. At first, all I knew was the person selling them was in Charleston. I have friends here and wanted to make sure they were safe. Let me put it this way, Cassidy isn't the only one with better connections than the CIA. They were just smart enough to hire her. My connections will never work for anyone. My grandmother's niece's youngest cousin's brother-in-law's school friend is a security guard for a powerful man in France. He told them about a beautiful ballet dancer he'd found in his office during a party. That, mixed with the rumors that a Russian agent is in Charleston, helped me narrow it down. I took a chance that the ballet dancer was the one who stole the secrets, not one of my friends. Looks like I'm not the only one who has done so."

Natalie swallowed hard. Arrows pointed to her, but it also didn't sound like they had actual proof she'd taken anything and she certainly wasn't selling anything. Maybe that was why she was still alive. They were trying to figure out if she was the spy. "And your family is worried there's something about them that might be sold?" Natalie asked.

"That's right. My grandparents might be retired, but other relatives are not. I'm not saying you are the one selling these secrets, but if you are, know I can help you act as a mediator to end this with your life still intact."

"That's good to know, Mr. Saccone. I would feel comfortable calling you for your assistance." Natalie realized it was true. While Nico was scary as hell but she saw something kind in his eyes. "The trouble is, I'm not selling anything. I wouldn't even know how to do that."

Nico cocked his head as if reading her truthfulness before pulling a business card from his pocket. "I'm staying in Charleston for a while. Here's my contact info. Call day or night if you need any assistance, Miss Novak."

Natalie took the card and didn't know if she'd been blessed by an angel or kissed by the devil.

17

Stone paced the office as he waited for Natalie to come back inside. He loved her and he wanted to tell her so, but first he needed to get to the bottom of this.

"How did practice go?" Natalie asked. She was clearly trying to divert the conversation she knew was coming.

"Belov is causing problems. My knee is great. I'll miss this game but start the next. Now you're updated on my day. Why don't you update me on what is going on?"

Natalie tried to look as if she didn't know what he was talking about, but it didn't work. "I don't know what you mean."

"Yes, you do, Nat. Why are your house, office, and you being searched? Why is there a man in your office who looks as if he walked off the set of a mafia movie? Please, Nat. Just trust me and tell me what's going on."

Stone watched as Natalie seemed to deflate in front of him. She closed the door and dropped onto her couch. Stone moved as quietly as he could as not to scare her. Natalie seemed to be lost in thought as he took a seat next to her.

It seemed time was slowly ticking by as Natalie rested her chin in her hands and stared at the floor, clearly lost in thought. Stone didn't press her. She looked ready to break as it was. Then, after a long silence, Natalie sat up and straightened her spine. She took a deep breath as if she were about to walk out on stage and turned to face him. "I was a CIA asset charged with bugging and stealing from politically important ballet benefactors."

Stone didn't know what to expect, but that wasn't it. "You're a spy?"

Natalie took a deep breath and shook her head. "Sort of, but not because I wanted to be. Agent Aaron Naylor, the man who made me do this, threatened my father. My dad was coaching in Russia and it was becoming progressively more and more dangerous for foreigners. Naylor said he'd tell the Russian authorities my father was an American spy if I didn't do what he told me."

Stone's hands clenched and he tried not to erupt with anger. He didn't want Natalie to think he was mad at her. "He extorted you."

"Yes. At first, it was little things. Drop a bug here or there. Then it got progressively more involved. Steal things, take pictures of things . . . stuff like that. At a gala, I ran into Archie Tupper. I planted the idea of my dad coaching here. Once my father was safe in America, I told Naylor to shove it and I left, but not before taking something I shouldn't have. I did it for insurance. I didn't want anyone coming after me and I stupidly thought it would protect me. Now, I think it put me in danger. Nico said his mafia family figured out I was the one who took it and a Russian agent is after it too."

Stone reached out and took Natalie's hand in his. "What is it that you have?"

Natalie grimaced. "I'm not exactly sure. I copied a folder

from a computer to a thumb drive. It was a detailed spreadsheet with names, orders, and money paid on it. I think the person I took it from is an illegal arms dealer or something and I have a copy of all his clients. I thought I could go up the chain and trade it for my freedom from the CIA if Naylor tried to push me back into working for him. I didn't think the person I took it from would ever know."

"And Cassidy?"

"She's a CIA agent sent to clean up the mess I made, but Naylor has pulled her from my detail and sent her back to DC. He's leaving me hanging as punishment for refusing to come back and work for him."

Natalie leaned back against the cushion of her couch and closed her eyes. "I don't know what to do. I didn't want any part of this to begin with, and now I'm in danger from either the person I stole it from, the mafia, the Russians, or possibly all three. This is such a mess."

Stone put his arm around Natalie's shoulders as she leaned forward and covered her face with her hands. "I don't know what to do or who to trust. Right now, you're the only person I trust. And now I probably put you in danger," her muffled voice said from behind her hands.

Stone's mind was racing a mile a minute, but it all came back to trust. "I trust my family, and that includes my brother-in-law. He's just a sheriff, but he might know something we can do to protect you. Hunter is military, and not just any military. He's the kind that can't talk about it. He might have some ideas too. Olivia knows all the laws to protect you. Kane was FBI, so he might have some insight too. I think it might be time for us to go back to Shadows Landing. Will you come with me?"

. . .

Natalie felt so defeated. She didn't know what to do or who to trust. Until she'd told Stone the truth. She knew she could trust him, but she hated putting him in that position. He knew her secret. He knew about the CIA. He knew about her spying. What if the people who were after her came after him?

"You still want me to come with you? I'm a whole heap of trouble waiting to happen, and I don't want you caught up in it." While she wanted to push Stone far away, she also still clung to his hand as if he were her only lifeline.

"Nat." Stone's voice was soft but full of command. "If I didn't want you in my life, I wouldn't have offered to help. I want you in my life, in my heart, and in my bed. If that means a little international incident, so be it. I've never run from anything in my life. I'm not going to start now. Not when I finally found something worth fighting for."

Natalie squeezed his hand and drew from his strength. If everything went sideways, she didn't want to have any regrets. She wanted Stone to know how she felt. "I would love to come home with you, Stone. Not because I'm scared or want your help, but because there's nowhere else I'd rather be than with you, in your arms." Natalie looked up into his eyes and saw her feelings reflected back in his gaze. "I love you, Stone. Not the star hockey player, but you. The knitter, the big brother who loves his family and friends and who is sweet to old ladies and children. That's who I have fallen in love with."

"I guess it's a good thing I fell in love with you before I knew you were off limits as my coach's daughter then." Stone gave her a wink that made her giggle, but then he turned serious. "I mean it, Nat. I don't say those words lightly and I do love you. In fact, I might have accidentally told your father after practice."

Natalie felt her mouth drop in surprise and then she slapped her hand over her mouth to try to stop the laughter from escaping. "Oh no. What did he say?"

"He's very pleased with himself, you know. Yeah, your father set us up and it worked. We owe him lots of grandchildren."

"Wow, you only just now told me you love me and we're onto having children?" Natalie felt as if she were walking on a cloud. Even with all the shit she was going through, Stone knew how to make her feel as if she were floating above it all.

"When I know what I want, I know. And I know I want you, Natalie. All of you. I'm so proud of you for the athlete and businesswoman you are, but also for how you're handling what that asshole put you through. Together, we're an unstoppable team. We have our future to live together and I won't let anything stop us from that. I love you, Natalie."

Stone leaned forward and kissed her before she could process all the feelings from what he'd just told her. The kiss wiped all thoughts of Naylor, the mafia, Russians, and the CIA from her mind. The pressure of his lips on hers, the sweep of his tongue, the way his fingers closed on the back of her neck, bringing her closer to him even as he cupped her cheek tenderly.

Stone ended the kiss and she sat clinging to him. "For now, we better figure out how to handle this. I guess that means we talk to your family."

"We can do that tomorrow. Coach says I don't need to go on the away game with the team so I'm all yours tomorrow."

"Then what do we do tonight?" Natalie asked with faux innocence.

"Oh, I have a very good idea of what we can do tonight." The way Stone's voice rumbled when he said that rocked her world and made it very clear what his plan was.

18

Stone never let women sleep over. Until Natalie. Now he couldn't imagine waking up without her in his arms. How quickly he'd gotten used to her being an integral part of his everyday life was shocking but not terrifying. Now he understood that saying about when it was right, you'd know it. Because he knew it.

"I know you have clients this morning," Stone said as Natalie snuggled closer to him. "But I was hoping we could meet with my family for breakfast."

"My first client isn't until ten, so I can do that."

Stone could tell she was trying not to be nervous, but the slight shiver down her naked body told him otherwise. She was scared about doing this. Stone sent out the text and reluctantly got up after brushing back her hair and kissing her neck. His family would be descending on them quickly. After what he put Olivia through, he wasn't so sure she wouldn't just walk in and sit down on the bed even if they were going to meet them at the diner in thirty minutes.

"Are you really sure we need to be doing this? I don't feel right dragging innocent people into my mess. I feel bad enough doing it to you," Natalie said as she pulled on her spandex athletic pants, a sports bra, and a Dri-Fit shirt with *N2 Training* on the front of it.

"I'm sure. They'll want to help, and I'll feel better knowing you're not alone in this." Stone frowned as he pushed his game-day suit aside and grabbed a Pirates T-shirt instead. He was missing game day and he didn't like it. He felt guilty not traveling with his team, but he'd be back on the ice in four more days. "Ready?" Stone asked as she slipped on his shoes.

Natalie raised her eyebrow from where she was sitting on the edge of the bed. She'd been ready for five minutes.

Stone held out his hand and loved how she instantly slipped hers into his. "So, do ballerinas eat grits?"

"This retired one does," Natalie joked as they walked downstairs and out into the garage.

Stone opened the garage door and saw two black boots on his driveway. He shoved Natalie behind him and reached for the closest weapon—a broom. The garage door continued up as jeans were revealed, then a tight black T-shirt, muscled arms crossed across a chest, and finally Damon's glowering face.

"Could you take any longer to get ready? I won't even insult Natalie by thinking it was her. You were always a little prima donna about your hair."

Natalie snickered behind Stone and leaned around to ruffle the top of his head with her fingers. "But it does look right-out-of-bed sexy."

Damon rolled his eyes, but when he was done his eyes went to her hand. "I don't see a ring. What's so important you called an emergency meeting?"

"I was wondering that, too."

Natalie screamed and jumped at the sound of Hunter behind them.

"Did you seriously break into my house just to sneak up on us?" Stone asked Hunter.

"I thought it might be a hostage situation."

"Stone's not holding me hostage. I promise," Natalie assured him.

"I figured you were holding him hostage. It's the only way he'd let a woman spend the night."

Stone gave his brother the middle finger as the sound of a siren growing closer drew their attention. Granger slid to a stop right behind where Damon stood. Olivia was out of the SUV so fast he didn't know how she was able to move on heels so quickly without falling over.

"What did I miss? I told Granger to drive faster. Are you pregnant? Is Stone dumping you? Are you dumping him? You're too good for him anyway," Olivia asked as if it were a cross-examination.

"Whoa, wait." Stone held up his hands. "I mean, I know she's too good for me. But come on, you're my sister. You should be on my side."

"When you make my prom date pee his tuxedo and ditch me at the last second, making me go to my prom alone, you no longer have me on your side for relationships." Olivia crossed her arms and glared at him.

"Is that true?" Natalie asked.

"Not entirely," Stone said stubbornly. "Damon was there, too."

"Damn right I was. I'm proud of my record. That's the only one I couldn't scare off." Damon tilted his head toward Granger without looking at him.

Granger smirked and reached out and tickled Damon's

stomach. "You're not so scary," he cooed as if Damon was a baby. "No, you're not. You're a big softy. Yes, you are."

Damon let out a low growl that sounded nothing like a cuddly baby. It only made Granger laugh, which is why Granger was now married to Olivia. Anyone else would have disappeared, never to be seen again.

"So, what's going on then?" Forrest asked as he walked up the driveway with Kane.

"Hold the phone up. We can't see." Came Rowan's voice even though Stone couldn't see him.

Kane held up his cell phone where Stone could see Rowan in scrubs, walking down the hallway of the hospital in Charleston and also Wilder who was signing something as a person was unloading a giant truck at the back of his nightclub, WET, in Charleston.

"I thought we were going to meet for breakfast?" Stone asked, stupidly knowing no breakfast was going to be forthcoming now that he and Nat were literally surrounded by his family.

"Brought it," Forrest said, holding up a bag from the diner. "It's why Kane and I were late."

"Did you get grits?" Natalie asked him.

"Yeah, but I got them for me along with a breakfast burrito," Kane told her. "I grabbed you an egg white omelet."

Olivia reached over and punched Kane's shoulder. "Why the hell would you do that?"

"She's a ballerina. Don't they like watch everything they eat?"

Natalie reached out and snagged the bag. "Retired. Thank you. Grits and a burrito sound great."

Olivia shook her head at Kane and walked inside with Natalie. "I'm so sorry for my brothers. I thought I did a better job raising them, but obviously I've been too soft on them the past couple of years."

"Oh shit," Kane whispered as Natalie and Olivia disappeared inside. "What does that mean? What's Liv going to do to us?"

"She's already getting revenge on me," Stone whispered as the brothers all huddled together staring at the door with something close to fear. Except Damon. Damon didn't fear anything. Although he should. He messed with Liv's love life more than all of them combined.

"How so?" Hunter asked, starting to look a little nervous.

"You know how we cock-blocked her and her dates? Let's just say she's getting payback. I'm constantly worried she's going to pop up in my bedroom. She came by the other day and didn't leave the entire night."

Hunter laughed. "She won't do that to me. My house is a fortress. She'd never get in."

"As if you'd get your head out of your ass long enough to see what, or who, is right in front of you to even bring home for Liv to interfere with," Damon said dryly.

"Who is right in front of me?" Hunter asked.

Stone rolled his eyes. Kane shook his head. Forrest dropped his head back and groaned. Rowan and Wilder stared at him as if he had two heads. Damon smacked the back of Hunter's head. "Open your freaking eyes, man! It's getting embarrassing."

"Are you all coming in or not?" Olivia asked, sticking her head around the door.

Stone left Hunter pondering what he was missing and headed inside. One problem at a time, and right now Hunter being too blind to see that Maggie was perfect for him wasn't the most important problem. It was how to keep Natalie safe so Stone could marry her.

Stone stopped walking and Granger slammed into his back. "What the hell?" Granger muttered and then looked at the shocked look on Stone's face as his brothers walked inside. Stone was having an existential crisis. He realized marriage was on his mind when Granger's hand came down on Stone's shoulder and squeezed. "I know that look. That's the look of a man who has realized his life will never be the same again. Remember where the jewelry store was downtown that you all came to help me pick Olivia's ring? Well, tried to help."

Stone might have said something, but it wasn't words as reality crashed down on him harder than any hit he'd had on the ice. He loved Natalie so much that he'd do anything and everything he could to make her his wife because he couldn't imagine life without her in it.

"Yeah, I'll text you the address. Now come on. I'm guessing something is going on and it's not the realization you love the woman." Granger shoved Stone from his trance.

"How did you know?" Stone whispered as they walked inside. Forrest was at the kitchen table handing out food as they walked slowly toward them.

"Had the same damn look on my face once. I know I'm not your brother and that you all don't particularly like me but tolerate me, so my opinion doesn't mean much. However, I like Natalie for you. She's smart, beautiful, independent, and doesn't put up with your shit. She's perfect for you."

Stone reached out and grabbed Granger's arm, stopping him before they reached the dining room. "You think we don't like you?"

Granger looked confused. "Is this a trick question?"

"We wouldn't let you marry our sister if we didn't like you."

Granger snorted. "You don't let Liv do anything. She does what she wants."

"Maybe, but she wouldn't have married you so quickly if she knew we disapproved. We're family and we look out for each other. Our opinions matter to her, just like hers does to me. We give each other crap, but it's our way of showing each other we care."

"Wow, you all must really love me then based on the amount of crap you give me," Granger said sarcastically.

Stone smiled and slapped Granger's shoulder. "Damn straight, bro." Stone paused as Granger shook his head at Stone's antics. "Seriously, you're a good guy and you're one of us now. I fully expect you to give Hunter crap, and I also fully expect you to scare the crap out of any guy Penelope brings home. It's your job as her big brother. Got it?"

A genuine smile lifted Granger's lips. "Yeah, I got it. Thanks Stone. Now, what's going on and how can I help my little brother out?"

Stone punched his shoulder as they joined the table. "So, the reason I called you all here is because Natalie is in trouble and I'm hoping you can help us figure a way out of it."

"Seriously?" Rowan asked over the phone. "I thought this was something stupid like we were all cock-blocking you or that a bunny showed up with a baby."

"I have never wanted to hunt bunnies more than I have in the last month," Natalie muttered, earning her a grin from Olivia.

"Seriously. It's why I also made sure Granger was here. Nat, want to tell them what's going on or do you want me to?" Stone asked.

19

Natalie took a deep breath as everyone turned to look at her. "I definitely need the burrito for this." Natalie snatched it from Kane and Olivia laughed as they all sat down.

The look on Kane's face as he looked down at the egg white omelet almost made Natalie feel bad, but not enough to switch back. "The CIA extorted me into becoming a spy for them by threatening to turn my father over to the Russian government as a spy when he never was one." Natalie blurted it out and took a bite of the burrito while everyone stared at her.

"I'm going to need some more details, please," Olivia stated, sounding every inch the professional attorney she was. Olivia pushed her breakfast aside and reached into her purse to pull out a notepad and pen. When she looked back up at Natalie, it was a silent order to continue.

Natalie told them about Agent Aaron Naylor, the threats, the jobs he had her do, the bugs, the thefts, the eavesdropping, and then ended by telling them about her last mission.

"Who owned the villa?" Olivia asked, not looking up from where she was scribbling notes.

"Emile Lavigne."

Olivia looked up with wide eyes. "The French vineyard owner who happens to have donated hundreds of millions of to the arts?"

"Yes, but that money comes from the black market. I think weapons. And I have that list of buyers and sellers. Oh, and some guy named Nico Saccone has offered to brokerage my life for the list with the Italian mafia."

Olivia raised an eyebrow. "Nico is involved?"

"You know him?" Natalie asked. "My CIA contact who Naylor sent home also knew him."

"Ryker and a friend of his in Keeneston have been helping Nico keep the family business legal. Nico's grandparents have been retired."

"Well, I think they retired to Italy with some long-lost family because he's been tapped to play intermediary."

"I'll talk to Ryker and see what he can find out." Olivia went back to writing notes.

"Were you ever paid by the government for your services?" Granger asked into the silence.

"No," Natalie answered immediately. "It was never an option. It was, do this or I turn your dad over to the Russian government."

"She was a foreign asset, even though she is an American citizen," Kane said with a frown. "That way Naylor can keep her off the books. She had Naylor and a rescue number, but I can guarantee if Naylor is having her do things that aren't sanctioned, I bet her file is bare bones if she even has one. The CIA gets away with a lot overseas. Most are ethical about it, but this Naylor guy clearly isn't, which tells me a lot."

"How so?" Natalie asked. Stone had told her that Kane had been a profiler for the FBI before becoming a private contractor, whatever that meant.

"Easy, the less transparent he is, the more unethical it is. That means the likelihood of this being an authorized mission is very low. I would bet if we dig into Naylor more, we might find enough rope to hang him with. Then you won't have to worry about the CIA dragging you back in. However, it also means he probably won't be there to back you up when you need it because he doesn't want any evidence of his crossing the line and messing up," Kane explained.

"He sent my CIA help back to DC," Natalie told him. "Also, she told me the file on me didn't say what I did for the CIA."

"That can't be good," Forrest muttered.

"He's leaving you to fend for yourself. He's covering his ass," Kane told her.

"I deal with a lot of CIA officers overseas," Hunter said. "As Kane said, most are good, but the bad ones . . . they can start a fucking war, blow up a village, kill thousands, and just walk away without looking back if it helps their career. It's a power trip for them."

"Can you ask around about this Naylor guy?" Granger asked Hunter.

"On it." Hunter turned around as he put his phone to his ear and left the room.

"What do you need us to do?" Damon asked.

"Know any way to keep me from being killed?" Natalie asked even as she was filled with dread because that was actually what she needed. She had tried to pretend it wasn't a big deal, that it was just a robbery. But it wasn't, and her life was in danger from more criminals than she could count.

"We can help with that," Olivia answered. "Kane and Hunter can work their resources to find out about Naylor. I have my own resources. Granger, you and Damon keep eyes on Natalie while we get this worked out."

"I know Emile. Let me see what I can find out," Wilder chimed in.

"How do you know him?" Stone asked him.

"We serve his champagne in the Paris club and a few others. He's a frequent visitor, along with his buddies. I'll catch the next flight out and let you know what I find out."

"Forrest, go with him and watch his back," Damon ordered. Wilder began to protest, but one glare from Damon had Wilder's protest subside into nodding.

"I don't know what I can do, but I'm on call if you need a doctor. If you think of anything, just tell me," Rowan said.

"Come to Shadows Landing at night. Just keeping a presence around Natalie will help prevent attacks," Granger said, easily fitting into the commander role as sheriff. "Also, I'll let the town know to be on the lookout for anything unusual. I can say you've been targeted by vandals, but not go into the specifics."

"The town? What can they do about it?" Natalie asked, not liking the idea of involving even more people.

"Oh, don't underestimate the people of this town. You wouldn't believe what damage can be inflicted with knitting needles," Stone told her. Natalie waited for him to laugh, but he didn't.

"The town was founded by pirates, and trust me when I say they still know how to fight like them," Granger said. "If anything happens, run for the church and ring the bell."

"You're kidding, right?" Natalie asked. "This isn't the

Middle Ages where churches were sanctuaries where the bad guys won't cross the threshold."

"No, but there are more weapons in that church and women who know how to use them than anyone expects. If you need to buy time until backup arrives, it also offers tons of places to hide or barricade yourself," Granger instructed. "Okay, everyone knows what to do. Get going. We'll meet back up for dinner at Harper's Bar and get an update."

Stone's house cleared faster than it filled until all that was left was himself, Natalie, and Damon. "So, what's on the agenda today?" Damon asked.

"I have to get to work," Natalie said, absently looking at her phone. Stone saw that her mind was elsewhere.

"Should you cancel your clients?" Stone asked.

"No!" Natalie practically shouted. "I worked so hard to get my business up and running. I won't let them scare me off. Besides, if I run and hide, doesn't it make me look guilty? Yes, I stole that information, but I'm not the one selling it. I want to show them I don't have any reason to hide."

Stone's eyes met Damon's and they shared a look that only siblings could read. They were both thinking the same thing. "That's a good point," Stone said out loud. "Who is selling these secrets?"

Damon was quiet for a moment as he frowned. "I'll see what I can find out. I know people who operate on the not-so-legal side of the law."

"No," Stone said quickly and in a tone that left no question that he was very serious. "You worked hard not to become part of that world when everyone tried to drag you into it. Don't reach out to them. I hate to say it, but I think we have another option."

"Who?" Damon asked.

Stone turned to look at Natalie. He didn't want to do this, but it was the better choice right now. "Do you know how to get in touch with Nico?"

Natalie nodded and pulled out a business card from her bag. She handed it over to Stone who pulled out his phone and dialed. "Nico, this is Stone Townsend. Could you meet us at Natalie's training center in an hour? I'll be upstairs."

20

Stone sat above the studio watching through the glass ceiling as Natalie worked with a client. They were normally in a private room, but with everything going on, Stone wanted eyes on her the entire time.

Damon stood next to him observing all the rooms in use below them. "This is a cool setup. When I used to take Penelope to ballet, I had to fight to see through a small sliver of a window in the classroom door. There is nothing more serious or dangerous than a dance mom trying to watch her kid."

Since it was daytime, no one was upstairs with them. Tonight, when dance classes and team sports training started, this area would be packed with parents. Right now, it was adults getting personal training, physical therapy, and taking private lessons. That was the exact reason Stone had asked Nico to meet them there and then.

The door opened at the exact time Stone had asked Nico to meet them. He strode in, looking as if he owned the place. He was completely at ease in this morally gray world he lived in.

He took in Damon standing where Natalie was expected, but there was no hint of a reaction other than to join them at the railing to look down at the class below. "You called?" he finally asked, turning away from the class to look at Stone and Damon.

"Yes. Thank you for coming. This is my brother, Damon."

Nico held out his hand. "Nico Saccone. Nice to meet you. So, does your brother want to invest in my Sacci Sportsbook franchise or is there another reason I'm here?" he asked Stone.

"The online sportsbook site that's starting to pop up in arenas?" Stone asked. "That's you?"

"It is."

"That's how you knew who I was so quickly." Now it was making sense. "Not that I'm not recognizable. But really, hockey players tend to be a little more incognito than say, pro basketball players."

"I'm in talks to open a lounge at your arena, yes." Nico didn't rush the conversation but simply gave a little information and let Damon and Stone churn it over. "Since I was right about not investing, Damon, what can I help you with?"

"I'm just a mechanic. This isn't about me." Damon crossed his arms and looked Nico in the eyes. Like recognized like.

Nico smiled then. "And I'm just a businessman. You have a very accomplished family for having started off with so little. You're all self-made. Damon, the oldest, started out as a motorcycle mechanic but then moved to customization and now has franchises all across the country. Now he picks his projects as a custom builder and has a waitlist several years long. Further, congratulations on being hired by the largest motorcycle manufacturer to design a limited edition for them. Then there's you, Stone. A pro hockey player who, while a bit of a player off the ice, is incredibly mature in your spending habits. No kids, no mansions, no obscenely flashy cars. Very responsible. Next up is Hunter. Now, he's interesting. Not a lot is known about him except he's in the military. I got shut down real fast when I began looking into him."

"And why are you looking into our family?" Stone demanded.

"I know Ryker. And when you know Ryker, you know Olivia. She's impressive. First in the family to go to college and more intimidating than Ryker's secretary who is a dominatrix. I looked into her and your family when I first met her. I've known about you all before you ever heard my name. I have found in my business that it's smart to know who you are dealing with, and that includes their family." Nico paused, but neither Stone or Damon commented. "Then there's Kane. Very interesting guy. He also went to college—something of a trend after Olivia and something I am guessing was made possible because of you two. Kane holds a master's in psychology and worked for the FBI behavioral unit as a profiler before quitting and opening his own private contracting company. A company that is actually rather large and sought after, but somehow most people will never know it exists."

"Most people aren't involved in ransom kidnappings," Stone pointed out.

"True. But he's earned a stellar reputation for negotiating very tense deals when lives are on the line. And if all else fails, he goes in and rescues the hostages, leaving no one alive to come back after them. That's the reason he's so successful. He's built a reputation of living up to the threats he makes. Then, in the seemingly complete opposite direction, is Wilder, who has a chain of the most successful night clubs across the globe. Yet, he also deals with many of the same people I do, or did in my former life. He's known as someone incredibly private, shrewd, and puts up with no shit from either the patrons or suppliers of his clubs. As a result, everyone scrambles to work with him. It's something of a theme in your family. You're straightforward, don't put up with nonsense, and always follow through with what you say you will do.

"Then there are the twins, Forrest and Rowan. Forrest is an environmental engineer who has started his own consulting and researching and development firm. Rowan became a pediatric surgeon. Both are highly respected in their fields. Forrest isn't afraid to tell either the government or the private companies who hire him to shove it and refuses to sign off on developments that hurt either people or the environment. I'm also hearing rumors of research that could be game-changing. Then there's Rowan who refuses to sit back and give up on a tough case. He'll make the incision no one else will with nerves of steel. His patients' parents love him, even when the outcome isn't favorable, because he refuses to give up on his patients.

"Last, there's Penelope, who I actually didn't know even existed until recently. Maybe it was because she's just out of college and still in Europe. Sometimes she works for Wilder at one of his nightclubs. But from what I can see, she hasn't settled on a career path. A bit of a black sheep in this family."

Damon finally moved, but it was only his lips as he smiled slowly. "If you think this either impresses me or intimidates me, you're mistaken. Mafia connection or not, I know who you are, too. If you looked into me, you know I've dealt with people who are considerably less ethical and have a weaker moral compass than your grandparents. They don't mess with me. That should tell you that I won't let you mess with my family either. I don't know where you fall in this mess. I don't actually give a damn. You hurt my family and it'll be the last thing you do. Your research can tell you the truth of it."

Nico smiled in return. "Oh, I know. I have great respect for your family and it's the only reason I'm here now. You're good people, not afraid to cross lines when necessary for the just outcome. That's the situation I am currently finding myself in as I change over the family business. Now, what can I help you with?"

"Natalie isn't selling secrets," Stone stated. Nico didn't look like he believed him. "We want to know why your sources are saying she is."

Nico looked at them and then glanced down to where Natalie was teaching. "Natalie was never mentioned by name. A woman selling secrets stolen from someone was. Through family gossip, I picked up on a ballerina who had been caught where she shouldn't be. I suspect I'm not the only one who has made that connection based on the break-ins she's had. I don't know if I really believe that she's not involved."

"I never said she wasn't involved. I'm saying she isn't the one selling secrets. Therefore, someone else is also involved or someone is betting on finding those secrets and selling them. What specific secrets are you hearing?" Stone asked.

Nico was quiet and Stone could see him thinking over everything he'd said and not said, weighing his options, and then finally making his decision. "If I put my cards on the table, will you do so as well?"

"Depends on the cards," Damon answered before Stone

could. "You lay down a two of clubs and we aren't giving you the ace of diamonds."

"I'm only doing this because of my respect for Olivia," Nico said, not sounding happy about it. "The new head of the family in Italy, a distant relative of mine, was called from an unknown number. A woman told the new head of the family they knew of their dealings with a certain black-market arms dealer. If the family didn't pay three million euros, they'd sell the info to the highest bidder, including allowing the government to have a shot at buying it."

"Wait," Stone said, stopping Nico. "That vague threat was it? It wasn't specific?"

"Besides the fact they knew we had dealings with him?"

"Emile Lavigne," Damon said. "Cards on the table."

"Yes, Lavigne," Nico confirmed as Damon and Stone shared a look and then shook their heads. "What?"

"They're conning you. By even considering paying them, you're proving that you've done work with Lavigne, who, by all accounts works with most of the world's biggest criminals. Real threats give a real taste of what they have so you know they're serious. They're fishing right now," Damon told him as Stone nodded his agreement.

"You know how many of those emails I get, threatening to expose naked photos or sex tapes if I don't pay?" Stone asked. "If they don't give you solid facts, they're full of it."

"This means the list of people after Natalie has just grown. Anyone who thinks Natalie has the list could be after her as well as anyone on it," Damon said, drawing Nico's attention.

"Does she have a list?"

"You laid down a four of spades. Not really sure we're on even footing." Damon crossed his arms and refused to budge on his disclosure. "Go talk to Nat and see how much she wants to say."

Stone tapped on the ceiling and Natalie looked up. He pointed to the door and she excused herself from class as he hurried down the stairs.

"What happened?" Natalie asked the second they were alone at the base of the stairwell.

"His family was catfished. The person is blackmailing them to keep their secret. If the family doesn't pay, they'll sell them to the highest bidder with the threat to include the governments in that bidding war. The problem is that they don't give a specific example of what they have. It's just a vague connection to Lavigne. This means it could be anyone on this list after you, or anyone who figured out what you were doing and is trying to steal it from you to back up their con if they get caught," Stone explained. "Can we tell Nico what you have and use him to talk to the others to let them know it's not you selling anything?"

"Do you trust him?" Natalie looked so pale he was worried she might faint, but she pulled herself together and took a deep breath. "Don't answer. This is my mess and I'll clean it up. Keep him upstairs for twenty minutes, then meet me out back."

"If that's what you want, that's what I'll do."

Natalie then smiled. "I'll remember that tonight." She winked and left him standing in the stairwell suddenly hard at the idea of her telling him exactly what she wanted.

Stone ran hockey stats through his mind until he could go back upstairs. When he looked back into the lesson room, Natalie was working below him. Nico moved off to the side to make phone calls but kept in sight.

Class ended, but the timer wasn't up. There was still ten minutes until they could go downstairs. "What do you think Natalie is up to?" Damon asked.

"I don't know." Stone didn't like it. He wanted to know her plan so he could protect her if things went bad.

Stone got a text ten minutes later from Natalie. It was time.

"Out back," Stone said, directing them to the back staircase and then down the stairs. He pushed open the back door and found Natalie leaning against her car. The doors to the car were open and music was blaring.

Stone approached with Damon and Nico close behind. The question in his eyes had Natalie responding without either saying a word. She put her finger to her lips and kept it there until all three men nodded their understanding. She reached into a large duffle bag and pulled out a stack of papers, rifled through them, and handed one sheet to Nico. Stone looked over at it and saw a spreadsheet.

Nico studied it. Then he reached into his pocket and pulled out his phone. He typed something and then held it up. *Is this the only copy?*

Natalie shook her head.

What do you want me to do? Nico typed.

Natalie held up her phone to show her reply. *Tell them it's not me.*

Then she grabbed a small metal trashcan from the duffle bag and tossed all the papers into it and lit a match. The papers went up in flames. She'd shown Nico how much she had by showing him the huge stack of papers. She'd also shown him what she had on his family. Then she burned it.

Let's talk in my car. Nico gestured to the front of the building. After the papers were burned, Natalie poured water over the embers, turned off her car, and followed Nico around front.

Stone slid into the back of the luxury car with Damon as Natalie sat up front with Nico.

"I told my family about the threats being vague. I know there was plenty to be specific about when issuing those threats since I've now seen the records. I'll call them and tell them. I'll try to get the hit taken off you," Nico told her. "If you allow me to act as an intermediary, that is."

Stone didn't like it. They were criminals. Was there really honor among thieves? "Does your family kill innocent people? Do they sell drugs? Traffic people? Because let's be honest, you're not going to save Natalie out of the goodness of your heart. You'll want something in return. Will she be making a deal with the devil?" Stone looked into the rearview mirror and made eye contact with Nico.

"You are correct. We'll want the family name scrubbed from the original document. As for what the family does, I'm not privy to the inner workings anymore. My branch of the family went straight, but it's not all drugs and prostitution. Sure, some families are into that, but there's a lot of money in construction and waste management. Don't underestimate the corruption or deadliness of government contracts," Nico told him. "I know that's the area my family is in. I don't want to know the specifics."

Natalie breathed in deeply as Stone saw her thinking about what Nico said. "Do I smell apple pie?" she asked suddenly.

Nico ignored the question. "Do we have a deal, Miss Novak?"

"What about the other names on the list?" Damon asked what Stone had been wondering.

"That's up to you. I'm here to prevent my family from

doing something stupid. However, I think it might be best to keep quiet that you have what you have. Let's find the person making these threats and pin them as the person who has the list. It's the only way to keep Natalie safe in the future," Nico told them. "Were you really never going to do anything with that information?"

Natalie bit her lip and Stone knew right then she'd had a plan to use the information. "I wasn't going to give it to Naylor. I don't trust him. I was going to get settled, let time pass, then the next time I go to New York City or Washington, D.C., I was going to drop it in the mail to the FBI."

Nico nodded. "Give it to Cassidy. You can trust her and there'll be no ties back to you."

"She said that about you, too. She also asked for apple pies before she left." Natalie looked pointedly at Nico.

"You have my number. I'll be in touch," Nico said instead of answering about the pies. Pies that left Stone confused. Miss Ruby and Miss Winnie baked amazing apple pies that men literally stripped for and posed nude just to get them. Did Natalie know that and suggest that Nico was one of those to strip for a pie? He didn't seem the type. He dismissed the whole notion of naked pie pics and focused on the matter at hand. He wondered just where things stood now because while they had some clarity, there were now even more questions that needed answering.

21

It was a long day as Natalie was simultaneously helping clients while not remembering a thing about it because she was focused on who was trying to sell the secrets she currently had hidden.

Stone seemed similarly lost in thought on the drive back to Shadows Landing. They drove in silence, yet he'd reached over and clasped her hand in his. He held it as they both were lost in their own thoughts.

"Are you still okay to go to the bar tonight to meet my family and watch the game?" Stone asked as they pulled onto Main Street.

"Yes, I'm anxious to hear what they've found. They're so kind for helping. I just can't figure out one thing. The person selling these secrets . . . do they even know I have them or are running a scam having no idea I am caught up in it?"

"I'm hoping we can find that out," Stone said, parking near the bar.

Natalie opened her own door even as Stone was running around to get it. She was partners with a man in the mafia whose family wanted to kill her. There were hundreds of criminals with a reason to kill her and some dumbass out there blackmailing them all and threatening to sell their secrets to the highest bidder.

Natalie was so lost in thought she didn't realize Stone had stopped walking until she ran into his back. "What?" Natalie then looked around Stone and saw two men standing there with guns tucked in their waistbands.

"Mademoiselle Novak, you need to come with us. Alone," the lead man said in a thick French accent.

"Martin? You work for Mr. Lavigne, right? What are you doing here?" Natalie asked with what she hoped was confusion. "Stone, this nice man helped me when someone got handsy at a gala I was at in France."

Martin looked momentarily surprised at being recognized. "You need to come with me." Martin reached for her. Stone moved so fast that Natalie didn't even see the punch he landed in Martin's face. She only saw the big man stagger back as his friend reached for a gun.

Natalie jumped in front of Stone, placing herself between him and the gun now aimed at him. "I'll go with you. But let him go."

From the corner of her eye, Natalie saw movement. Then suddenly a turtle shell in a red and black sweater sailed through the air in front of her. A head snapped out from the shell and latched onto the hand holding the gun. At the same time a man dressed in overalls and a COCKS baseball cap slammed into Martin, taking him down hard.

The man with the sweatered turtle now attached to his finger screamed and dropped the gun. Stone pushed Natalie aside and grabbed the gun while the man jumped around trying to shake the turtle from his hand. The high-pitched yelling brought people streaming out from the bar. Granger and another man in a sheriff's uniform stood with their hands on their hips and smiles on their lips.

"You hog-tied him up good, Gator," Granger said as he pulled out his handcuffs. "Kord, why don't you get that one?"

The deputy was tall with wide shoulders, dark skin, and a tight trim to his natural black hair. The smile on his face was one of pure amusement. "Scared of a little snapping turtle?" he teased Granger.

"I've seen one hanging from a pecker. I've seen more than one hanging from a finger. What I've never seen is one hanging from me." Natalie was amazed that Granger and the entire town just took this all in. There was no panicking. No questioning what was going on. Instead, it was pure amusement as they watched the show. Natalie felt her mouth opening and closing as she couldn't really decide what to think in this situation.

"At least he didn't add to my bullet collection in the door," Harper, the owner of the bar, said before turning and heading back inside. "Game starts in five minutes!"

That cleared most of the sidewalk, leaving just the Townsend family, a couple of other people, including Maggie Bell, and a surprising number of children.

A little girl with braided pigtails came up to the man still hog-tied on the sidewalk. Before Natalie could stop her, the little girl pulled back her leg and kicked the man on his side. "Mr. Stone reads me stories. He's nice and you're mean." Then she stuck out her tongue at him before skipping back to her brothers and sisters.

"Thanks for sticking up for me, Lindsey." Stone was barely containing the laughter in his voice as he still held the man at gunpoint. Turtle and Kord worked to get the snapping turtle to let go of the man now sitting on the curb and crying.

"Does the FBI need to be here?" a man asked as he strode up the sidewalk.

"Peter Castle, meet Natalie Novak. She's dating Stone. Natalie, this is FBI Agent in Charge of the Charleston office, Peter Castle," Granger introduced.

"Damn. I wasn't even going to ask if you need ATF," the huge man leaning against the wall said. Natalie remembered his name—Dare. He was married to Harper.

"Actually, ATF might be handy here," Natalie muttered, thinking out loud.

"Ha ha! Sucker!" Peter said, hurrying inside. "Three minutes until game time!"

Dare gave him the middle finger but turned to Natalie. "Why would you need ATF?"

"Because they have illegal guns," Granger answered for her, giving Natalie a wink only she could see. He was keeping her cover. "Now, help me get this guy into my SUV."

"Come on, Tank. Let go for Daddy," Turtle cooed as he stroked the turtle's head.

"*Oui*, listen to Papa," the man cried with his French accent.

"I've got an idea," Kord said, turning and rushing inside the bar. He came out a minute later with a fried fish sandwich. "Here you go, Tank." Kord held the fish sandwich close to Tank's head.

Natalie saw the turtle make up his mind. Quicker than a flash he let go of the man's finger and snapped into the sandwich. The man tried to bolt up from the sidewalk, but Stone shoved him back down and wagged his finger at him as Kord tossed Hunter his cuffs. Hunter placed them on the man before handing him off to Granger.

"You're a hero, yes you are," Turtle said to Tank who was happily eating the fried fish Kord was holding.

"Who are you?" one of the many children asked Natalie. He looked on the cusp of becoming a teenager with a little bit of pudge that would quickly change to muscle as soon as he hit his impending growth spurt.

"I'm Natalie."

"She's my girlfriend," Stone called out as he helped place the man currently crying with blood running down his hand into the back of the SUV.

"I'll get Gavin to sew him up," Kord called out, heading back into the bar to get the town doctor.

"Girlfriend." The boy said accusingly as he crossed his arms and scowled. "I thought you said girls could distract you from your game."

The oldest boy, clearly in his gangly teen years, sighed with classic sibling frustration. "Levi, he said don't let girls distract you from your goals. Not that you couldn't have a girlfriend."

"She looks pretty distracting to me," Levi muttered and glared at her. "Stone is teaching me how to skate. Are you the reason he hasn't been able to recently?"

"Levi," Stone said, clearly sending a message with his tone. "I told you I couldn't teach you because I wasn't cleared to be on the ice. I am now and already told your mom we're on for next week's lesson. Men also know how to use their manners. Maybe you need a lesson in that as well?"

The boy looked deflated as a woman who had the same hair color and face shape as the kids came outside with a baby on her hip. "Stone, are they causing problems?"

"Not at all," Stone replied. "Lydia, this is my girlfriend, Natalie Novak. Nat, this is Lydia and her family. From oldest to youngest, Landry Junior, Lacy, Levi, Leah, Lindsey, Lyle, Leo, and this little one is Lennie."

"You have a whole hockey team," Natalie said, holding out her hand to shake Lydia's. "It's nice to meet you."

"You're pretty," the one Natalie thought was Leah said.

"Thank you."

"She's a distraction," Levi muttered.

"Actually, I'm a ballerina who owns her own training facility where I teach ballet and help athletes like Stone recover from injuries. I also work on conditioning athletes to be at their peak athletic abilities."

"I've always wanted to be a ballerina!" Lindsey said, twirling around.

"Me too!" Leah said before breaking out into spins down the sidewalk.

"I like basketball," Landry said.

"I work with several basketball players," Natalie told him.

"She works with Quad," Stone added, and suddenly all the boys were paying attention.

"What about hockey players?" Levi asked, still looking unconvinced at her status in Stone's life.

"I worked with Stone and helped him get back on the ice for the game on Saturday," she answered.

"Several guys from the team want to start working with Natalie after seeing how much I'm improving." Stone hadn't told her that, but that was great. It was exactly what she wanted N2 to be.

"Really?" Natalie asked quietly, trying to hold down her excitement until she knew more.

Stone nodded. "Already got your dad's permission."

Natalie looked away to keep herself from screaming and jumping up and down. She glanced at the oldest daughter standing with her arms crossed. "Do you also want to do ballet?" Natalie asked the eldest girl, Lacy.

"No. I want to fence. I'm really good with swords."

"You must have great balance, footwork, and concentration." Natalie had never worked with a fencer, but she'd always found a lot of graceful similarities between ballet and fencing.

"She does, but there's always room for improvement. Does N2 do anything with fencing?" Lydia asked. Lacy was interested but also in clear teenage mode she wasn't going to show said interest.

"I already have tons of ideas. Fencing is so graceful and fluid in the movement. I'd love to work with her if Lacy's ever interested."

"Until Landry, that's my husband," Lydia told her, "comes home from his last deployment, we're pretty tight on money. Maybe next year?"

Natalie looked at Lacy and crossed her own arms to mimic the teenager. "Are you any good?"

"Duh." Lacy rolled her eyes even as her mother swatted her arm.

"Manners, missy," Lydia hissed.

"Duh, ma'am. I'm really good."

"How about this?" Natalie looked uninterested. If this teenager thought she had anything on a diva ballerina she was fooling herself. "We trade. I'll train you to improve your footwork and eye-hand coordination. And you teach me to fence."

"What about us?" Leah asked as she and Lindsey stopped twirling.

"I have an open class every Saturday morning for ballet. It's open to anyone who wants to learn. And, I happen to have some chores around the place that your brothers could help me with while you're in class. And then I can work with them to thank them for their help. How does that sound?"

"Like Saturdays will be a long day for you, but that would be great if you have time," Lydia looked so excited and so did the kids, even the teenagers.

"Good. I'll see you Saturday morning."

"You're going to work hard, but it's so much fun," Stone whispered to them as he placed his hand on the small of her back. "But now we need to meet my family for dinner."

Natalie smiled at them, handed her business card to Lydia, then headed inside. All Natalie wanted was to explore her feelings with Stone, grow her business, and live. Someone, or a lot of someones, were trying to make that impossible. She hoped Stone's family found out something to end this. The sooner, the better. She had a future waiting for her, and she wasn't about to give up on it.

22

Stone pulled out a chair for Natalie as cheering rang through the bar. The game was on the big screen and it pained Stone not to be there. Olivia sat at the table with Ryker Faulkner, Damon, Hunter, and Kane. They had just sat down when Rowan joined them, still wearing scrubs.

"Damon texted there was some excitement just now," Rowan said, looking tired as he reached over to take Damon's bourbon and coke and tossed it back.

"Bad day?" Stone asked his brother.

Rowan just nodded. He wouldn't talk about it. He never did. It couldn't be easy taking the cases no one else would. It meant losing a lot of young patients and that did a number on Rowan. But, the ones he saved? They made the pain worth it.

"Who were those guys?" Hunter asked. "You seemed to know them."

"I knew the one Gator tackled. He was the head of security for Emile Lavigne." Natalie glanced at the bar and caught Kyler's attention. He reluctantly came over to the table and orders were placed. "I want to buy Gator and Turtle two beers. Not cider. Just regular beer."

Kyler looked insulted. "No cap?"

"No cap," Natalie said, looking serious. "I don't want any herbs or fruit included. Just regular beer from the tap."

Kyler looked insulted, but he gave her a nod. "That kills my vibe, but bet." Then he sauntered off behind the bar.

"He's leaving this weekend," Damon said with relief. "He put essence of lavender and passion fruit in my bourbon. When I told him I didn't want any of that, he called me basic."

Stone put his arm around Natalie's chair. His fingers caressed her arm as he glanced at the television. Belov landed a cheap shot, stole the puck, refused to pass, and skated it down for a goal. No one on the team cheered. This was a mess. There was a team dinner tomorrow for a family night. A chance to bond, both on the ice and off. Part of that was getting to know each other's families. He'd corner Belov there and see if he could fix this problem. By the way Coach Novak was dressing Belov down, it looked as if Coach was almost out of options. Belov completely ignored him, refused to get off the ice, and skated away as Coach yelled.

Natalie hissed in the air on a sharp intake of breath. "Dad is not going to like that."

"He's asked me to try to help. I don't know what to do. Archie Tupper wants Belov and it's Archie's team. But the guys won't put up with it much longer."

"Then let's figure this out so you can get back to focusing on hockey." Natalie turned her attention to the table. "What did you all find out? And why is there a billionaire at the table?"

"Ryker Faulkner." Ryker held out his hand. "I don't think we've properly met yet."

"Natalie Novak." Natalie shook his hand but then placed her hand on Stone's knee under the table. How did something so small make him feel like the biggest guy around? Just that touch and Stone felt his whole body swell with pride.

"I thought I might be of assistance as we're neighbors. I believe my shipping yard is near your training center," Ryker said, as if that answered the question.

"Ryker came to me offering his assistance. It's always helpful to have powerful people on your side. Anything we can't find out, Ryker can," Olivia explained.

"Well, Wilder and Forrest landed in Paris in two hours ago. They're heading to the club to see what they can find out right now," Damon said, starting off the debriefing as Granger walked in and joined them.

"Those are two pissed-off Frenchmen in our cells. We'll let the ghosts at 'em overnight and see what we can learn in the morning." Granger looked up at Kyler and frowned. "I guess I'll just have water. He served me something with cactus in it last time. I mean, it was good, but it just isn't my thing. I asked for a straight bourbon and he called me basic. It kinda hurt."

Olivia rolled her eyes. "That hurt you? My brothers called you a lot worse and it never hurt you."

"Yeah, but I can punch them. I can't punch Kyler. He would cry."

"Wait," Stone asked, going back to what Granger said. "What do you mean let the ghosts at them?"

"The holding cells in the basement of the courthouse are haunted. They don't like people who come into town and cause trouble. Scared the crap out of a guy giving Georgie trouble when her family sent him to bring her home." Granger shrugged like it was no big deal. You couldn't walk down the street in Shadows Landing without a ghost story, so it shouldn't come as a surprise the cells were haunted.

Kane leaned forward and frowned. "A ghost won't fix this problem. I asked around my criminal contacts. Lavigne is an underworld kingpin who has a stellar reputation in both the underworld and the legit world. My FBI contacts don't have him on their radar at all. That should tell you how good he is."

"Did you hear about the person selling secrets?" Stone asked him.

Kane nodded. "Yeah. It's common knowledge in the criminal world that a woman stole Lavigne's black book and if people don't pay, she's selling their secrets. The Russians are pissed. I guess they have a lot to lose. So are several drug cartels and weapons dealers." Kane paused. "Basically, everyone is pissed and wants this woman to disappear forever."

"What about Naylor?" Natalie asked.

"Not much on him. My FBI contacts knew him. He's been making waves as he climbs the CIA ladder. Apparently, he's not a team player and doesn't care who he knocks off on his way up."

Hunter leaned forward then. "That's what my military contacts have said. They didn't know anything about Lavigne or someone selling anything, but they had plenty to say about Naylor being an asshole. He worked his way up during the war from a field officer to one running ops out of Langley. It was only the older guys who had first-hand knowledge of him, and none of it was good. He cut corners, gave orders that were questionable to follow, and threatened their careers if they didn't do what he said. They were all happy when he got promoted and moved out of the field."

"So, what do I do now? It's clear I can't ask Naylor for help." By the way Natalie slumped against Stone's side, he could tell she was feeling defeated.

"We need to find out who these Russians are who have been sent," Stone answered. "Any idea on how we can do that?"

"Cassidy," Ryker answered. "I'll have her look into that."

"No!" Natalie sat up quickly. "She'll tell Naylor."

Ryker shook his head. "She won't. She doesn't have to play the DC shuffle. She has more powerful contacts than Naylor ever could. Plus, she's really good at her job. I'm also going to have a friend look into Naylor's record. He might also be able to hack the Russian government to find out who they sent."

"How would Cassidy know this?" Hunter asked. Ryker didn't answer. Natalie didn't answer. "Ah," Hunter said with a smile. "Got it."

"Maybe I should look over this *black book* you have," Ryker suggested. "I might know a lot of people in it."

Natalie shook her head. "I haven't even read it all. I don't want to put any of you in danger. You're already doing too much. That file is a grenade about to go off and I don't want any of you holding it when it does."

"Thanks, Natalie!" A cheer rang out from the bar. Stone turned to see Gator and Turtle toasting with regular ol' beer and Kyler looking rather put out about it.

"Thank you both!" Natalie replied before turning back to the table. Stone looked to where she was looking and saw she was watching Hunter watching Maggie. "You could just get out of your own way and ask her out."

"What?" Hunter said, totally busted.

"Ask Maggie out. If you haven't messed up your chance

by being an arrogant jerk," Natalie said, clearly relieved to be off the subject of her problems.

"I'm not the arrogant jerk. She is. She always walks around like she knows something I don't. Besides, someone like her wouldn't be able to handle the things I have to do." Hunter still was casting glances towards Maggie's table.

"Like her?"

"Yeah," he said with a shrug. "Such a girl. Pink everywhere. And monograms. Everywhere. Like, everywhere. Does she forget her name? Plus, she'd probably cry when I left for missions. I need a strong woman who isn't scared of a gun or the color black."

"Maybe she'd surprise you," Olivia said, sharing a look with Natalie that made Stone both happy and scared. He loved that his sister seemed to like the woman he loved, but it also petrified him that they could team up against him.

"Yeah, not going to happen. Now, what's our next step with you so we can keep Natalie alive."

Harsh reality crashed down on them. It had been a nice thirty seconds without it.

Natalie sniffed the air and leaned forward across the table, getting close to Ryker. "Why do I keep smelling apple pie?"

Ryker shrugged and Stone frowned. That's twice apple pie has come up. One with Nico and once with Ryker. Then both of them just appeared out of the blue to help?

Natalie looked down at her phone and Stone felt her sag against him. She turned her phone so he could see the text from Nico: *You're on good terms with the family*.

"What does that mean?" Stone asked.

"The hit has been called off. Nico did it." Natalie turned to Ryker. "Okay, work your magic, mystery man. Let's see if we can find out who this Russian is who is after me and more importantly who is trying to sell off this list. We can turn the heat up on her and get it off of me."

"It would help if I could see the list you have," Ryker said in such a soft but dangerous tone that Stone could see why Ryker had the reputation of being ruthless in business. He didn't need to beat anyone up. He just had to look at them with narrowed eyes and use that tone.

"No. Not until I know I can trust you and your . . . friends." Natalie crossed her arms and glared back.

Ryker relented by leaning back and pulling out his cell phone. He sent a quick text and then stood. "I'll let you know when I have something."

"I think Granger and I should stay with you two for the night," Olivia said with a sweet smile. "You know, to look out for you two and keep you safe." Hunter snorted and Olivia's scary sweet smile turned to him. "Don't worry. When you get your head out of your ass, I'll make sure to box you out, too."

"Two beavers make a bigger dam," Natalie said, earning a fist bump from Olivia.

It was happening. They were teaming up. Stone looked over at Damon to see a moment of fear flash across his face before he hid it. "Natalie, I'll drive you to work tomorrow since Stone has team meetings." Stone gave a little dip of his chin in appreciation to his brother. Damon might be the tough-as-nails big brother, but he was a good one.

Stone glanced at the TV when the sound of the whistle went off. Belov was sent to the penalty box. The replay showed the dirty hack job he did when the Pirates were already up 2-0.

Suddenly the mood on the ice transformed. The Pirates

were skating as a team. They were communicating. They were high-fiving each other. And just like that they scored. The entire team celebrated. Belov was too busy mouthing off to the opposing team to notice.

23

The rest of the evening was filled with bar food, beer, cheering on the Pirates, and growing more and more irate with Belov. The last of the setting sun had long ago dipped below the horizon as Stone and Natalie walked out to his pool wearing nothing but towels. They both needed to get their minds off their problems and focus on the positive. The positive was that Stone had somehow fallen in love with the perfect woman for him. And by some stroke of luck, she loved him, too.

"Are you sure your neighbors can't see?" Natalie asked into the darkness slowly surrounding them.

"I'm sure. No pool lights, no patio lights, and tons of trees and thick bushes separating us from the neighbors." Stone dropped the towel and grinned when he saw the flash of Natalie's towel drop.

"Wait, what's that in the pool?" Natalie asked stopping at the edge of the pool. He had a heater for it to extend his use of it well into October and sometimes into November.

Stone squinted to look into the darkness settling around them. "Oh, it's just a pool float."

Stone stepped into the water and sighed as he sunk down. It was warm and felt so nice after the tense day. There was the sound of a slight splash, and then he felt Natalie's arms around him. She leaned against his back and hugged him. "Can I help with Belov?"

Stone reached up and placed his hands on hers as they snuggled in the water. "Maybe. I've heard his wife can also cause problems. Maybe you can get a read on her while I work on Belov at the family get-together tomorrow night."

Stone was met with silence for a good thirty seconds. "You want me to go to that?"

"Well, you are my girlfriend and the woman I love, so yeah."

"I'm also your coach's daughter. Some of your teammates might think you're getting special treatment because of me. Specifically, being made team captain."

"I'm not worried," Stone said, turning so he could hold her in his arms. "I was actually voted team captain by my team and your dad just signed off on it. I want you there. If you want to be there, that is."

Natalie laced her fingers behind his neck and pressed her body against his for a moment before placing a soft kiss on his lips. "I would love to be there with you."

This time when she kissed him, it wasn't soft, but hot, deep, and demanding. Stone pulled her tight against him, grinding his hips into hers as they quickly got carried away in the softness, hardness, love, demand, and passion that heated them and the pool.

Natalie broke from the kiss with a gasp. "Stop poking me in the ass. I get it. You're an ass man. But it's not happening."

Stone pressed his hips forward again and Natalie inhaled as his cock pressed against her. "Yeah, that's not your ass I'm poking."

Natalie went stiff in his arms. That wasn't the usual reaction he got. "If you're not poking me in the ass, then what is?" she whispered as to not move at all.

Stone looked over Natalie's head and tried to make out the shape in the shadow he saw. Then he started laughing. "It's just my pool float." Natalie relaxed and Stone reached around her to give the float a shove.

Hisssssss.

"Holy shit! Not a float!" Stone grabbed Natalie who screamed as the alligator flicked its tail in annoyance of being moved. Stone didn't bother racing to the steps of the pool. He lifted Natalie straight out of the deep end and onto the patio.

"It's coming!" she yelled at the top of her lungs.

"Not what I had in mind for tonight," Stone grumbled as he pulled himself out of the pool, but not soon enough. Alligators could use their tails as weapons and this one flicked its tail, sending it slapping onto Stone's backside.

Natalie was there, yanking him the rest of the way out of the pool as Stone's butt cheek absorbed the hit that was as hard as one from a top pro-hockey defender.

Lights were thrown on in the distance. People stormed through bushes and trees at the sound of Natalie's screams. Stone was hopping around naked, holding onto his butt cheek and groaning. Natalie, also naked, was on top of the patio table, screaming for Stone to stop grabbing his ass and to get on the table.

There were pictures. There were videos. Stone would kill them all, but later. Right now, his butt cheek was throbbing and so not in a good way, and he was trying to keep an eye on the alligator in his pool.

"Put this on," a soft but calmly commanding voice said from behind him. Stone turned to see Savannah, Ridge

Faulkner's wife and a neighbor from down the street, shoving a towel at Natalie. "Don't worry. It's just Bubba."

"What's Bubba?" Natalie asked frantically, grabbing the towel and wrapping it around herself but still not getting down from the table.

"The alligator. His name is Bubba. He's the friendly one. Well, except for that one guy he ate. But he was a bad guy, so it doesn't count," Savannah answered as her husband Ridge tossed a towel at Stone.

"Put that thing away. You're likely to make Miss Ruby and Miss Winnie faint and hit their heads," Ridge said with a nod of his head to the two elderly women who had appeared on the scene.

Stone didn't think they'd faint, considering they were videoing him with their cell phones. He saw them wave as his brothers joined the spectators.

Hunter was laughing his butt off. There was even a smirk on Damon's lips. "You all going to help me with this?" Stone asked them as he pointed to Bubba who was back to happily floating in Stone's pool.

"Hell no," Hunter said, still laughing.

"Don't worry," Tinsley Faulkner Kendry said, getting everyone's attention as she walked over with her husband, Paxton, and joined the fray. "I knew that scream as soon as I heard it. Sounded like Paxton's when he met Bubba for the first time. I called Gator to remove Bubba." Tinsley looked in the pool at the alligator floating. "Really, you don't need to scream that much for Bubba. He's only killed one person and he was bad so it doesn't count."

"That doesn't make it better!" Natalie squeaked from the tabletop.

"Sure it does. Did he bite you in the pool? No, because you're good. He knows the difference between good people and bad. Now Bertha, she's a real bitch. She would have bitten you just for fun."

Stone stared at Tinsley but then leaped back as Bubba lifted his snout in the air and sniffed. Then he swam to the concrete stairs and sauntered up onto the patio. Natalie froze. Stone froze. No one else seemed to mind that an alligator was now walking toward Tinsley. He stopped in front of her and lifted up his snout that came surprisingly high up on Tinsley—to about her waist. Then he inhaled deeply and shoved his snout against her lower stomach. He blew out the air from his nostrils and Tinsley giggled.

"Sweetheart," Paxton said, looking way more nervous than Tinsley. "Do you think it's a good idea to have the alligator sniffing the baby? We don't want him thinking you're baking a chicken nugget."

Miss Ruby and Miss Winnie stopped videoing and instantly turned their focus on Tinsley and Paxton. Tinsley's family, Savannah and Ridge, didn't look surprised, so they must have already known.

"Congratulations on the baby," Natalie said from the top of the table where she was holding onto the umbrella. "But could we please get the alligator to leave?"

"Don't worry none, Miss Natalie." Gator strode in carrying a bag of beef jerky. "Bubba is right friendly, especially if you feed him."

"Except for the one guy he bit," Natalie said sarcastically.

"Ate," Gator corrected. "But he was not a nice man so it doesn't count." Gator shook the bag of jerky and Bubba immediately turned from Tinsley and hurried toward the sound. "My job has gotten so much easier after Kenzie got Bubba hooked on jerky."

Gator walked off, tossing little pieces of jerky onto the

ground. Bubba scooped them up as he trotted happily after Gator.

"Well, that's good to know. I guess I need to buy some jerky," Hunter said as he slipped a gun Stone hadn't even seen back into his waistband. "Well, now that no one is in danger, I'm going to bed." Hunter held out his arms to Miss Ruby and Miss Winnie. "Ladies, it would be an honor to escort you home." Then he dropped his voice, but it was still enough for Stone to hear. "And I'll need you to send me the videos you took of my brother."

"Hunter!" Stone warned, but it was too late. The three of them had their heads together, watching the video on Miss Ruby's phone as they walked off into the night.

Slowly his neighbors all cleared out, leaving Natalie slumped against the umbrella. "Maybe it would have been better to be killed by Bubba than deal with the embarrassment," she said, sliding down to sit on the table with her legs dangling over the side.

Stone walked over and stood in front of her. He stepped closer so that her legs were between his and his hands were on her arms as the lights from neighboring houses all turned off, leaving them cast in darkness once again. "I bet I can make you forget."

Then he threaded his fingers through her hair, pulled her lips toward hers, and kissed her. In that kiss was all the built-up adrenaline of swimming with an alligator, becoming exhibitionists, and a very real possibility of ending up completely nude and holding his ass on an apple pie banner at the next fair.

Natalie's hands came around his back. She pressed her fingers into his muscles to let him know she was enjoying it. Like magic, Stone's towel dropped. No hands needed. The kiss deepened, and all thoughts of Bubba faded.

Natalie wrapped her legs around his waist, locking her heels together so that Stone could easily pick her up. "Inside. Now."

"Yes, ma'am." Stone had one hand under her ass and the other was already reaching for the door. Natalie kissed his neck and Stone almost stumbled when she bit him just enough to send a *zing* of lust shooting straight to his cock.

Stone tried to run up the stairs, but Natalie kept distracting him. Pictures were now askew through the house from where they'd stop and he'd press her against the wall to kiss her deeply, to nip her bottom lip, or to squeeze her ass. Eventually, they made it to his room, and finally, he had Natalie exactly where he wanted her. Naked in his bed.

"I love you," he whispered as he crawled onto the bed, his arms framing her head.

"I love you too." Natalie traced her fingers through his hair as she looked him in the eyes and Stone was lost. Lost in love. Lost in Natalie. Lost in living. Lost in dreaming.

24

Ballerinas tend to have a lot of confidence. Sometimes it can come off as snobby, bitchy, or having a big ego. It's not wrong, but it's also not the whole story. Natalie was used to being judged on everything from her hair to her feet. Her literal feet were harshly judged because dancers "had to have good feet." Of course, any dancer actually has horrid-looking feet for the amount of work put in to make you a dancer.

Then, you had to wear a skimpy outfit, be picked up by guys in tights, spun around, and leaping higher than ever. And it all had to be perfect. The expression in your eyes, the tilt of your lips, the softness of your hands even as you're leaping five feet in the air across a stage . . . it all had to look effortless in front of thousands of people.

So, yeah, sometimes she looked snobby sailing into a room of non-dancers because dancers just move differently. Posture was a religion. Even retired, Natalie couldn't shake the ballet dancer's walk. Natalie had always found strength in it. She knew she could walk into a room and command it. However, this was not a room of dancers or patrons of the arts. This was a backyard cookout with hockey players and their families.

Instead of the looks of adoration she was used to, she received glares as the WAGs closed ranks against the new girl who dared to break into their world. This time Natalie was the outsider.

Also, apparently the fall dress she wore was not the appropriate attire. The WAGs all had jeans, booties, and T-shirt tops that were not your regular T-shirts. They were the cool in-style T-shirts that all the celebrities were wearing.

Natalie squared her shoulders, smiled politely, and walked into the lionesses' den.

"Hello, ladies. I'm Natalie." Natalie held out her hand. No one took it. She was about to pull it back when a shy woman with a baby on her hip held out her hand.

"I'm Hilary. Everyone calls me Hilly. I'm married to Dan Jones, the goalie. It's nice to meet you." Hilly had blonde hair, which most of the wives seemed to have. Some natural, most not. Another point against Natalie with her brunette hair, but Hilly at least had a genuine smile.

Natalie shook her hand with a good amount of relief. At least someone was nice. "It's nice to meet you."

"This one won't last long. Why bother with her name?" The supermodel looking woman with the Swedish accent barely looked at her.

"Who are you here with? They should know better than bringing someone to family night who is not even engaged. Run along little bunny." The Russian accent gave Galina Belov away, along with the attitude of one who was the Queen B out of meanness and not out of leadership.

"There's my baby girl!"

Galina's skeptical eyebrow rose. "You doing the coach?

You think that makes you one of us? No. You nothing but a slut bunny."

Her father slung his arm around Natalie's shoulder and kissed her temple. "Thank you, ladies, for welcoming my daughter. Nat, this is Hilly Jones, she's married to our goalie, Dan. Then Ellen is Karl Berg's wife," her father said about the supermodel. "And lastly, this is Galina. She's married to Igor Belov." The way her father said Igor's name told Natalie what her father thought of the man. He didn't respect him or his wife. "Well, I'll let you ladies chat. I need to check on the burgers. Glad you made it, Nat."

Her father left and Ellen immediately tried to redeem herself. Her husband was the second line center and sucking up to the coach's daughter might help him start if Natalie put in a good word. Too bad for Ellen, Natalie never got involved in her father's lineup. Especially when Stone was the starting center.

Galina didn't try to redeem herself. "You'd be more interesting if you were doing the coach. You're not even a slut bunny, just a boring one."

Natalie smiled as Stone walked out of the house. He instantly scanned the backyard, his eyes stopping when they found her. "No, I'm doing him instead. I'll leave the daddy issues to you. After all, you must have some for putting up with Igor and his sleeping around. And then there's your own behavior to consider, so I think we know who the real slut bunny is." Natalie dropped that bomb with a smile and gave a little shoulder shrug. She knew how this game was played and she didn't want to play. "I hope for your sake he's not as selfish in bed as he is on the ice. Or is that why you sleep around so much, you adulterous little bunny, you? Excuse me, ladies. I'm going to kiss my boyfriend who has an ass tight enough to bounce an alligator's tail off of."

"Is that some American expression? Alligator tail? I don't understand," Ellen asked Hilly as Hilly struggled to smother her laughter. Galina, on the other hand, was *fuming*.

Natalie met Stone halfway across her father's lawn and loved how he instantly put his arm around her and kissed her. The entire team went dead silent.

"Bruh, that's the coach's daughter," Theo Larson whispered.

"She's also an incredible ballet dancer, a badass trainer, a businesswoman, and I'm lucky enough to be her boyfriend," Stone said, not bothering to whisper.

"But Coach—" Bless Theo's heart. He was trying to look out for Stone.

"Coach knows. Don't worry. Now, who wants some burgers?" her father called out. Conversation started again, but Natalie and Stone hung back as others stared at them while they lined up for food.

"Making friends?" Stone asked with amusement.

"Making enemies. I can see Belov married a woman just like him. How is that going, by the way?"

Stone frowned. "Horrible. I pulled him aside to talk to him about being a teammate and it went nowhere. I could make Bubba a better teammate than Igor. How was Galina?"

"Let's just say Bubba has a better personality. She's vicious, and I'm afraid I might have made things worse."

"How so?" Stone asked. Natalie could see it was with amusement and not anger. That was confirmed after she told him what she'd said to Galina and Stone burst out laughing. "Nah, you're good. It needed to be said. I honestly don't know what to do about them. Maybe if we don't back down from them, the rest of the team won't either, and they'll get the hint and move on."

"Hi, Natalie," Hilly said softly as she joined them with

her husband, Dan, who was now holding the baby. "I wanted you to meet my husband, Dan. I told him how you stood up to Galina. We're all scared of her. Being the coach's daughter, you don't have to be. I almost applauded when you said what we've all been dying to."

Natalie shook Dan's hand and let the baby grab her finger and shove it in her mouth. "I appreciate it too," Dan told her, glancing around to make sure they weren't overheard. "I know you're the coach's daughter, so I don't want to put you in a bad place. There aren't many wives on this team and Galina has made them all cry. We talked to Igor and he laughed. It's as if that's his favorite trait in his wife."

Stone answered before she could. "No, she's cool. Besides, they're a team problem and we'll handle them as a team, both as players and as wives or girlfriends."

"You're a good captain, Stone." Dan paused and then gave a little smirk. "Okay, I have to know. How did you two get together?"

"Her dad," Stone said, putting his arm around her and pulling her to his side. "He suggested I see her for rehab. Between the sweat and tears she put me through and the fact she made me wear ballet tights, I fell in love."

"That's really sweet," Hilly said to them.

Natalie leaned against Stone and smiled up at him. "It is. I even have pictures of him in the tights. I think I might make it my phone screen saver."

Dan burst out laughing, drawing several of the other guys over. Natalie batted her lashes at Stone and he just grinned. He wasn't bothered by her teasing and she loved that. "Guys, Natalie got Stone to wear ballet tights and has pictures!"

All the players begged to see it. Stone shook his head

and teased them back. "You see me naked in the shower. Why would tights make a difference?"

"Please tell us he wore tutu!" Elias Laakso yelled in his Finnish accent.

"Listen," Natalie said, drawing their attention. She was having so much fun. "I'll make a deal with you. You all win the championship and I'll put it on the jumbotron. Dad, I can do that, right?"

"My captain in tights? Of course, you can put that up. It would be good for him to have people laugh at him every now and then. Keeps him humble." Natalie knew her father would be game. He was always up for a good prank.

"If you saw me in tights, you'd know there's nothing for me to be humble about," Stone said with a cocky grin. Natalie's eyes went wide as she smacked his arm. Her dad rolled his eyes and groaned.

"Are you trying to get yourself benched? Keep it up. Dating my daughter is not an advantage in my book." The team suddenly looked nervous. Her father's bark was scary enough, but there was truth there too. However, Natalie saw the twinkle in his eye and relaxed. "I think you in tights on a billboard is called for to really make you suffer. Maybe a team press release to all the sports channels too."

Stone was the first to realize Natalie's father was teasing him. "If it means I get to keep dating Nat, you have a deal, Coach. I'll look good on that big billboard by the bridge. Although, I might be such a distraction, cars might end up in the river."

Her father snorted with laughter. The team all looked confused. When Stone cracked up and her father did the same, they realized they were just teasing each other. They looked nervously at each other but began chuckling along with them.

"Come on, Nat. Come meet the rest of the team." Her father then took her off on the grand circuit.

The rumors of her standing up to Galina had already made their rounds and several of the wives lowered their voices and thanked her. "Look," she told Tucker Webb's wife, Joslyn, "I'm in a unique position as the coach's daughter. If she's making trouble, let me know. I don't have to worry about my husband's playing time or upsetting the team."

"But you're one of us now too. You have to worry about Stone's playing time," she said, looking nervous as her husband talked to Natalie's dad.

Natalie shook her head. "No, I don't. And really you don't either. My dad knows wives are a big part of the team and respects their opinions. I also know it's scary to walk in and talk to a coach, so feel free to call me if you need me to do it."

The poor woman looked so relieved Natalie began to wonder just how much damage Galina had done in the month they'd been here.

Her father rejoined her and steered her away as they went to meet the last of the coaching staff. "How bad have Igor and Galina been to the team?" she asked to get his perspective.

"So bad I'm worried we won't have one left by Christmas," he replied.

Natalie frowned. This was not good. "Can you talk to Archie?" she asked about the team owner.

"I did. He's loving the free publicity we're getting because of Belov's antics. I'll try again. I don't really know what else to do."

"Can you bench him?" Natalie asked.

"Archie already told me I couldn't. I don't like not being

able to run my team my way, but this is the only area Archie has put down his foot."

Natalie put her arm around her dad. "We'll figure something out. I could break his leg if all else fails."

Her father laughed, but she wasn't entirely joking. She saw the way he and his wife were poisoning the team. A team that had been perfect just a month ago. There was no way she would let her father become vulnerable again and risk him ending up back in Russia.

"Well, if I get fired, I can just move in with you and Stone."

"We'd have to live together first."

"Oh, so is that where you've been recently . . . home?"

Busted.

"I . . . we . . . that is . . ." Natalie tried to come up with something to say besides she'd been too busy skinning dipping and having sex with Stone to be home.

Her father held up his hands to stop her. "I don't want to know. I'm just happy you're happy."

Natalie smiled then. "I am happy. He loves me."

"I know," her father told her. "He told me before he told you. Now, here's our medical staff."

Natalie was thrown into daughter-of-the-coach mode. By the time she made it home . . . well, back to Stone's, she was too distracted to remember to talk to him about how much her father knew. Stone's tongue had a way of making her forget everything, including her own name.

25

Natalie was under no delusion the threat was gone. Not when Damon was in her parking lot, fixing motorcycles for some scary-looking bikers while she saw clients on Thursday.

Stone was at practice and Damon had been a constant in her life when Stone was absent. Even Rowan had stopped by today between surgeries to have lunch with her.

"Okay, you have got to spill about these men in your life," Rita said as she slipped on a sweatshirt in the lobby after her appointment. "First, that sexy man in his scrubs was leaving when I got here and now Mr. Dark and Dangerous is in your parking lot."

"They're friends of mine." Natalie didn't know why, but she didn't want to say more. By the way Rita was eyeing them, they might want her to so they could get laid, though.

"How does your boyfriend feel about that?"

Natalie shrugged. "He likes them, so he's cool with it." Stone loved them like brothers.

"I need to start hanging out with you more." Natalie laughed at Rita, but she was distracted by the clock. Stone would be done with practice soon and she was excited to get back to Shadows Landing. They were going out to eat tonight at a place called The Pink Pig. "Actually, I was wondering, can you get me two tickets to Saturday's game?" Rita asked a little nervously.

"Oh, sure." Natalie smiled and sent a quick text to her dad. "Okay, you have two tickets at will call under your name."

Rita picked up her bag and smiled. "Excellent. I'm really excited to go. It's my first hockey game. Are you coming?" She rolled her eyes and laughed. "Of course, you're going. Your man is making his big comeback. I'll see you there!"

"Yes, see you there," Natalie called out, leaning against the door to keep it open. As soon as Rita drove off, she called out to Damon. "I'm going to dance a little before Stone gets here. Should I leave the front door unlocked?"

Damon turned from a beefy man in a leather vest. "Yeah, I'll be here for a little longer working on this bike. You and Stone will probably leave before I do."

Natalie smiled at the big biker and then at Damon. "Thanks, Damon." Growing up as an only child, she was loving having a big brother. It was a strange feeling, but the Townsends were turning into family and she loved it.

Natalie lost herself in the music for forty-five minutes. She heard Stone enter the lobby and call out to her. Sweat covered her body as she pulled off her ballet slippers and toweled the sweat from her body.

"This is my favorite room."

Instantly her body heated at Stone's words. "Mine too. Do we have time to stop at your house for a shower before dinner?"

"Only if we take it together. You know, to save time and water." Natalie threw the towel at him and he caught it with a laugh before placing a kiss on her lips. "How was your day?"

"Really good, actually. I'm also looking forward to dinner. What's the plan for tomorrow? I don't know your pre-game rituals, but I'm sure you have them. Most athletes do." Natalie turned off the lights and they walked to the lobby and began locking everything up and turning off the lights for the night.

"Friday night the team stays at a hotel. No wives or girlfriends. I can try to get your dad to include a room for you."

"Nope. I don't want to mess with your ritual. I'll be fine for one night."

"I was actually thinking of asking Olivia if you could stay with her and Granger for the night."

"Is that really necessary?" Natalie asked as she locked the front door.

Damon was still working on the bike, but there were fewer things lying on the ground, so he must be getting close to finishing.

"Damon," Stone said, stopping by his brother. "What do you think about Nat staying with Olivia and Granger tomorrow night?"

"Sure. Or she can stay with Hunter or me. But she'd probably be more comfortable with Liv. Plus, Granger can fill you in on the Frenchmen."

"What about them?" Natalie asked.

"Don't know. Granger only said he's holding them until a special team gets here to interrogate them on Saturday. Until then, they're not logged anywhere. They're ghosts." Damon then chuckled. "Speaking of ghosts, apparently the guys are freaked out by ghosts and have begged for transport. Granger got some information from them in exchange for moving them to a different, above ground cell."

Natalie was relieved to hear they were still in custody. She never wanted to see Martin again. "Thanks for everything, Damon. I really appreciate it."

Damon gave a grunt before getting back to work. Stone opened the car door and as they were driving toward Shadows Landing, got back on topic of pre-game rituals. "Friday, we stay at the hotel and have team meetings. Saturday, we have breakfast together, more meetings, and a light skate to loosen up. Then we get ready for the game. Everyone has their own superstitions, so the locker room pre-game is a very interesting place."

"What are your superstitions?" Natalie asked. She had her own pre-dance superstitions and wondered how they compared.

"I put my gear on in a certain order. I also tape my stick a certain way and once it's taped, no one can touch it."

"I wouldn't let anyone touch my pointe slippers either," Natalie told him. "That and I had to put my right slipper on first. That meant the show would start off on the right foot." She laughed at how silly it sounded, but it was what it was. "I also always drank exactly thirteen ounces of water for good luck."

"I eat three bananas," Stone told her. One first thing in the morning. One before our warm-up, and one right before the game."

They talked about their rituals and the strangest rituals they'd ever witnessed as they drove home. Maybe her father had a point. Where was her home now because she hadn't been to hers in days?

"Are you sure you want me to come home with you? I

can stay at my place if you want your space back," Natalie told Stone as they turned into his driveway. She didn't want to be that girlfriend who moved right in, making assumptions about a relationship without talking it through with Stone.

Stone parked the car and turned to her. He looked very serious and her heart dropped. She had been right to ask. "If I didn't want you here, you wouldn't be here. We haven't talked about it, and I know you have your place in Charleston, but I love having you here. I didn't realize the difference between having a house and a home until I had you in it. Now it's a home because you're here with me."

"Oh." The words took the breath from her body as she somehow fell even more in love with Stone. "Then, maybe I can get a toothbrush for your place."

"Sweetheart, it's been our place since the moment your foot first crossed the threshold."

Natalie was not going to have sex in a car. Well, she wasn't until he said that. Now there was a good chance of it. They made it as far as the threshold before Natalie had to kiss Stone. It wasn't just need, not just lust. It was everything. Love, lust, passion, compassion, appreciation, and respect all wrapped up into a kiss that changed her world. She'd never been a woman afraid to be alone. She'd rather be alone than waste her time on the wrong man. Not that she hadn't fallen into that trap a time or two, but now she was part of a couple. She had someone to trust, to lean on, to depend on, and to share her life with. This just felt different. It felt as if she were becoming whole, not by giving up a part of her to blend with a man, but by them both joining together to lift each other up with love.

Natalie could feel the difference in the kiss and the way they made love. Stone was reverent with her. He worshiped her. They were in perfect harmonization as they climbed that mountain and jumped off into their future amid an explosion that crumbled all walls and rocked her to her core.

Stone never thought he'd see the day he not only asked a woman to move in with him, but actually couldn't wait for her to do so. It was the best way to spend the day before his game. They'd had practice that morning, and while Damon was watching Natalie, Stone was running a quick errand before picking her up at N2.

"Here you go, sir."

Stone held out his hand and looked down in it. He was doing this and he couldn't wait. "Thank you."

Stone drove to N2 and saw Damon in his now regular spot—a corner of the front parking lot. His trailer's tailgate was down and inside music was playing as he worked on his pet project. It was a 1951 Vincent Black Lightning he'd found in a barn in rural upstate New York. It was all original and he was slowly bringing it back to life. He'd bought it for $300,000. But when he was done, he could probably sell it for a million.

"How's it going?" Stone asked.

Damon looked up from where he was cleaning every single nut and bolt of the motorcycle. "I have both wheels cleaned. Now I'm working on the handlebar before I take it all the way apart to clean the engine."

"Do you think it'll run?"

"Don't know yet. I'll know better when I get it cleaned and then put back together. I'll see what works and what needs to be replaced. Considering only thirty-one of these bikes were made, I'll probably end up making any parts to try to keep it as original as I can. Otherwise, I'll be off hunting for classic parts. Is that what I think it is?"

Stone looked down at his hand. "Yeah. It is. You think I'm moving too fast?"

"Nope. I like her. She fits our family. She can put up with the teasing and dish it out. I was worried when you said ballerina, but she's defied all the stereotypes. Although, Natalie and Olivia joining forces scares me a little."

Stone shuddered. "Totally. I'm going to give this to her, then I have to go to the hotel. Can you take care of everything from here?"

"Sure can." Damon stood up and before Stone knew it, Damon was hugging him. "Go get 'em tomorrow. It's going to be fun watching you on the ice."

Damon may tease him, but this was family. "Thanks, big bro. It means a lot to have you there."

"That's what we Townsends do." Damon slapped him on the back and then got back to work on his bike.

Stone headed inside to find Natalie working with an injured dancer. The floor barre looked familiar as she put the dancer through a routine with a wrap on her lower leg. He didn't interrupt. He stepped back from the open door and went to wait in the lobby. He didn't have to check into the hotel for another hour.

Fifteen minutes later, Natalie and her dancer walked out. Natalie gave him a smile but focused her attention on the dancer as they set up their future appointments.

"I didn't think I'd see you this afternoon. Don't you have to check in at the hotel soon?" Natalie asked as she walked over to where he was sitting. He patted his lap and she took a seat on his thigh. "Is everything okay?"

He was nervous. He'd never done this before. The metal felt hot in his hand as he opened his fist.

"Cute key chain," Natalie said as she looked at the ballet slipper key chain.

Stone took a breath and looked up at her. "It's for you. It's a key to my place. I'd like you to have it."

Stone didn't breathe as Natalie looked from the key chain to him. "You're asking me to move in with you?"

"Officially. Last night I told you I want you in my home and my heart but I want to show you it wasn't just talk. I really mean it. I love you, Nat. But I also know you're an independent woman with her own house and goals. I want you to have the key to my house and you can decide how much to use it. The door is always open to you, whether it's for one night or forever."

"You say that, but how will you feel when your bathroom has tampons in it?"

"I've heard they're good for nosebleeds. Hockey players get a lot of nosebleeds. Guys can be a little slow on the uptake, but when I see them out, I'll know when you need a little extra TLC. Remember, I did grow up with two sisters."

"Not your mother?" Natalie teased.

"My mom had nine kids. She didn't have time to have a period. But geez, living through Olivia's time of month until I moved out has turned me into a battle-hardened male who has no trouble going to the store to get those super absorbency tampons, those maxi pads with wings, agreeing with whatever you're saying, and buying a two-pound bag of chocolate."

"I like boxes of assorted chocolates, but I might cry if I bite into one that I don't want." Natalie took the key from his hand and Stone felt like a superhero. The most amazing woman he'd ever met chose him. Instead of being fearful of picking the wrong chocolate, he couldn't wait to be the one to find out which chocolates were her favorite and to learn all of Natalie's ins and outs.

Stone cupped her cheek and then slid his hand behind her neck to pull her down to his lips. "I love you," he whispered a moment before his lips took hers in a kiss that he hoped showed her how much it meant to him that she'd be willing to share herself with him.

"Mmm. I love you too. How much time do you have until hotel check-in?"

Stone groaned and plucked her from his lap. "Not enough and I sure as hell am not going to explain to your father why I was late."

Natalie smirked in such a sexy way he became instantly hard. "Wanna bet?"

"No! No sex before a game."

Stone stood up and Natalie slid from his lap and laughed. "Are you scared of me?"

Natalie advanced on him and bit her lip as Stone backed away nervously. "It's a ritual. Every time I had sex the night before a game we lost." One time he had sex before a game they lost 6-1. They'd become a meme. Never again would he risk it.

"But you've never had sex with me, the woman you love, before a game," Natalie pointed out.

Stone looked at her and swore. He loved her, but he couldn't risk it. "Do whatever you'd like to the house. I love you! I'll call you later," Stone called as he rushed out the door.

Natalie had gathered a suitcase worth of things and loaded them into Damon's car before he drove her to Stone's house. She unlocked the door with her new key as Damon insisted on carrying her bag up to Stone's room.

"You're a good guy, aren't you?" Natalie asked.

Damon set her bag down and turned to her, definitely not looking like a good guy. "I am not a good guy. Don't let my love for my family confuse you."

Natalie should have been intimidated, but she wasn't. Instead, she opened her bag, pulled out a couple of outfits to take to Olivia's, and put them in a small backpack. "Don't worry, Damon. I won't spill your secret."

"What secret?" he practically growled.

Natalie reached over and tickled his rock-hard stomach. "That you're nothing but a teddy bear under all that growling."

Damon slapped her hand away and she laughed. "Seriously, do you know the type of men I'm around as a ballerina?" Damon just raised an eyebrow. "Trust me when I say I know bad men. You, Damon, are a good man. You can try to hide it, but I see it. Someday, someone special will see it too. And you bet your ass when that day comes, Olivia and I will run her through the wringer."

Natalie tried not to laugh when an involuntary shiver went through Damon's body. She went to the closet and looked inside. There was Stone's jersey in a smaller size. He had told her he'd gotten her one at practice earlier this week. Natalie took it off the hanger and carefully folded it. "Okay, I'm ready."

Natalie grabbed the freshly packed backpack and bounded down the stairs leaving Damon growling behind her. So, this is what it's like to have siblings? Oh man, she was going to have so much fun.

Natalie and Olivia were sipping wine on the screened-in back porch when Granger got home. But Granger wasn't alone. He was with Damon, Kane, and Hunter. He was also with Ryker and a woman Natalie hadn't met yet. She had a nice smile, and while Ryker was in a clearly custom suit with even more expensive leather shoes, she was in scrubs with no makeup on.

"Hi," she said with a big smile for Natalie. "I hope you don't mind that I came along, but I've wanted to meet you. I'm Kenzie Faulkner, this one's wife." She gave a tilt of her head to indicate Ryker. There was zero pretense about her and Natalie instantly liked her.

"Natalie Novak," she replied. "It's nice to meet you."

"I have to admit, meeting Stone's girlfriend wasn't the only reason I wanted to come. I heard you're the owner of N2. I'm a nurse practitioner here in town with Dr. Gavin Faulkner, my cousin-in-law. Quad Clemmons told me he was seeing you so I looked into your training and rehab philosophy. It's so unique, yet not. The techniques have been around forever. I'm surprised they're not used more often."

"Sweetheart," Ryker said, taking a seat next to his wife. "Let me update Natalie, then I'll let you interrogate her for the rest of the night."

Natalie smiled as she saw the love between them. Ryker had been pretty scary and when she'd looked him up on the internet all she saw were business articles of how cutthroat he was. But this side of him was nice to see. Damon and his brothers couldn't see it, but this was exactly how they were. Ruthless on the outside, teddy bears on the inside.

"What have you learned?" Natalie asked the group now filling the porch.

Granger leaned forward to take the lead. "Martin and his friend aren't talking much. But they did tell us you had stolen something from their boss. They were simply asking for it back, which in itself isn't a crime. Luckily, you were right about the weapons. Dare ran them through ATF and they're black-market weapons. It's why we can hold them. Ryker contacted one of his cousins who works with the president. Greer is sending a special team to take over and investigate. They'll be here tomorrow."

Natalie shook her head. "They'll just report back to Naylor. He's pretty high up in the CIA, isn't he?"

"Yes and no," Ryker answered. "I got his employment records. While he's worked his way up, he's also never achieved the true higher ranks of leadership that he's been trying to reach for the past twenty years. Someone up the chain doesn't like him and he's been capped out. He hasn't advanced in years. So, yes, he has a lot of control over some field officers and assets, but he actually doesn't have much power in the politics and running of the CIA."

"That lines up with what I've heard from my contacts," Hunter said, taking a beer from Granger and leaning back in his chair.

"Wilder called from Paris," Damon told them. "Lavigne has reserved the VIP section of the club tonight. He's asked Wilder to stop by and say hello."

Olivia frowned. "I don't like that. He must know we have his two guys by now."

"Forrest is with him, but I don't know what else we can do," Damon said.

Natalie's stomach knotted. She didn't want anything to happen to them because of her. "Tell him not to meet with Lavigne. I can't have him in danger. Besides, we have his men. Surely Wilder can't learn any more than we can learn from them."

"That's why I sent Tristan to Paris this morning," Granger said.

"Who is Tristan?" Natalie asked. He had to be good since everyone seemed relieved.

"He's my deputy. But prior to becoming a deputy, he was an assassin for the government of Millevia, a small country that borders France on the Mediterranean Sea. He's fluent in French and still has a lot of contacts in the region. Plus, if anything goes sideways, they'll be safe in Millevia," Granger explained.

No one looked surprised. Natalie knew her mouth was hanging open as she looked around. "Why is there an assassin in Shadows Landing?" she finally asked.

"He fell in love with Edie. Now he's a deputy," Granger said with a shrug. "I've found it's really helpful to have an assassin in town. Between him and Maggie, we're covered if we need any long-distance shots. And Tristian is really good at hand-to-hand combat. He can snap a neck—sorry. Not important."

Hunter set down his beer and cocked his head. "What do you mean between him and Maggie? The only thing Maggie can shoot are drinks on her sorority girls' nights out."

Granger just shook his head. Olivia hid a smile behind her wine glass. Natalie looked around. Not a single one of them was going to tell him the truth.

"What do we do next?" Ryker asked.

"We have Lavigne accounted for in Paris. We have his men in the jail. Nico had the hit from his family called off," Granger said before sighing. "Now, I guess we wait for the next move. Unless your guys could find anything on the Russians?"

Ryker shook his head. "Nothing yet. Seen any Russians around?" he asked Natalie sarcastically.

Natalie paused and frowned. No, it couldn't be. "Actually, yeah, I have. Igor and Galina Belov."

"The hockey player?" Ryker asked.

"Yeah. His wife is a piece of work and he's been giving the team hell. However, she was not trying to be my friend and no one talked about secrets when I saw them on Wednesday at the team dinner," Natalie told them. "They're the only Russians I know."

"A pro hockey player probably isn't a spy," Kane stopped himself and frowned. "Actually, it's worth looking into. Natalie was a pro dancer and was tapped by the CIA. Maybe a pro hockey player would be spy gold for the Russians. He can get in anywhere. Into any club, he can travel the States, and attend events, just like Natalie did."

"I'll pass along the idea to Cassidy and have her look into it," Ryker said as he sent a text.

"Okay," Kenzie said into the silence as everyone was thinking about Igor being the spy, "is there anything else to discuss?"

"I don't think so," Granger answered.

"Good. Then you guys run out and grab some dinner for us while Olivia, Natalie, and I talk. I can't wait to hear about your training center," Kenzie said, shooing the guys off with both hands.

Granger insisted on staying but went into the kitchen where he could keep an eye on them through the large window. The Townsends went back to Damon's house and that left the billionaire to go get dinner. Natalie loved it. She also loved that there was absolutely no snobbery in Kenzie. She was funny and such the girl-next-door.

"Okay," Kenzie said, leaning forward. "Now that they're gone, tell us everything about Stone."

"Not everything," Olivia said, refilling her wine. "Just the stuff I can tease him about mercilessly for the rest of his life."

Stone was ready for bed. They'd turned in their phones as soon as they checked in and started the team meeting. Then they watched film, ate dinner, had breakout meetings with each position, and meetings for the offense and defense. Finally, they were all together watching a movie.

"Any luck with Belov?" Coach asked as the team broke up, heading back to their rooms.

"I tried at the dinner and again just now." Stone felt his hand tighten in a fist. "I've never wanted to punch someone so badly and he's my own teammate."

"I guess that answers how it went." Coach Novak ran a hand through his hair with frustration.

"He's the most conceited person I've ever met. How does he land all these ad campaigns and get invited to these big events? He's headlining the annual sports gala hosted in New York. He made sure to rub that in since I'm only an invited guest. He also took an athletic apparel ad from me." Stone had to take a breath to calm down. "I talked to him numerous times. He doesn't care about the team. He only cares about himself. And with companies rewarding him for his behavior with ads and invites, he's not going to change."

"Archie Tupper has told me I'm out of a job if I bench him. My hands are tied."

Stone walked to the elevator with Coach and stabbed the button. "Why is the team owner so in favor of a player that will tear his team apart?"

"Like you said, people love a villain. Merch and ticket sales are through the roof. They can't wait to see what Belov does next. That's what Tupper told me when I said I wanted him off the team."

They rode the rest of the way in silence. "I'll let you know if I come up with anything. Right now, all I got is poisoning him or breaking his leg. I'm tempted, but I also don't want to miss the rest of the season because I'm in jail." Stone stopped at his door with Coach.

"Trust me when I say I've thought about those ideas too. Good night, Stone. I'm glad you're back. It'll be good to have you on the ice again."

Stone thanked his coach and then used his key card to enter his hotel room. He pulled off his sweatshirt and walked down the short hallway. He tossed it onto the chair and stopped after kicking off his shoes. The hair stood up on his arm as he turned slowly to look at the bed.

"Don't stop on my account," Galina purred.

"What the hell are you doing in my room?" He didn't bother asking nicely. His tone was clear. He was pissed off. What made him even more pissed was the fact Galina Belov was wearing nothing but a black lace bra and panties as she reclined on his bed.

"It's tradition. I sleep with every team captain and in return you get to win the championship."

"Get the fuck out. Now." Stone was so mad he'd turned to literal stone to prevent himself from reaching out and grabbing a woman, dragging her to the door, and physically tossing her out on her ass.

Galina made a clucking noise as she shook her head, not taking his anger seriously at all. "No. You come," she patted the bed, but Stone didn't move. "Don't tell me your coach's daughter is satisfying you? What does she do anyway? Why don't you tell me about her while I do other things to occupy my mouth than talk?"

"You're not to speak of Natalie. Galina, I'm serious. Get out of my room now or I'll go get your husband."

Galina shrugged. "Go ahead. I'll tell him you forced me here to take advantage of me."

Stone laughed, but there was no humor to it. "What do you want, Galina? We both know there's no way I'm going to touch you. You're not dumb. You have to know your husband is a pariah on the team and we don't want him. Are you trying to suck up? Or just screw me so I'll stop my war against him?"

Galina just smirked. Gone were the false pretenses and all that was left was a cold, calculating woman. "What war? You're no threat to my husband. I wouldn't be so sure he isn't stealing your woman right now just to say he did it. Just to put you in your place. Now," she said, turning back into a seductress, "come to bed. I'll make you forget that woman before you can even say her name."

Stone gave a smile with no warmth. "Natalie really got to you, didn't she? She doesn't give a shit about who you are or who you're married to, and she wasn't intimidated by your bitchiness. You're trying to get revenge on her. You, Galina, are pathetic."

Galina screeched and leaped at him, but Stone was already moving to the door. He was out in the hallway and knocking on Coach Novak's door before Galina could make it to the hall.

"Stone? Is everything okay?" Coach asked as Stone practically pushed his way into coach's hotel room.

"I had an unwanted visitor in my room."

Novak cursed and called security. "We have a bunny in room 507 that needs to be removed."

Stone waited until Coach hung up before telling him the rest. "It wasn't a bunny. It was Galina Belov trying to seduce me."

"You're kidding," Coach said, clearly stunned.

"Nope. She's mad that your daughter didn't bend the knee to her rule over the WAGs." Stone leaned against the desk as they waited for security to secure his room.

"Poisoning is moving up the list," Novak muttered before he ordered Stone's room to be moved next to his in hopes of Galina not finding him again.

There was a knock on the door and security was there to report that the room was clean. Galina wasn't in there when they'd gone to look. They had packed up Stone's things and handed him the key to the room next door.

"I think I was going about this the wrong way," Stone said before leaving. "How much leeway can you give me before I get suspended?"

"What do you have in mind?" Coach asked but didn't answer.

"I'll have a more forceful word with him tomorrow. In front of everyone. If that doesn't work, I have one more trick up my sleeve. I don't want you to know, because I want you to have deniability since Tupper's already given you orders."

"If you can get our team back, I'll do everything I can to keep you on it. Goodnight, Stone."

"Night, Coach."

Stone walked next door and was relieved to have the silence of his own room again. He had a plan, and he had to think about the best way to execute it.

27

Natalie was drinking a calming tea with Olivia when Granger's phone rang at midnight. Granger walked into the room and set the phone down on the kitchen table.

"Wilder, what happened?" Granger asked.

"Nothing," Wilder sighed over speakerphone. "A couple of guys did the normal chit-chat thing and the girls were flirty, but nothing outside of the usual," Wilder told them.

"Flirty, how?" Natalie asked, as an idea began to form.

Wilder chuckled. "It may surprise you, but I'm something of a catch. I get flirted with all the time. They talk, they giggle, they give suggestive touches to let me know they're interested in me. You know, the normal."

"What is it?" Olivia could see the wheels turning in her mind. Why? Because it might be the normal flirting or . . .

"Hang up, leave your phone, shoes, and clothes in a different room, then call us on a landline," Natalie ordered before ending the call.

"What's going on?" Granger asked, looking down at his phone.

"It could be normal flirting, but those were all techniques I used to plant bugs on people and things. I just want to be careful," Natalie explained as they waited several minutes and then finally, Granger's phone rang again.

Granger answered it and put it on speaker. "Will someone please tell me why I am naked in the storage room?"

"Wilder, I'm sure you're a catch, but those are the same tactics I was instructed to use to plant bugs on things or people. When we hang up, check every item of clothing and your phone. If you have a phone case, open it and make sure a bug isn't hiding there. Check everything, including the cameras to make sure no one came into your office and planted something." Natalie was worried he'd think she was paranoid when he was quiet for a moment.

"Yeah, I can see that's a possibility now. I'll get back to you all."

The calming tea did nothing to calm her nerves as they waited over thirty minutes for Wilder to call them back. "I found three bugs on my things. One on my phone, one on my shoe, and one on my belt. I pulled security tapes and saw a girl sweet talk her way past security and enter my office. I don't know how to sweep for bugs, so I'm just not going in there until Tristan gets back."

"This isn't good," Olivia said with a sigh. "This means they have enough eyes here in Charleston to know not only who and where Natalie is but also that she's dating Stone, thus making Wilder a contact. Did they see Forrest?"

"Yeah, they did. He was at the bar, but I saw Lavigne take a good, long look at him. What do I do now?" Wilder asked.

"Stay there and act normal. Just make it a routine visit. Then visit another of your clubs in Europe before coming home. Make Forrest check for bugs too and get a burner phone," Granger instructed. "Did Lavigne even talk to you?"

"Lavigne came in, chatted, sold me some champagne, danced, drank, and then left. He didn't ask about my family, Charleston, sports, secrets, blackmail, nothing. Tristan trailed him to see if he could find anything else out. I checked my cell and Tristan texted that Lavigne went back to his penthouse, no other stops. I don't know how we can catch him and even if we do, what we can learn."

"Send photos back of anyone he was with. I'll see if Ryker can find any Russian connections. That might help us know who to be on the lookout for here," Granger told him before ending the call.

They were still sitting together, mulling over this news when Granger's phone got several text messages from a French number. Wilder must be sending everything through his new burner phone. When Natalie looked at the clock, she was surprised it was two in the morning.

"I feel as if we know more but are in an even tighter spot since there's less we can do. We still don't know who is after us, but we can conclude multiple organizations think it's me blackmailing and selling secrets." Natalie slammed her hand on the table in frustration. "I don't know what to do."

"You do have the actual proof, right? And it's someplace very safe?" Olivia asked.

"Yes and yes."

"Then we wait," Olivia said, not sounding any happier about it than Natalie felt.

∾

Stone was pissed. This was his comeback and instead of being excited to be out on the ice, he had to deal with the

Belovs. He slammed his way into the locker room, startling his team.

They were all in various positions of getting ready. Some had full equipment on. Some were still wrapping their sticks. Others were relaxing and playing video games. However, they were all now staring at him.

"Where's Igor?" Stone asked loud enough for everyone to hear.

"Not here yet," Kallee Aho answered with what sounded like both annoyance and relief.

"Good. Team meeting," Stone said before putting his fingers to his lips and letting loose a sharp whistle to get his team's attention. "I haven't been playing, but I'm tired of his shit. Is anyone else?"

The entire team either tapped their sticks or clapped in agreement.

"We've missed you, Cap," Andrew Kenny said and the clapping intensified.

Stone held up his hands to quiet them. "I don't have much time, but I need your help to put Igor in his place."

An hour later, Stone stopped at the end of the walkway, getting ready to lead his team onto the ice. He glanced around the stadium, looking for Natalie before he got on the ice. There, across from the bench, right in the middle of the rink at the glass, was Natalie.

Stone jumped onto the ice. The second he began to skate on the ice the arena erupted with cheers. Damn, it felt good to be back. Stone put his hands over his heart and then applauded the fans to let them know he was touched. The response was overwhelming. The arena was near deafening as his teammates all rallied around him. All except Igor who had been especially cocky tonight. He'd laughed when Stone had slammed him into the locker. Stone learned why shortly after.

Archie Tupper, the team owner, had come into the locker room just moments ago. He clasped Stone on the shoulder and said he was glad Stone was back but then went to tell everyone how integral Igor was to the team and how lucky they were to have him. It soured the mood, knowing the team owner didn't care about the friction Igor was causing.

But now, with his team around him on the ice, he didn't care about Igor or Tupper. He only cared about his team. "As we talked about, men. There's no one I would rather be on the ice with than you all."

Together, on the ice, with Belov skating around talking shit to the other team, the Charleston Pirates decided it was time for him to walk the plank.

Natalie arrived at the arena with the Townsend family. They'd gotten there early and went up to the owner's suite. Granger was glued to his phone as some "team" came to get Martin and his buddy, not three hours ago.

There'd been no news since.

Not only was Natalie anxious, but so was Granger. The others were tired of it and decided to get to the game early. Natalie didn't want to break Stone's concentration, so instead of going to see the team, they headed for the owner's suite. The wives and family had a private interior room across from the suite. There the wives could relax and their children could play. Natalie wanted to say hello to Hilly and check on Galina.

Damon led his brothers and Granger into the owner's suite while Natalie took Olivia into the wives' room. "You've never been?" Natalie asked.

"Not a wife. Besides, I like being at ice level better than in a suite. I want to see it live, not on television," Olivia answered.

"Ready for this? Stone is working on Igor, but it's time we free these poor women of Galina's reign of terror. I can't wait to execute our plans."

Olivia smiled serenely and Natalie shivered. She was a shark and Natalie both loved it and was in awe of it. Also, she was slightly terrified. "Let's have some fun," Olivia answered.

Natalie nodded to the security guard who opened the door. Hilly Jones was in tears as her baby similarly cried. Joslyn Webb was hiding in the corner behind a potted plant. Ellen Berg, who had been rather rude at first, looked as her red-rimmed eyes filled with relief when she saw that Natalie knew whatever happened had to be bad.

"Hilly," Natalie said with a soft smile. "Let me hold that sweet little angel. What happened?" she asked, taking her baby from her. She began to bounce the baby on her hip as Olivia handed a tissue to Hilly.

"Galina said she's been sleeping with our husbands. That Dan was desperate for someone who was not a stretched-out mother. She said she even slept with Stone. I'm so sorry, Natalie," Hilly said between gulps.

First, fear struck. Pain ripped her heart in two. But then Natalie looked at Galina standing there, sipping champagne with a huge smile on her face surrounded by the WAGs who looked too scared to move.

"Tell me little bird, did you really think you could keep up with a man like Stone?" Galina asked with a laugh before coming over to her. Natalie could feel Olivia practically vibrating with anger. Natalie took a deep breath. She trusted Stone. There was no way he'd sleep with her. Ever. So instead of tears, Natalie just smiled. "Oh, you like that idea? You want to watch a real woman satisfy your man? Does it hurt that he told me all your secrets while I blew him?"

Olivia stiffened next to her. Natalie wasn't the only one who picked up on that. Could it be Galina? Was she the one blackmailing everyone?

Natalie laughed. The entire room went quiet. "Wow, you are even more pathetic than I realized. What did you do in Russia, Galina? I would say you could be a spy for them, seducing men for information, but you're not very good at it."

"Stone would say something different," Galina tried to challenge.

"No, he'd laugh at you for trying to sleep with him. He's not interested, just like I bet Dan and Karl turned you down too. Ouchy. That's got to hurt. Now, get the fuck out of here, Galina. Your husband might be part of the team, but you're not part of us." Natalie turned and opened the door. "Security, please escort Ms. Belov from the room. She's no longer allowed in here."

"You can't do that!"

"What's going on here?" Natalie looked over at Archie Tupper standing at the door to his suite with two men. One was a tall, serious looking man with dark hair, an impeccable suit and a frown. Next to the mystery man was Nico Saccone.

"Galina was just leaving," Natalie said, not backing down.

"Ah, the beautiful Galina, join us. I was just telling my friends about what a great player your husband is." Archie opened the door to the owner's suite for Galina. Galina threw a smirk over her shoulder at the roomful of WAGs before disappearing into the suite. "Natalie," Archie said, stopping her from returning to the room. "Let's get together after the game."

It was said as if it were a suggestion, but she doubted it would be. "I'd love that, Archie. It's been too long since we've seen each other." Then she shut the door and turned to the WAGs. "Ladies, I think we can say enough is enough. Who wants Galina and Igor out of the Pirates?"

Everyone raised their hands.

Olivia smiled. "I'm Stone's sister, Olivia, and I'm here to help."

"Yeah, we know who you are. The team credits you with most of their wins for chirping the other team so badly they can't play," Hilly said.

"That's me. Now, we have a plan."

An hour later, the wives and girlfriends were in place and Natalie couldn't sit still. She was standing at the glass, waiting for Stone to make an appearance. Then, finally, he came out of the tunnel leading his team.

The moment he caught her eye, Natalie blew him a kiss. There was more than one way to handle a situation. If the team couldn't do anything about it, then the wives and girlfriends would.

The crowd was deafening and next to her Olivia swiped at a tear. "It's so good to see him back on the ice."

Natalie couldn't agree more. As the team got ready, Belov skated around pumping himself up by hitting the number eighteen on his jersey. The team ignored him. She could see Stone whipping his team into a frenzy. Tennessee was going to get hammered tonight. They just didn't know it yet.

"Natalie!" Nat turned to see Rita and a man take the last two seats in the row. "Oh my gosh, these tickets are amazing! When you said you could get me some, I thought we'd be in the nosebleeds."

Natalie smiled, but before she could say more the game was being whistled into action. Time for action. She and Olivia stepped to the glass. They looked at each other and smiled.

Natalie saw Hunter make the sign of the cross as he shivered, watching them. Poor Kane went pale. Damon's eyes widened slightly, but then he smiled. Dear Lord, Damon Townsend's smile was enough to make half the women there pass out.

Natalie caught the eye of Hilly who was a quarter of the way around the arena near her husband's goal, to the right. She gave Hilly and Joslyn next to her a nod. Then Natalie looked to the left at Ellen leading a small team of women near the opposite team's goalie, and gave her a nod.

Natalie and Olivia were banging on the glass the second the player skated by. "Hey number eighteen, you won't play with your team, but your wife will," Natalie shouted. Belov stumbled and a Tennessee player intercepted the puck.

The audience around them went silent. Natalie could hear the whispers, but now Olivia was at the glass, pounding on it. "Hey eighteen, you can't score if you skate like that. Don't worry, your wife scores enough for both of you."

People started gasping around them and a couple of the players from both teams looked over at them with surprise. They were chirping their own player.

Belov glared at them but skated down the ice where

Tennessee was about to shoot on the Pirate's goal. Natalie gripped Olivia's arm at the sound of the stick hitting the puck. The puck sailed through the air, but Dan Jones's large glove snatched it from the air.

"Denied!" Hilly screamed so loud Natalie could hear it even as Hilly slammed on the glass. "Don't worry, Belov's wife knows the feeling. Dan denied her, too."

Dan's head whipped back with surprise to look at his normally shy wife who just smiled and blew him a kiss as the other girlfriends on that end of the ice began chirping, not only against Tennessee, but also against Belov.

Stone almost fell off his skates when sweet little Hilly Jones started chirping. Tennessee players were so shocked Stone was able to steal the puck and break away down the ice. His wingmen, Andrew, Kenny, and Theo Larson were in position. Stone could shoot or pass.

"Razzle Dazzle!" Theo shouted and Stone passed the puck to Theo. The defense shifted toward Theo, who spun and passed the puck mid-spin back to Stone.

Stone had a clear shot. He pulled back his stick and slammed it into the puck. The puck sailed through the air and into the net. The arena went absolutely electric. His team, minus Belov, slammed him into the boards by the team bench and celebrated.

"Keep your chin up, Belov!" Ellen called out in her Swedish accent. "There's always the beer league!"

"What is going on?" Elias Laakso asked. Kalle Aho, who was on the bench since Belov started in his place, looked stunned.

"They're chirping Belov," Stone said, realizing exactly

what was going on. "Let's do it men. No more waiting. Time to start my plan."

They cheered and then went back on the ice with more excitement than ever. Stone caught Coach Novak's questioning look and winked. If Igor didn't want to be part of the team, they wouldn't treat him as such.

"Hey Belov, nice dive. Next time, play in a Speedo!" Natalie yelled when Belov missed a steal. He might have fallen and hit the ice because Laakso's skate happened to trip him, but it didn't matter. They were almost done with the second period and Belov was such a mess he was missing every play.

He also wasn't getting any touches since the team totally iced him out. They wouldn't pass to him and when he got the puck, Stone stole it from him and went on offense. Belov broke his stick over that one and the tide began to turn in the arena. They were seeing that antics don't win games, teamwork does.

Olivia slammed on the glass. "This isn't a game of catch, Belov. The point is to get it past the goalie, not toss him the puck!"

Hilly got Belov's attention by pounding on the glass screaming his name after he missed a wide-open shot. "How do you tie your skates with no hands?"

The clock to the second period was counting down and Tennessee had the puck. They were charging the goal. Belov made a move to intercept the puck instead of defending the goal. Laakso moved to protect Dan and Stone kicked up the speed. He slammed into Belov's back, sending him flying into the Tennessee player. The shot went wide and Laakso cleared it from the goal with a pass to Kenny.

"Hey eighteen! Are you wearing a rainbow wig under your helmet?" Ellen yelled as she banged the glass. "Because you look like a clown out there!"

Belov started to go for Ellen so Natalie banged the glass calling out his name. "Oh! Belov! That's some real small stick energy, bud! You must be pregnant since you missed the last two periods!"

Belov turned to Natalie and glared. "You chirp like a dead bird. Maybe you need to be one."

Stone must have heard because suddenly he was racing towards Belov. "If we're birds, you're the cuckold bird!" Natalie yelled.

"Cuckold! Cuckold!" Olivia called out as if she were singing *cuckoo-cuckoo*, like the clock. The other wives caught on and soon a chorus of bird chirps saying "cuckold" rang out.

Belov turned and apparently said something to Stone. Natalie gasped as Stone threw his gloves to the ice as the second period came to an end and slammed his fist into Belov's face. The team cleared the bench, but it wasn't to break up the fight. It was to prevent anyone else from breaking it up.

The refs couldn't get to them as Stone and Belov traded punches. The fans were silent, not knowing what to do. A good fight was always welcome, but this time it was teammates. Stone got Belov on the chin and he went down. Stone said something to him and then turned to skate away. Belov bounced up and before the team could restrain him, Belov got a sucker punch in. Stone fell backward, but his team caught him. No longer were they a circle around them. Now they all stood behind Stone. The sucker punch also snapped the crowd out of their trance. They started booing as Belov held up his hands as if he were victorious.

"Is Stone hurt?" Natalie asked as she held Olivia's arm.

"He has a hard head. He'll be fine," Olivia assured her.

Stone turned and found her in the stands and winked. Then Natalie knew Stone was okay.

Stone led his team, minus Belov, off the ice and into the dressing room. They had fifteen minutes to solve the Belov problem. It was going to be another dogfight in the locker room by the look on Coach's face.

"Tupper is on his way down and he's not happy," Coach Novak told him. "I, on the other hand, loved every chirp and that really nice uppercut."

"I didn't know about the chirping," Stone admitted with a smile. "But that has Nat and my sister written all over it."

"Did you hear Hilly?" Dan said, his chest puffed up with pride. "I've never heard her talk so loudly before. And she got him good. So did Ellen!"

Karl high-fived Dan as the team started sharing their favorite chirps. That was, until Igor stomped in with the team owner next to him. Someone tattled.

"What is going on? This is an embarrassment!" Tupper screamed. Coach began to open his mouth, but Tupper cut him off. "One word from you and I'll fire you on the spot."

Stone couldn't let that happen. He knew how important it was for Coach Novak to be in Charleston. To be in the United States. It's what kept Naylor's threat invalid. If he needed a job and was sent back out of the safety of the US, all of this would be for nothing.

Stone stood up before Coach Novak could explode. His face was red, his mouth was moving to say something, but Stone stopped him. "No, what's embarrassing is the fact that the team owner supports this team about as much as Belov does, which is not at all. That's embarrassing. What else is embarrassing is what it will look like when your entire team refuses to take the ice if Belov does."

Archie Tupper's face turned molten. His hands tightened, but Stone didn't back down. "The question is, whose back do you have?" Stone asked.

The room was quiet, even Belov didn't speak. Tupper turned to Belov, and frowned. "I'm sorry, Igor. Let's sit you out this period."

Belov slammed his stick against the locker, splintering it.

"This isn't over. We'll discuss it after the game." The threat from Tupper to Coach Novak was clear. Tupper slammed the door closed and the team turned to Stone. He was their captain. He needed to lead them.

Natalie sat down for the first time as the entertainment came out on the ice. Her heart was pumping, her hands were sweating, and she was so worried her actions might reflect badly on Stone or her father. She knew their hands were tied, so maybe she could do what they wanted to do but couldn't. If Tupper wanted the PR nightmare of kicking out the wives and girlfriends of all the players, so be it, as long as the players weren't punished.

"I can't believe this side of you," Rita said. The man next to her nodded in agreement. Natalie hadn't met him yet. She'd been so busy chirping she hadn't been a very good hostess. "You're an expert on trash-talking. I have to say I'm impressed."

The team came back out onto the ice and slightly confused cheers went up. Belov wasn't out on the ice. It was Kalle Aho who was on the ice instead when the team lined up for a face-off. The whistle blew and the chirping turned solely against the Tennessee team. The wives and girlfriends all smiled at each other in victory. Belov had been benched. The difference was noticeable.

The Pirates played as a unified team. They passed, they scored, they repeated. By the time Olivia and Rowan got up for one final beer, people were starting to leave the arena since the Pirates were wiping the ice with Tennessee. Natalie couldn't be any prouder. She stood up and cheered until her voice was gone when Stone scored his third goal, completing a hat trick for his first game back.

Rita was cheering next to her, but then Natalie flinched when Rita hit her in the ribs. "Ow." Natalie looked over to where Rita was smiling and cheering. Only it wasn't her elbow that hit her. There was something poking her in the ribs. "What is that?"

Natalie tried to move but Rita pressed it harder against her. "Let's go help Olivia carry those drinks," Rita said loudly so that Granger and the remaining Townsends heard her.

"Rita, what's going on?" Natalie asked again.

"This is a gun. I will shoot you if you alert anyone. Not only that, but my friend here will kill anyone with the last name Townsend if you don't do exactly as I say." Rita said it all with a smile on her face as she gave out a whistle here and there as the team celebrated.

Natalie was so surprised she couldn't compute. Rita was holding a gun to her? "How did you get a gun inside?"

Rita rolled her eyes. "Amazing what you can do with a 3-D printer. Now, stop stalling. We're leaving." Rita threw an arm around her as if they were besties. "Let's catch up to Olivia. I need a beer after that!"

"I'll go with you," Granger said, standing up to join them.

"Do you want a beer?" Rita asked. "We'll bring one back for you." Then she dropped her voice so only Natalie could hear. "My partner will kill him if he tries to come. Get him to sit back down."

Natalie swallowed hard before turning a smile to Granger and hoping Granger would get the hint. "We want a little girl time, just like Wilder and Forrest got their guy time. They wouldn't be happy if Tristan interrupted that. I'll bring you back a beer just like Rita's bringing her friend one back."

Natalie felt the gun against her rib and stopped talking. Granger didn't miss a beat. He sat back down. "Great. I don't want any light beer though. I like a full-bodied beer that races up and knocks you on your ass. What about you, man?" Granger asked. The man looked confused, but Granger kept talking as Rita navigated Natalie out of the row. "Our bartender tried to put mango in beer. Can you believe that?" Granger was saying as Natalie began to climb the stairs.

"You don't even sound Russian," Natalie blurted out halfway up the stairs.

"That's the point," Rita said with a roll of her eyes. "Ever heard of sleeper agents? Now, you have evidence my government wants back. If you give it to me, I'll kill you quickly. If not, you'll die slowly and painfully after I kill your boyfriend and father and possibly anyone with the last name Townsend. Now, move."

.   .   .

Stone finished celebrating and glanced over to where Natalie was sitting. He couldn't wait to celebrate with her. She helped him achieve this tonight. Except, Natalie wasn't in her seat. Neither was Olivia. They must be together. Stone looked up the stairs and saw Natalie and her client, Rita, almost to the top of the stairs. He was about to look back to his coach when he saw Hunter stand up and moved out into the stairway by Damon when Olivia and Rowan came back to their seats.

Except Hunter didn't just stand there. He raced up the stairs three rows and then held his fingers to his lips as he pushed by the people sitting there.

"Townsend, you listening to me," Coach Novak snapped.

"Yeah, Coach." Except he wasn't. The whistle blew and he skated out for a face-off. He leaned over the puck but, at the last minute, cast a glance at the stands. Hunter jumped from a seat and onto the man who was attending the game with Olivia's client. They hit the floor hard, and because they were in the first row, the boards now blocked them from view, but Stone could hear Granger shouting, "Sheriff!" as Damon and Kane took off up the stairs to the concourse.

"They have Natalie!" he heard Olivia yell a split second before the whistle sounded.

Fear propelled him forward. He lowered his shoulder and knocked the Tennessee player on his ass. Stone took possession of the puck and skated full tilt to the boards across from the bench. He aimed for the weakest point of the glass and slap-shot the hell out of the puck. The puck flew at over a hundred miles per hour into the spot Stone had aimed for about a third of the way down from the top, right in the middle of the glass. The tempered glass shattered and Stone didn't slow down as he leaped through the glass.

Stone hit Hunter, but also the man who had been reaching for what looked like a weirdly shaped white plastic toy gun. "Get the gun!" Hunter yelled as pandemonium erupted around them.

Stone reached out, grabbed the gun, then used his skate as a weapon. He kicked the man in the chest, feeling the blade of his skate sink into the man's pectoral muscle. The man yelled out in pain and security rushed toward them.

"Where is she?" Stone yelled over the noise.

"That woman took her," Hunter grunted as he yanked the laces free of the skate now stuck in the man's chest.

Stone ripped off his other skate and didn't wait for Hunter. Granger was securing the man while Rowan was already providing medical aid as Stone raced up the stairs. He pushed fans out of the way as he kept his eye on the last place he saw Natalie.

"Townsend!" he heard his coach yell.

"Natalie is in danger!" Stone bellowed over his shoulder as he raced up the stairs. He saw Coach Novak jump out onto the ice and raced after him before he looked forward again.

"Natalie!" Stone yelled. He had to find her.

"I'm a sheriff! Lock down every exit! Now, now, now!" Granger was yelling to security.

Natalie was strong. She was smart. She would fight. She just had to hang on until they could find her.

29

Natalie didn't fight. She couldn't let anything happen to the Townsends. She would bide her time until they were away from Rita's partner and then she'd fight. Until then, she could distract her.

"Why is Russia after me? I don't have anything of theirs."

Rita laughed with no humor. "You blackmail us for five hundred million after threatening to sell our secrets, then say you don't have anything?"

"I didn't blackmail anyone! I'm not selling any secrets. Rita, you know me. When would I be doing this? I wouldn't even know who to contact."

Rita shoved her onto the concourse then walked them to the private elevator reserved for VIPs. "Use your card. We're going down to parking. Say anything or tip security off and I'll shoot him and have my partner shoot anyone with the name Townsend or Novak."

Natalie nodded and showed her pass to the security guard. The doors were about to close when a hand stopped the doors. Rita pressed the gun tight against Natalie's side as

Galina pushed her way in. Right now, Rita was preferable to Galina.

"Trying to escape the mess you made?" Galina asked, looking at the parking lot level button that was pressed. She pressed the button for the suite level before reaching into her designer bag. Suddenly Natalie was deaf. The bang of a gun was so loud in the small elevator her eardrums were ringing.

The pain in her eardrums caused a moment to pass before Natalie realized it wasn't her who had been shot, but Rita. Galina reached over and grabbed Natalie's arm, pressing a real gun, not a 3-D printed plastic one, to her forehead. "Sorry, you're mine. See what happens when you piss off everyone?"

The door to the elevator opened in the parking garage and Galina pressed the upper floor again. Natalie cast a glance to find Rita dead on the floor with a bullet hole in her forehead. "You're Russian. Rita's Russian. Did you kill your partner?"

"*Pfft*. She's not my partner. She's a government agent in my way. The arena is being shut down so I need to stash you in the one place they won't find you."

"How did you get a gun?" Natalie asked, still surprised to have a real one pointed at her.

"They never search the wives of the players."

The door opened to the suite level and Galina tightened her hold on Natalie's left arm with her own left arm. Then Natalie felt the gun pressed into her back as Galina pulled her out of the elevator, using Natalie almost as a shield. Natalie didn't know what to do. Would Rita's partner kill Stone, her father, and the Townsends if Rita didn't check in?

The door to the owner's suite opened and Natalie felt

her heart beat faster. Was this the help she needed to escape? The mysterious man and Nico stepped out with Archie Tupper. "This way, gentleman. Let's get you safe in my office while we figure out what's going on."

"Miss Novak," Nico said, pulling away from Archie. "Come with us."

"No," Galina answered for her. "Wives and girlfriends are going to the family room," she said, giving a nod of her head to the door across the hall from the owner's suite.

Natalie's heart was beating so hard she was afraid she'd miss what Nico was saying as all kinds of thoughts ran through her head on ways to signal for help. "Miss Novak," Nico snapped, his words finally cutting through her near panic. "Would you like to come with us or go to the family room?"

Galina pressed the gun hard into her back. "No thank you, Nico. But, please tell your friend, Cassidy, it was nice meeting her and I can't wait to see her soon."

Nico didn't miss a beat as he dipped his head and walked away. The mysterious man who looked to be in his early forties with dark hair and an expensive suit cast one last glance her way before turning on his heel and following Nico.

Did Nico understand the message? Did he know it was a cry for help? She just hoped help would come. If Galina put them in the family room, suddenly the number of hostages grew to several defenseless children. Then Natalie wouldn't be in position to take a chance to escape. Not when children were in danger.

However, once Archie disappeared from the hall with his guests, Galina didn't push Natalie into the family room, she pushed her into the cavernous owner's suite. Natalie was expecting to see the suite filled with people. If not guests, at least staff. There should be a bartender, waitstaff, and kitchen staff. The suite was comprised of a bar area, a food service area, a sitting area with a massive television, and actually only a smaller part that looked out over the ice. Unfortunately, there was no one in the suite as Galina shoved her over to the sitting area that had a live feed of the ice, but was completely hidden from sight.

Galina pushed her down into one of the plush leather chairs and stood in front of her, pointing the gun down at her.

"I don't understand, Galina. What are you doing?"

"Where is the information you stole from Lavigne?"

Pieces were starting to fall into place. "You're not with the Russians, are you?" Natalie asked.

"Not this time, but I'm flexible. You know how I enjoy more than one partner. Now, where is it? Or do you want me to hurt you a little first? I'd enjoy that after the shit you pulled today with my husband."

"I'm a ballet dancer. I don't feel pain." It wasn't too far from the truth. She'd danced with broken toes and pulled muscles before. What could Galina do besides shoot her? But then she wouldn't get the location of the drive. Natalie's heart began to slow. Galina might have a gun, but it was Natalie who was in control. "How did you know who to blackmail and sell secrets to if you didn't have the list?"

Galina rolled her eyes. "Men. They're so stupid. I had someone who helped me put together a list of known criminals and I threatened them. They never thought a woman would bluff them out of millions, but I have. The Russians and an old Italian family are dragging their feet, but when I give them a little taste of what I have, they'll happily pay. Then I'll go after the lesser-known ones and make a fortune."

"Igor already makes a fortune."

"Ten million from the club and another ten million from endorsements. I'm talking billions, not millions."

The door opened to the suite and Galina looked over her shoulder. Natalie leaned forward. "Archie, run!" Natalie yelled. Galina drew her hand back before swinging it forward. The butt of the gun in her hand cracked against Natalie's cheekbone as Galina hit her. Pain shot across her face. Her eyes watered, her nose ran, and all she could do was suck in air as she fought through the burst of pain.

Through tear-filled eyes, Natalie saw Archie close and lock the doors to the suite. "Do you have the location of the list yet?" he asked Galina, ignoring Natalie and the pain she was in.

Stone raced up the stairs. He shoved people out of his way as he ran out onto the concourse. The doors were locked and the concourse was filling with people who had been trying to exit, but were now stuck.

"Stone Townsend!" People were calling his name and trying to grab selfies as Stone looked around, trying to find Natalie.

"Back off!" Damon shouted, shoving people out of the way. "They went to the VIP elevator."

Kane was pushing his way to the elevator as the guard began to look overwhelmed. "Where did the two women go?" Kane was demanding when Stone and Damon finally made it to Kane.

"I don't know, man. This crowd has been nuts, but there

were three women. One got on right before the doors closed." The guard was trying to keep fans away from Stone.

"My card isn't working," Kane cursed before turning to the guard. "Open the elevator. Now!"

The guard used his card to override the security lockdown. The elevator doors opened and then there were the sounds of horrified screams. Stone looked down to see a woman lying on the floor of the elevator in a pool of blood. His first, terrified thought was that it must be Natalie, but this woman wasn't wearing Stone's jersey like Nat was.

"Stone!" A deep booming voice was yelling as the crowd seemed to part.

Stone turned to see Nico Saccone and a man he didn't recognize rushing toward them. Well, Nico was rushing. The other man strode as if he owned the arena. "Nico?"

"Galina Belov is holding Natalie hostage upstairs in the owner's suite," Nico said as soon as he joined them. He glanced down at the body but didn't seem as shocked as everyone around them did.

"Galina Belov? Are you sure?" That couldn't be right. Was she pissed because of the chirping?

"I'm positive. Archie Tupper evacuated the suite and was taking Sebastian and me," Nico said, nodding his head to the silent man in the suit next to him, "to his private office for our security. Natalie passed me a message that she couldn't wait to see Cassidy again. We went with Archie, but when he went to check on what happened, we left. Galina said they were going to the family room, but when we asked the guard, they never went in. They went into the owner's suite."

"I'll get Igor Belov and fill Natalie's dad in," Damon said. No sooner than he did, Coach Novak came pushing through the crowd. "I got this. Go."

"There's a team on their way to handle this. They'll get Natalie out. They're fifteen minutes out," the man identified as Sebastian told them.

"Who are you?" Stone asked. "How do you know that?"

"Sebastian Abel."

"The billionaire? What team?" Stone shook his head. "I don't care. I'm not waiting."

"I'll go with you. And here's Hunter," Kane said as they pushed into the elevator. Hunter easily sidestepped the blood as Stone pressed the floor for the owner's suite.

"What's going on?" Hunter asked as if it were normal to have a dead body between them. Kane filled him in and Hunter gave a little nod. "Got it. Just leave it to me."

"I got this." Stone said, shoving the fake-looking gun he'd gotten from Rita's body into the back of his compression shorts waistband under his pads. Stupid toy, but it was evidence and he might be able to bluff his way to getting Natalie free with it.

The elevator opened and the security guard moved forward to stop them, but instantly stopped as he saw Stone. "Is everything okay, Mr. Townsend?"

"Are the families still inside?" Kane asked.

"Yes, sir. The mothers and children have made their way up from the rink, but several of the wives and girlfriends are not here. Miss Galina and Miss Natalie are across the hall."

"I want you to lock the mothers and children inside and slide the key under the door so no one can get in. Then pull your weapon and tase anyone who tries to get in that isn't one of the mothers, including Galina or the police chief himself. Got it?" Kane asked.

"Yes, sir." The man opened the door and slipped inside.

Stone could hear him explain to the mothers what was going on before coming back out into the hall, locking the door, and sliding the key under it to the women inside. As soon as he pulled his taser they started for the owner's suite.

Hunter looked to Kane who gave a silent nod. Hunter moved to the left of the door, Kane to the right. Stone knew he wasn't the trained man here, but the woman he loved was inside and he'd put Hunter to shame if someone tried to hurt her.

Kane slowly reached to the handle and tried to pull it open. The door didn't move. Kane frowned and turned to the guard. He put his finger to his lips and pointed at the lock. The guard nodded and handed over a key.

Kane was about to unlock the door when his phone vibrated. It wasn't loud, but Stone heard it. Kane reached into his pocket and looked at the text. His frown told him everything he needed to know. Whatever it was, it wasn't good.

Kane turned to phone to show Hunter and Stone. *Belov is missing.*

Stone looked down the hall, but there was no one. The sound of yelling coming from inside changed everything. He wasn't going to wait another second.

"Tell me where it is!" Galina yelled, reaching down, and grabbing Natalie's hair. She gave it a hard yank and Natalie grunted in pain. She wouldn't give Galina the satisfaction of knowing it hurt.

"How did you know I had it?" Natalie asked through gritted teeth.

"I have my sources."

"The same sources that told you who to blackmail?" Natalie asked, rubbing her scalp after Galina let go.

"Enough. We don't have much time until they check on

us," Archie hissed. "Get the location or kill her."

"Archie? How are you involved in this?" Natalie wondered. "Galina's a bitch. I can see her blackmailing people. But you? You're a billionaire. You don't need any money."

"Blackmail goes both ways. Or maybe it's just patriotic duty. Now, where is it?" Archie demanded. When she didn't answer, he stomped forward and didn't stop until his fist punched the air from her lungs.

Natalie gasped for air. The punch to the stomach hadn't been expected. Galina was getting agitated. Archie was clearly already agitated. But Natalie had to stall. Maybe someone would find her. "If you kill me, you'll never find it. It was you all searching my home and office, wasn't it?"

Galina laughed, with no trace of humor in it. "We weren't the only ones. That Russian bitch got there before us, and that's after whoever got there first. Now, where is it, you traitor? Tell me or I'll start shooting. I think I'll start with your feet." Galina cocked her head and frowned as she put her hands on the arms of the chair. She shoved her pouty, mocking face in hers. "How will you dance then? Don't worry, I'll keep Stone company while you're in the hospital. That is, unless you tell me where the list is. Then I won't screw him over and over again in your bed." Anger made Natalie want to lash out, but she had to keep it together. "Fine. I'll tell you where it is if you promise not to sleep with Stone."

"Eh." Galina was toying with her now that she found Natalie's weakness.

"Galina!" Archie snapped. "Get to the point. Where is it, Natalie?"

"It's in a bank vault," Natalie whispered so quietly Galina missed it.

"What?" she asked, leaning forward to hear.

That's when Natalie made her move. She slammed her forehead into the bridge of Galina's nose. Galina screamed, Archie yelled, and the door to the suite crashed open.

Natalie didn't dare look to see who was there. She had to get the gun from Galina. The gun that was still in her hand currently trying to stop the flow of blood from her very broken nose.

Natalie launched herself forward. She wrapped her arms around Galina's ribs and shoved *hard*, as if she were a linebacker making a tackle. Galina stumbled and fell on her back, her arms going wide, and her gun falling from her hand when she hit the floor. Natalie couldn't get a good handle on the gun from where she was straddling Galina, but she could push it farther away. She curled her hand into a fist and then quickly flexed her fingers open. It didn't move the gun much, but it moved it out of Galina's reach and under the nearby couch. Unfortunately, it also gave Galina time to wrap her fist in Natalie's hair.

"You going to dance your way out of this?" Galina taunted and then yanked. When she yanked, Natalie's head turned to the side to see Stone and his brothers rushing inside.

Natalie pulled her hand back and punched Galina's face over and over again. "You forgot I grew up playing hockey. Girls make guys' fights look like child's play."

"Get Natalie!" she heard Stone yell, and a second later, two feet appeared on each side of a now unconscious Galina.

"I think you got her, Nat." Two hands reached down, hooked under her armpits, and then Kane was lifting her up and off Galina. But Natalie wasn't done. She got in one more kick to Galina's side before Kane dangled her off the ground. "Damn, Nat. You could give Stone some pointers."

Stone! The fight went out of her as she looked by the door to find Stone holding Archie by the throat and slamming his fist into Archie's face.

"They even fight alike. Now that must be true love," Hunter said with amusement. "If I can find someone who can shoot at least a quarter as good as I can, I'll marry her!"

Natalie opened her mouth to tell him about Maggie, but Kane shook his head. "Let him figure it out on his own," he whispered as Hunter finally moved to pull Stone off Archie.

Stone let Archie Tupper drop to the floor. Hunter would take care of him, just like Kane was securing Galina's weapon and hands. "Nat! Are you hurt? What happened? Please tell me you aren't hurt." The adrenaline was preventing him from hearing anything but the rush of blood in his ears as he ran a thumb over her bloody cheek and down her arms.

"Stone, I'm okay. I knew someone would come."

"The woman has a better jab than you do," Kane taunted.

"Who did that to your cheek?" Stone demanded, ignoring his brother.

"Galina, but I got her back." Damn, Nat was something.

She was shaking, but she was holding it together. Stone wrapped her in a tight hug as he heard Hunter call Granger and update him.

"Hey! What are you . . .?" Stone heard the guard start to yell from out in the hall a second before Igor Belov stormed into the room with a gun pointing at them.

Stone turned to face Igor and shoved Natalie behind

him. Stone saw Kane prop Galina up as if he were about to hug her before he turned around. One hand was on the top of her head. The other was on her chin.

"Hand it over, Natalie, and I'll walk out of here and you'll never see me again," Igor said with zero emotion.

"He's behind it?" Stone asked. "I thought it was a woman who had been contacting people."

"Galina made the calls, but I know all about it. I won't go back to Russia. So, you either give me what I need or I'll kill you right now," Igor said.

Go back to Russia? None of this was making sense.

"Put your gun down or I'll kill your wife," Kane said, mirroring Igor's complete lack of emotion.

"Go ahead. She's an adulterous bitch." He turned the gun to point it at Stone. "I bet I can kill you both with one shot."

Suddenly Stone felt something pulled from the back of his waistband. "Not if I kill you first." Stone turned to look to see Natalie holding the strangely shaped white toy gun aimed right at Igor.

Igor laughed and Stone knew their time was about up. "You're going to shoot Igor with a toy? Go ahead. Shoot," he taunted.

Stone looked to Hunter who was inching closer to Igor, but then there was a slight shadow coming from the door. Damon. The question was now if one of them could get to Igor before he fired.

"Okay," Natalie said and pulled the trigger.

Stone jumped in surprise when a bullet actually shot out of the gun and slammed into Igor's shoulder. Damon and Hunter converged on Igor, but he wouldn't go down easy.

"I won't go back! You'll have to kill Igor!" Igor yelled as he battled to aim his gun at Natalie.

Stone turned and tackled her to the ground. He shielded her body with his as the sounds of a fight waged on and two more shots went off.

30

The sound of the shots echoed in the room. Parts of the ceiling showered down on them as Stone protected her with his body. Then there was a *zzzzzzzzt* noise and things went quiet.

Cassidy stood with a taser to Belov's neck. "I couldn't let y'all have all the fun." Stone looked behind Cassidy to find someone helping the guard up off the floor and two others running in to secure Belov. "Who am I arresting?"

"I'm a government asset!" Archie Tupper yelled from where he sat, bloody, in the corner, finally looking relieved. "You can't arrest me."

Galina began to moan as she became fully conscious. "Yes, government asset. We work for the CIA."

Stone rolled off of Natalie and stood up. He reached down and helped her to stand. Cassidy motioned for all three to be placed on the couch in handcuffs. There was some fighting and wrestling, but with four armed men aiming guns at them, Galina, Igor, and Archie finally gave up.

"If you are with the CIA," Cassidy said calmly as she

took a seat on the coffee table in front of them. "What is your mission?"

"I was to find out where the traitor hid the list she stole with all the black-market criminals on it when she refused to turn it over to the CIA. Then she moved to Charleston and I was called in to help recover it," Galina explained.

"That's when I was approached," Archie said, picking up the story. "I was told I was doing my patriotic duty by bringing a CIA asset—Galina—to the United States. I was told to sign Igor and allow Galina complete access to the arena."

"And you?" Cassidy said, turning to Igor.

"I didn't want to be traded, but I was approached and told if I didn't accept the trade to Charleston and if I didn't assist Galina, I would be sent back to Russia. I was fine with that, but then I was told I would be sent along with the thanks of the U.S. government. Russia would kill me." Igor explained. It was the first time Igor had looked fearful.

Next to Stone, Natalie stiffened, but Cassidy spoke first. "And the blackmail and selling of secrets on that list? Where did that fit in?"

"I was told there was a rumor going around that Natalie was doing that. The plan was for me to take over and make the contacts in hopes of drawing Natalie out and exposing where the list was," Galina explained.

"Bullshit. You said you were going to keep the money," Natalie accused her.

Now Galina looked a little nervous. "I deserve to be paid, yes? I bring in a government traitor and make the CIA look good. What harm in keeping a little money?"

"I bet you didn't tell the CIA that part," Cassidy said with a little laugh. "Got it. Now, who is your CIA contact?"

"We can't tell you. It's a secret," Archie Tupper said. "But

I have the right to call my attorney and I'll have your job for detaining us."

Cassidy smiled sweetly as she relaxed in the chair and crossed her legs. "Do I seem worried? That should tell you about who I am working for. Who is your contact at the CIA, who approved this mission, and who recruited you?"

"You don't scare me." Galina decided to go full diva. "I want a phone right now."

Cassidy leaned forward and dropped her voice. "I can kill a person eight ways with a spoon. Imagine what I can do with a knife. Would you like to find out? Who. Is. Your. Contact?"

"I know who it is," Natalie said suddenly. Everyone turned to look at her, including Stone. "It's Aaron Naylor, isn't it?"

Stone looked back at the group. There was some reaction there. Cassidy didn't seem as surprised as Stone or the rest of the group.

"See," Natalie said, moving to sit next to Cassidy. "I didn't mean to become a traitor if I am even that. I was forced into becoming a government asset, just like Igor. I was told if I didn't do these things for Naylor, he would tell the Russians my father was a spy. My father was coaching in Russia at the time. I was left with no option but to plant bugs, spy on people, and steal things. I saw that list and took it. Not to be a traitor, but to keep it as insurance to prevent me from being dragged back into the spy world. I was going to trade it for my freedom if Naylor ever came calling again. Does this sound familiar to you?"

Now the three were looking nervous. It was Igor who broke first. "Yes. It was Agent Naylor. He threatened me like Coach."

Galina let out a deep breath. "I might have worked for

the Russian FSB."

"Worked for or currently work with?" Cassidy asked for clarification.

"How do you say it? As needed." Galina shrugged. "Agent Naylor knew and threatened to have me arrested as a spy."

"And you?" Cassidy asked Archie.

"I won't say a word without my attorney and a signed immunity agreement."

"We don't need you. I know why."

Stone turned to see the man in the suite who was with Nico. He was standing at the door looking bored as he fixed his cuff while Nico stood behind him.

"Hey, Sebastian," Cassidy called out, not looking behind her but instead at the fear on Archie's face. "Archie, want to tell me yourself?"

Archie shook his head. "Immunity first."

Sebastian Abel laughed. It was freaking scary. Stone wished he knew how to do that. He wouldn't even need to hit someone on the ice if he could just laugh like that.

"Yeah, you're not going to get that immunity. Archie here made most of his money having children make designer knockoffs and stealing intellectual property. That's why he was so easy to blackmail into helping," Sebastian explained. "My guess is Naylor promised to keep his name off the list if he did what Naylor told him to."

"Prove it," Archie said, his voice sounding defiant.

"Okay," Natalie said with a shrug before turning to Sebastian. "Not that I'm upset you're here since you're helping out, but who are you and what are you doing here?"

"Sebastian Abel. I'm Cassidy's cousin by marriage. I'm just here visiting a friend," he said nodding to Nico.

"Looks like I got here too late. Need me for anything?"

Granger asked, joining the group as Natalie's father pushed through to wrap her up in a tight hug.

"Yes," Cassidy said, standing up. "I need to have a chat with Agent Naylor. Would you mind showing these three your extra special holding cell in Shadows Landing?"

Granger raised an eyebrow. "With or without the help of the local police?"

"Without please. And preferably with no photos taken either." Cassidy said, walking out of the sitting area and frowning as she saw the action below.

"The game is on a thirty-minute delay," Coach Novak said, "as police clear the scene and the glass gets fixed."

"Crazed fan," Granger explained.

"Who is a Russian spy working with Rita, who is now dead," Natalie explained.

Cassidy gave one of the guys a nod of her head and off he went to collect said spy.

"What happened, Nat?" her father whispered. She gave him a very short explanation and Stone was worried his coach might have a heart attack by the shade of red he was turning.

"There's a private elevator in this suite," Coach said, walking to the far side of the room and opening a door that revealed a small elevator. "It goes down to the locker room level. Take them down in it and use hockey bags to carry them out."

"We can help with that," Hunter said, plucking Archie up from the couch and tossing him over his shoulder.

"Thank you, Coach." Cassidy gave him a wink and grabbed Galina while Damon took Igor. "I expect a wedding invitation soon," Cassidy called out over her shoulder as she, Galina, and one of her men went down in the elevator.

"Stone, go get changed. Nat, get your cheek looked at,"

Coach Novak ordered as he glanced down at his watch. "I have to figure this shit-show out."

"I believe we can help," Olivia said, indicating a very stressed, somewhat rumpled man next to her. "This is Detective Chambers. He's here to take Natalie's statement about a crazed couple who were stalking Stone and attacked Natalie. Stone rescued her, and in the process, the man was injured and the woman was shot by security after holding Natalie at gunpoint. That should wrap up things nicely for your investigation, right?"

The detective shook his head but pulled out his notebook and began to write. "I still can't believe the president's advisor called me and ordered my cooperation in the matter. How is it a national security threat?"

Rowan approached with a small first aid kit as the detective wrote in his notebook. Damon and Igor went down next and then Hunter and Archie. Wives, girlfriends, and children had been cleared from their room and now the hall was empty while Natalie's face was patched up. After they were cleared to go, they made their way down the private elevator with Coach Novak.

"I'll wait here," Natalie said as she leaned against the wall. Hunter and Damon were already there and were standing protectively on both sides of her. Kane had gone with Cassidy and Granger to secure Archie, Galina, and Igor in the Shadows Landing jail. "Stone, I think you should play. Show everyone that we're okay."

Dan Jones burst out of the locker room and Damon and Hunter jumped to protect Natalie before seeing it was the goalie. He pushed them aside and wrapped his arms around Natalie and hugged her tightly. "Hilly was so worried about you. She told me what you did. How you organized the wives and girlfriends, and you were hurt in the process. And you," Dan turned to Stone and his brothers before wrapping Stone up in a big hug. "Keenan, the family room security guard, told us how you helped protect our babies. The families are all inside and want to thank you all."

Dan opened the door and inside the locker room were all the players with their wives, children, and girlfriends.

"Natalie!" Hilly cried, running forward with her baby laughing in her arms. Soon Natalie and Stone were engulfed with hugs from the entire team and their families.

"The Charleston Pirates are a family, and family takes care of each other," Coach Novak said, wiping away a tear as he hugged Stone. "Thank you for keeping her safe," he whispered. "Now,"—Coach turned to his team—"everyone, give your extra jerseys to your wife or girlfriend. We're walking out as a family."

Coach Novak led the team with Stone and Natalie directly behind him. Holding hands, the wives walked their husbands and boyfriends out onto the ice to the cheering crowd.

The players skated around their women and blew them all a kiss or two before Natalie led the women and children to the row right behind the bench. After what had happened to Natalie and Stone, even though the team didn't know the true extent of it, only the story they'd put out about a stalker, it had scared them. They wanted the people they loved close.

The glass had been replaced, the blood had been cleaned, and it was time to play. Stone won the first face-off but was pulled soon after to the resounding cheers of the fans. It was over. His knee was healed. Natalie was safe. He could actually look toward a future with them together.

It was so late at night that Natalie was about to fall over from exhaustion, but her mission wasn't complete yet. Stone didn't talk in the short ride to her training center, but neither of them could keep their hands off each other. They were either holding hands or resting their hands on the other's leg at all times. Both were worried they might lose each other even though the threat was over.

A sleek black sports car was already parked by the front door. As soon as Natalie had taken a seat behind the bench, she'd sent a text to Nico. She'd given him her word. Nico stepped out of one vehicle and waited for Stone to park. He opened Natalie's door for her. "You've had quite a day, haven't you, Miss Novak? Why am I here?"

"I made you a deal, didn't I? I thought you'd want to verify it for your family."

"Wait, the list is here?" Stone asked. "But this place has been searched several times."

Natalie grinned as she unlocked the door. They walked inside and she stopped, turning to the door. "Can you reach those for me?"

"Your old pointe shoes?" Stone asked. They were hanging over the front door like a good luck charm.

Natalie nodded and Stone went up on his toes and pulled them down. He looked them over and frowned when no thumb drive fell out. He handed them over. "Follow me, gentlemen."

Natalie led them into her office. She turned on her computer and pulled out the sewing kit from her drawer. "Do you have any idea how much sewing a ballerina does just on her shoes? We can go through multiple pairs during just one performance. We sew on the ribbons ourselves and we break the shank of the shoe causing the inside to pop open. We cut the satin from the tip of the platform and we smash the toe box and more just to get a pair to fit right. This is the pair I used in Giselle."

Natalie took the small scissors and cut off the small threads holding the insole to the slipper. The one she'd torn when she broke the shank of her slipper. Then she pulled the inside sole free, exposing a small flash drive. She slipped it into her computer and opened the large file.

"Nico, here." Nico walked around and she pointed to the section with his family's name. She highlighted it and then deleted it. Then saved the file and ejected the flash drive. "Thank your family for believing me enough to stop the hit. But tell them they might want to clean up their act." Natalie giggled at her pun. They were in the waste management business after all.

"It's been a pleasure, Miss Novak." Nico shook her hand, then left them in the office.

"Ready to go home?" Stone asked.

"One more stop. Then I don't want to leave your bed for at least twenty-four hours."

The last stop was to hand the flash drive over to Cassidy at the jail where she was interrogating Tupper and the Belovs. The drive would be turned in as having been found in Galina Belov's apartment. Igor had already asked for a divorce and was in negotiations to turn over official evidence on Agent Naylor, Archie Tupper, and his soon-to-be ex-wife. Cassidy didn't stick around. She took the drive and left town to go arrest Naylor.

When Natalie curled up in Stone's arms that night, sleep instantly took her. But in her dreams, she was happy. She was loved and she was free.

EPILOGUE

Stone sat in the locker room, reading the news article on his phone. Olivia had sent him a link to the story that the media was living and breathing at the moment. *Billionaire Archie Tupper and Hockey Wife Sentenced After Pleading Guilty to Conspiracy Charges.* The article went on to say how Archie Tupper and Galina Belov were going to spend fifty years in jail while Igor would spend fifteen but not be deported back to Russia. What the article didn't say was that Aaron Naylor was now at an undisclosed location serving out his own sentence. Cassidy had caught him trying to sneak out of the country the day after the hockey game. No one had heard from him since, but Cassidy assured them that he wouldn't be back.

Naylor had confessed he'd learned about the list being stolen from a bug he'd had Natalie plant at Lavigne's villa. He knew it had to be Natalie. The plan had never been to turn Natalie in but to get the list and turn it over to President Birch in return for a directorship. He was tired of being passed over for high-ranking jobs. The trouble was, he'd never gotten permission to make Natalie an asset and certainly not through extortion. Her file stated she was in contact with some people the CIA would want to get close to. It further said that Naylor had approached Natalie to gauge her interest in helping gather information for the CIA. Same with his extortion of Archie, Igor, and Galina, and who knew how many others. He used them to find the list, keeping his hands clean, but would then claim all the glory to become a director at the CIA, where the real power was.

Igor divorced Galina and threatened to testify against her and Archie. It had been what forced them to take the plea bargains, avoiding a public trial, and keeping key details secret.

Meanwhile, there was a small note at the bottom of the article that Lavigne's vineyard had been sold since he had been arrested after the flash drive found at Galina's showed him to be a black-market dealer. He'd been arrested by an agent of Millevia when he was fleeing France.

That night was months ago, yet it seemed as if it were both yesterday and forever ago since the news was on it from the moment of their official arrest to this plea bargain. The hockey season was in full swing. Stone had been traveling and missing Natalie like crazy when he was on the road. It wasn't as stressful to leave Natalie anymore. It helped that his family already treated her as one of them and always looked out for her, even months later. Well, tonight he'd make it official. She would be family for real.

"You ready for tonight?" Coach Novak asked him.

"I am. Thanks for your blessing, Coach."

"I think it's time you called me Nate." He slapped Stone's shoulder before turning to the team. "Men, I know this season started off bumpy, but things are going to change. First, does everyone know the plan for tonight?"

"Yes, Coach!" the team called out, all getting up to high-five or fist bump Stone.

"Good. Now I have some more news. The league forced Archie Tupper to sell the team. The papers were signed this morning."

Stone's heart stuttered in shock. Everyone froze in their celebrations. Would they move the team? Would they get rid of the players? Would they fire Coach? After Belov was arrested, the team played like a family. Passes were completed as easily as if they had the ice to themselves and they'd been winning. Surely a new owner wouldn't come in and break them up.

"The new owners, Pirate Holdings, are here tonight. Let's give them a warm welcome." Coach nodded to his assistant who opened the door to the silent locker room.

Stone blinked, having trouble processing the people walking into the locker room. Ryker and Kenzie Faulkner led the group. Kenzie came in carrying freshly baked apple pies that had the men making some very strange moaning sounds.

"No! Don't take your clothes off yet! We have a game to win!" Stone shouted, jumping up and grabbing the pies from Kenzie, who was struggling to hold onto them because she was laughing so hard.

"Hello, guys!" she said, handing the pies to Stone. "He's not lying. We promised our minority owners, Miss Ruby and Miss Winnie, who own 0.001% of the team," she said, indicating the two elderly women who were beaming, pinching cheeks, and snapping photos, "that the team would help them out and pose with their pies for the Spring Festival later this year. Would that be okay?"

"If they're half as good as they smell, will you marry me?" Kalle Aho asked, dropping to his knee in front of Miss

Ruby and Miss Winnie. The team fawned over the two elderly women, completely ignoring the billionaires in the room, but no one stopped them. Even Ryker was smiling at their antics.

"We don't have much time, but we thought I could tell you about Pirate Holdings," Kenzie said, getting everyone's attention. "I'm Kenzie Faulkner and this is my husband, Ryker. We own fifty-one percent of the team. Also, I'm a nurse practitioner and while you all have immediate medical care when you join the team, I am available for your families either permanently or to hold them over until they get settled. My husband does a lot of things, but the one you'll probably know is Faulkner Shipping, the big shipping yard a little over that way," she said, pointing to a wall.

There were a lot of murmurs and nods then as the team registered who Ryker was.

"Then, owning forty-five percent is Ryker's cousin, Greer, and her husband, Sebastian Abel of SA Tech and SA Hotels. He's going to be building a hotel where that condemned old parking garage is next door," Kenzie told them, and that got a lot of attention since SA Hotels were some of the most luxurious in the world. However, Stone was pretty sure Sebastian did a lot more than that. There'd been no explanation as to why Sebastian had been with Nico, except to say they were friends. There was something definitely mysterious about him.

"Then, owning three percent is Greyson King Family Enterprises, which is made up of Dell Greyson, his granddaughter, Georgina"—Stone smiled as Georgie, the former bartender at Harper's bar, stepped forward with her grandfather and her new husband—"and Georgie's husband, Kord King." Kord was the sheriff's deputy in

Shadows Landing. It didn't matter that his wife reconnected with her wealthy grandfather and inherited the family money. He loved the law and he loved Shadows Landing. Kord never thought about stepping down from his job, just like Kenzie became a nurse practitioner when she married Ryker instead of stepping away from her career.

The men were incredibly respectful to Dell, and Georgie was nothing but a sweetheart. Kord was psyched. He was high-fiving the players and pumping them up as he met them.

"We're also blessed with Charleston royalty, who now own 0.7% of the team," Kenzie said, stepping aside to reveal an elderly man in a black suit with a crisp white shirt, red tie, and red cane. The elderly woman next to him was in a red dress and a black hat that seemed more suited for a garden party, but it still worked. "Mr. Elijah F. Cummings and his wife, Miss Tibbie."

Stone smiled at his team. The men fawned over the elderly couple, just as they did Miss Ruby, Miss Winnie, and Dell. The team was already becoming a family with the owners, just like it should be.

"When we formed Pirate Holdings, we wanted the majority of the owners to be locals who would understand what this team means to this city," Kenzie told the team. "We have new Charleston," she said, gesturing to Georgie and Dell. "We have old Charleston," she said, gesturing to Miss Ruby, Miss Winnie, Miss Tibbie, and Mr. Elijah. "We have tech, security, advancement, and business experience," she said, gesturing to Ryker, Sebastian, and Greer. "But there was one thing missing. True fandom. Someone who lives and breathes hockey. Someone who has been around it their whole life. Someone who truly terrifies opposing teams. With 0.299 percent ownership . . ." Kenzie gestured to the door and Kord opened it.

"Hello, boys. Let's show Minnesota they came all this way to go home with a participation trophy."

The guys cheered and Stone just stared at his sister. Granger walked around the crowd and sat on the bench next to Stone.

"I thought she was bad before. Now they literally can't throw her out since she owns part of the team. I'm going to have to start carrying my weapon and zip ties to arrest all the opposing teams' fans who try to punch her at the game," Granger said with a sigh. "But look how happy she is."

"My sister is now my boss. Damn."

"Hello, big brother." Olivia stopped in front of him after the team carried her around the locker room like a good luck charm. "Told you I'd get you back for interfering with my love life. Now, I think you need this for tonight." Olivia handed him a bag and winked. "It's an order from your boss. And good luck. I'm proud of you."

Olivia leaned down and kissed his cheek. Damn, he couldn't even be mad. He was lucky. Damon had come to Shadows Landing to scare Ryker off, thinking he was dating Olivia and now the man bought the damn team to help keep them all here. Stone was touched and the only way he could show them what that meant was to win. And win he would.

The team left the locker room on a high to the cheers of their new owners and with the promise there would be no change in players or coaches.

Stone skated out on the ice as the team warmed up. A red carpet was laid out on the ice and the announcer introduced the new team owners. The crowd went wild, all of them recognizing several of the owners, but especially Olivia. Not because of her legal prowess but because in this arena she was known as the Queen of Chirping.

Ryker took the microphone. "As the proud new owners of the team we want to start a new tradition thanking the community who supports the Pirates. Team captain Stone Townsend, will help with our first thank you."

It was time. This had been planned, but he'd not known about the new owners being behind it. Stone skated over and took the microphone. "Every year the Pirates will give a four-year college scholarship to a Pirates fan." Stone paused as the crowd cheered. "For our first recipient, we couldn't have picked a better person, a better fan, and someone who is going to make a difference in hockey. This is a surprise to her, so let's give a big congratulations to Miss Charlie McKinley on her future career as a sports agent!"

The camera panned to Charlie's shocked face, and even better, her father's. He was a single dad working two jobs to pay for his daughter's dream. They'd met Charlie and her father last year and Stone had helped as much as he could because Charlie was worth it. She was smart, determined, and passionate about hockey. Tears were forming in her father's eyes as the announcer urged Charlie to come down to the ice. It took her several minutes to make it to the ice, but once there the composed Charlie Stone had met last season was in full force. "Just a couple more years until I'm your agent," she said when Stone hugged her. "And thank you for the internship with your agent, Finn Williams. I learned so much. I can't wait to start college in the fall."

"The team is here for you. We're all cheering you on, but if you need academic help, call Olivia," Stone said with a wink.

· · ·

Natalie was cheering so loudly she about lost her voice. Between the announcement of the new team owners, the scholarship to that sweet girl, and the Pirates beating number one Minnesota, tonight couldn't get any better.

"Hey," Olivia said as the second period ended and production got set up on the ice for the intermission show. "Let's go over behind the team bench. Miss Ruby and Miss Winnie are there."

"I think they're becoming good luck charms for the boys," Natalie said, standing up. They leaned over to get a high five from the two pie-baking elders each time a player scored. They even gave out pieces of pie between the first and second periods.

Natalie had just sat down with them when the lights dimmed.

"Ladies and gentlemen, please direct your attention to the ice for a special show," the announcer said. "Welcome the ballet dancers from N2 Dance, owned by Coach Novak's daughter, Natalie Novak!"

The jumbotron suddenly had her face on it. "What is this? Why are my dancers here?" she asked as all her little Saturday dancers came running out in black leotards, pink tights, and pink tutus. The boys were all in black leggings with matching black T-shirts. A wooden floor had been laid out on top of a large rectangular square of carpet and they began the routine she had taught them.

"Oh, look how adorable Leah and Lindsey are!" Miss Ruby cried as they cheered on the tiny dancers.

"Now welcome our special guest," the announcer called out. "Stone Townsend!"

"What?" Any further question died on Natalie's lips as Stone ran out in black tights, a tight black dancer's top, and a pink tutu.

"The tutu was my touch," Olivia said with a smile as she began filming on her phone.

Stone joined the group of dancers and had a dance-off with her boy students that left her in near tears. But it was when he picked up each little girl for a leap that had the tears falling. The girls leaped with Stone's assistance. Then they crouched down along the back of the stage, giving the floor to the next dancer. When the last girl was finished, the boys made their own leaps before joining the girls crouched down in a row until only Stone was left standing.

And then he began to really dance. The crowd grew quiet as he moved around the floor, leaping, spinning, and conveying the emotion of the routine. Natalie was so engrossed she missed that the team had filed out of the locker room to watch.

Stone danced his way to the far right of the stage. He bent down and spun the little girl, still crouched, to face the bench. The girl spun along with a big white board in her hands. Stone went down the row, turning each child. When he was done, he gave them a nod and then spun across the floor, only stopping when he went down on one knee. Natalie stood up and cheered, but when the crowd went silent, she noticed she'd been so busy watching Stone she hadn't noticed the children. They weren't holding blank boards anymore. Instead, they were each holding a piece of a sentence that read: *Natalie, will you marry me?*

Natalie blinked, reading it again before looking to where Stone was now holding a ring in his fingers and waiting.

"Dear," Miss Winnie said. "They're all waiting for an answer and I'm afraid that poor boy will keel over if you don't answer him soon."

"And then we won't have a centerfold for our picture," Miss Ruby added.

"Don't keep my son-in-law waiting." Her father kissed her cheek, and then the tears really began.

Natalie stepped out of the row and down to the bench leading to the ice. She had to run through the team cheering her on to reach the ice. "Give me a pair of skates!" Natalie said to the assistant coach who reached behind the bench and grabbed a pair.

"They're going to be huge," he warned.

Natalie shoved each foot, shoes and all, into the skates. The crowd, and Stone, were wondering what was going on. She snagged an extra stick and a puck as she teetered her way out onto the ice. The crowd cheered. Stone looked confused.

She raised her hands to quiet them. "Since Stone danced for you, I thought I should skate for him. If I make the shot, it's a yes."

The team skated out onto the ice, getting into the proposal too. The skates were a little wobbly, but she'd been raised on the ice. The stick was practically as tall as she was, but she knew how to handle it. She circled around the stage, getting a feel for the skates, and blew Stone a kiss.

"Don't miss!" he yelled and the crowd ate it up, but she could hear the fear in his voice.

His team lined up as if they were pretend defenders. Natalie skated and spun around them as she skated closer to the goal. Dan and Karl were blocking the goal, but the wink from Dan left her with no worries. Each teammate she skated by, then spun out and skated around the goal to line up on both sides until it was her versus the goalies. They probably thought she'd tap it in and that made her laugh.

Dan and Karl separated until their gloves touched leaving the center of the goal open. They'd move when she took her shot. She knew that. But she didn't need them too.

Just like she knew the rest of the team was lined up to provide an assist if she missed.

Natalie pulled back the stick and swung from way farther away than they expected. The sound of the stick hitting the puck echoed in the arena as everyone gasped. They thought she'd skate up to the goal and tap it in too. The puck sailed through the air so fast Dan and Karl didn't even move, they were so surprised. The puck flew right between them and into the back of the net. The buzzer sounded and the crowd erupted. The team skated over, and suddenly Natalie was on their shoulders as they carried her over to Stone.

"Theo, get my skates, please," she asked. Her skates and shoes were pulled off with a yank and she was placed on the stage.

Stone was still on one knee, holding out the ring. "So, Natalie, the woman I love with all my heart and all my soul, will you marry me?" he asked with a huge smile.

"Yes, a million times over!"

Natalie held out a now-shaking hand as Stone slipped the ring on her finger. The second it was on, he scooped her up and kissed her to the cheers of the crowd, their friends, and their families.

"And this is just the beginning," Stone told her. And what a beginning it was.

Damon was wondering if he needed to beat Hunter over the head with his own gun. His brother was staring longingly at Maggie who was sitting across from them at the arena. He didn't know how much longer he could stand Hunter not opening his eyes and seeing that Maggie was so much more than a beautiful woman in a cute dress. The woman was the team leader for the U.S. Olympic Shooting team for crying out loud.

Damon looked over to where Olivia had rejoined the row of Townsends after helping with Stone's proposal. She kissed Granger and leaned against his shoulder. She was happy. Damon had done his job as the eldest brother.

Stone was the surprise. Natalie was perfect for him. Damon had expected Stone to mess it up. But Stone had realized right away she was his soul mate and jumped into love with both feet. Now look at them. Engaged to be married and happier than Damon had ever seen him.

Damon let out a sigh as he glanced at Hunter. His brother was staring at Maggie again. Hunter might not realize it, but his time was coming. The only question was whether he'd be as smart as Stone and realize his true love when she shot him in the heart. At this rate, it was a fifty-fifty chance whether Cupid or Maggie would shoot Hunter. He didn't know who would win out, but it sure would be interesting to watch.

Hunter Townsend sat with his brothers as Stone carried his fiancée off the ice. Granger was next to him and now Natalie would be joining the family. The Townsends were growing.

His attention drifted further down the arena to the section where most of Shadows Landing was seated. Why his eyes went to the one woman who drove him crazy? He didn't know. Probably just making sure Maggie Bell stayed over there and away from him.

Liar.

Hunter took a deep breath and forced his eyes from Maggie. Fine, he could admit to himself that she was beautiful, but that was it. She was too bright. Too monogramy. Too debutantish. She'd never understand what he did for a living. He was part of an elite military team. His gun could be his best friend. They spent so much time together.

He did dark, dangerous things to keep the country safe. She helped plan events and weddings. They couldn't be more opposite. But why did he have to keep reminding himself of that? Because he enjoyed their verbal sparring. It was surprising, coming from a blonde-haired, brightly dressed, pearl-wearing lady.

"Just ask her out already," Damon whispered.

"What? Who?" Hunter asked, knowing he'd gotten busted staring at Maggie again.

Damon just stared at him as if he were stupid.

"She's not my type," Hunter said, knowing that excuse was wearing thin.

"So," Damon said, crossing his arms over his chest. "What is your type?"

"Smart, funny, beautiful, tough, independent, doesn't scare easy, and can hit a bullseye at four hundred yards," Hunter said, checking off the list he'd come up with for himself.

"And you'd marry her the second you found a woman like that?" Damon asked.

"Hell yeah, but women like that don't grow on trees. I'll probably find someone on base. A general's daughter or another soldier. Not in my unit of course since we're all guys. Hey, I should check out the base's gun range. I leave next week for a couple of months. Maybe I'll find someone there." Hunter was growing optimistic.

He had to admit that watching his sister and brother fall in love was leaving him feeling a little empty. He didn't have trouble finding dates or someone to warm his bed, but keeping them around was a little harder. Not many people understood his schedule or the secrecy of his job.

Maggie did. She always told him to be safe and come home, yet never pushed for information he couldn't give. Hunter shook his head and forced his eyes back to the ice. When had they wandered back over to Maggie anyway?

"Or maybe she's been right in front of you the whole time?" Damon questioned ominously.

Hunter shivered as if feeling a bullet wiz by his heart. "I highly doubt that," he muttered, yet suddenly he felt like a marked man. Maybe the sooner he got out of Shadows Landing, the better. He was starting to believe in those ghost stories Skeeter told.

ALSO BY KATHLEEN BROOKS

Forever Driven

Forever Secret

Forever Surprised

Forever Concealed

Forever Devoted

Forever Hunted

Forever Guarded

Forever Notorious

Forever Ventured

Forever Freed

Forever Saved

Forever Bold

Forever Thrown

Forever Lies

Forever Protected

Forever Paired

Forever Connected

Forever Covert (coming Jan/Feb 2024)

Shadows Landing Series

Saving Shadows

Sunken Shadows

Lasting Shadows

Fierce Shadows

Broken Shadows

Framed Shadows

Endless Shadows

Fading Shadows

Damaged Shadows

Escaping Shadows

<u>*Shadows Landing: The Townsends*</u>

Face-Off

Targeted (coming April/May 2024)

<u>Women of Power Series</u>

Chosen for Power

Built for Power

Fashioned for Power

Destined for Power

<u>*Web of Lies Series*</u>

Whispered Lies

Rogue Lies

Shattered Lies

<u>*Moonshine Hollow Series*</u>

Moonshine & Murder

Moonshine & Malice

Moonshine & Mayhem

Moonshine & Mischief

Moonshine & Menace

Moonshine & Masquerades

ABOUT THE AUTHOR

Kathleen Brooks is a New York Times, Wall Street Journal, and USA Today bestselling author. Kathleen's stories are romantic suspense featuring strong female heroines, humor, and happily-ever-afters. Her Bluegrass Series and follow-up Bluegrass Brothers Series feature small town charm with quirky characters that have captured the hearts of readers around the world.

Kathleen is an animal lover who supports rescue organizations and other non-profit organizations such as Friends and Vets Helping Pets whose goals are to protect and save our four-legged family members.

Email Notice of New Releases

https://kathleen-brooks.com/new-release-notifications

Kathleen's Website
www.kathleen-brooks.com
Facebook Page
www.facebook.com/KathleenBrooksAuthor
Twitter
www.twitter.com/BluegrassBrooks
Goodreads
www.goodreads.com

Made in United States
Orlando, FL
08 March 2024

44554966R00178